Praise for Ashton Lee and his Cherry Cola Book Club series!

The Cherry Cola Book Club

"If Fannie Flagg and Jan Karon's Mitford were to come together, the end result might very well be Cherico, Mississippi. Ashton Lee has created a magical town with characters who will inspire readers and bring them back to a simpler time and place. With both humor and moving passages, Lee has captured the quirkiness and warmhearted people of the small-town south to a T. Fix yourself a Cherry Coke and savor this fun and moving book."
— Michael Morris, author of *Man in the Blue Moon* and *A Place Called Wiregrass*

"Down-home and delicious, *The Cherry Cola Book Club* combines everything we love about Southern cuisine, small-town grit and the transformative power of books."
— Beth Harbison, *New York Times* best-selling author

The Reading Circle

"Charm, wit and a cast of characters so real they could be your next-door neighbors make *The Reading Circle* a sure-fire winner. Ashton Lee's authentic Southern voice shines in the latest addition to *The Cherry Cola Book Club.*"
— Peggy Webb, *USA Today* best-selling author

"Lee has crafted another pleasurable and diverting tale."
— *RT Book Reviews*

The Wedding Circle

"I have loved immersing myself in the charm of Cherico's small-town doings and feel as if all the characters are people I know well. What a happy read!"
— Gloria Loring, singer, actress, and author

A Cherry Cola Christmas

"*A Cherry Cola Christmas* is filled with the quirky, funny, and charming characters we've grown to love and whose poignant tales become the true blessings of Christmas. This book belongs under every tree this season."
— Christa Allan

Books by Ashton Lee

THE CHERRY COLA BOOK CLUB

THE READING CIRCLE

THE WEDDING CIRCLE

A CHERRY COLA CHRISTMAS

QUEEN OF THE COOKBOOKS

BOOK CLUB BABIES

Published by Kensington Publishing Corporation

Book Club Babies

ASHTON LEE

k

KENSINGTON BOOKS

www.kensingtonbooks.com

KENSINGTON BOOKS are published by

Kensington Publishing Corp.
119 West 40th Street
New York, NY 10018

Copyright © 2017 by Ashton Lee

All Kensington titles, imprints, and distributed lines are available at special quantity discounts for bulk purchases for sales promotion, premiums, fund-raising, educational, or institutional use.

Special book excerpts or customized printings can also be created to fit specific needs. For details, write or phone the office of the Kensington Sales Manager: Kensington Publishing Corp., 119 West 40th Street, New York, NY 10018. Attn. Sales Department. Phone: 1-800-221-2647.

Kensington and the K logo Reg. U.S. Pat. & TM Off.

eISBN-13: 978-1-4967-0581-5
eISBN-10: 1-4967-0581-5
First Kensington Electronic Edition: December 2017

ISBN-13: 978-1-4967-0580-8
ISBN-10: 1-4967-0580-7
First Kensington Trade Paperback Printing: December 2017

10 9 8 7 6 5 4 3 2 1

Printed in the United States of America

To my wonderful sweetheart and soul mate, Will

Acknowledgments

As in the past with all of my Cherry Cola Book Club novels, I must give credit to my team of New York professionals who guide my work from beginning to end: my agents, Christina Hogrebe and Meg Ruley, of the Jane Rotrosen Agency; and my editor, John Scognamiglio, at Kensington Books. I always take their advice and counsel to heart.

This time out, I am also indebted to Katherine Coleman Babin for her feedback on certain aspects of pregnancy and to Katherine (Kay) Banks for her historical anecdote on her high school experiences. Also, to my cousin Selah Ann Saterstrom for permission to use her name for my imaginary small press in Denver (and congratulations to her on her marriage to HR!). And always to my librarian friends around the country who support me. Of course, I do advise them to be on guard around me, as what they say could always end up in one of my novels—but never without their permission.

1

"We" Are Pregnant

How perfect was it that Maura Beth McShay had at her fingertips the complete resources of her brand-new library on the shores of Lake Cherico once her pregnancy was under way? She only had to go to work and sit in her director's office in her comfortable leather chair every day to look out over the sunlit water and read up on every conceivable aspect of "being with child." The oppressive Mississippi summer had finally given way to the inevitable tilt of the planet, bringing with it chilly nights and clear-blue days that looked like paintings, and the library's deck jutting out over the water was tailor-made for taking it all in. More than once throughout her busy workday, Maura Beth would venture out for a breather, inhaling the cooler air, sensing nature getting ready to retreat, folding in upon itself until the renewal of spring; even as she was in the gradual process of percolating new life within.

Of course, Maura Beth had her solicitous, grandfatherly obstetrician in Memphis, Dr. Joel Lively, for her prenatal foundation: what to eat, what not to eat, what supplements to take, how much rest to get, what activities to avoid, how to deal with morning sickness and all the outside-the-box cravings that inevitably would appear. He was a soft-spoken, tremendously reassuring man with a bedside manner few could equal, able to squash her doubts and insecurities with a couple of concise sentences and a thoughtful stroking of his gray mustache.

"You are textbook right now," he had told her during her last visit. "Your sonogram is picture-perfect."

Even more reassuring was the fact that the pregnancy collection in the new Charles Durden Sparks, Crumpton, and Duddney Public Library was now state-of-the-art, thanks to the monumental weeding project that Maura Beth had undertaken before moving into the new building. It was a labor of tough love she thought would never end—there were some ancient pub dates gathering dust on the shelves that made her practically shriek—but end it finally did.

One of the most amusing snippets Maura Beth had been able to glean from her new collection was a paragraph from something titled *Pregnancy for Laughs*. Imagine that. Someone writing a book on the hilarity of it all. A woman who had been put through her paces had somehow managed to look back upon it all fondly and find her audience by putting pen to paper.

"Just as women supposedly have their penis envy," Mandy Perkins, the author, had pontificated, "so do men perhaps secretly have their envy of bringing new life into the world. Not that they don't enjoy their spurt of masculine energy thoroughly. They always do, even when it doesn't lead to pregnancy. But that is hardly the same as building a baby, molecule by molecule, meal by meal. Both, in fact, ultimately contribute to reproduction, but in very different ways. Can the two genders ever really understand each other until they experience the physicality unique to each? As for myself, I realize that my husband is probably doing the best he can with *his* hormones and all that they demand of him. After all, women shave begrudgingly, while men make a macho ritual of it and even grow strange patterns on their faces deliberately to prove it."

At first, Maura Beth was ready to dismiss those glib musings as fluff invented for book sales, entertaining as they were. But then, as if on cue, a seismic shift began to appear in her relationship with her husband, Jeremy. It wasn't just that he intended to use her experience as the muse for the Great American Novel he had been struggling to write for some time now, or that his lone-wolf, feminist sister Elise had taken a sabbatical from her teaching at the University of Evansville to come South to live with their relatives out on the lake, Connie and Douglas McShay, while awaiting the birth of her baby. It wasn't even the uncomfortable feeling that Elise's mother and father in Brentwood, Tennessee, had not even been told about their daughter's life-altering decision so far. It was more that Jeremy himself began to mimic Maura Beth's pregnancy in every conceivable way. When she had cramps, he had cramps. When she had her first cravings, he had them, too—zipping out of their cottage on Painter Street to head to The Cherico Market for the flavor of the moment or other crazy, specific ingredients. And there were many as the later weeks of the first trimester tumbled by: Gummi Bears, red hots, snow cones, pistachio ice cream, wilted spinach with vinegar and boiled eggs, pieces of dark chocolate with whipped cream, Vienna sausages and crackers with mustard—and finally, fresh-squeezed lemonade. Not store-bought, mind you—it had to be made from scratch out of lemons Maura Beth could hold in her hand and then roll back and forth on the butcher block to produce the most juice. No reason to justify that at all—it just had to be done that way.

For the record, Maura Beth was certainly appreciative of Jeremy's willingness to wait on her hand and foot, but her hormones also seemed to be producing a territorial effect regarding her pregnancy as she began to gain the first hint of weight. They seemed to be whispering in her ear all the time: "Now you know good and well that he is not the one who is actually pregnant, don't you? You can't let him think he really understands what you're going through, can you? Stand your ground, girl, and put him in his place. That's your birthright, pun intended."

Which led to their first showdown toward the tail end of the first trimester. It took place in their bright yellow kitchen with the potted palms, and Maura Beth had just finished squeezing the life out of half a dozen lemons at the counter, noisily stirring and mixing up a batch of her lemonade with the biggest spoon she could find in the silverware drawer. After taking a big swig of her precious concoction, she put down her glass, looked Jeremy straight in the eye, and unloaded.

"There's something I've been meaning to discuss with you, sweetheart," she began, her voice soft and syrupy at the start. But it rose a decibel level and became a shade snarky soon enough. "You have just got to stop this. I don't even think you know you're doing it, but I want you to stop. There, I've said it. Stop."

Jeremy's handsome but skeptical face went all full of creases, his eyes approaching a squint. It was the typical "high school English teacher" face he used when one of his less-motivated students answered some question with jaw-dropping, D- or even F-inducing ineptitude. "You want me to stop what?"

She took another swallow of lemonade and drew back slightly with an imperious pose. "Oh, don't play so innocent with me, Jeremy McShay. You know good and well what you're doing."

Jeremy managed a smile in spite of it all. "Wait . . . what? You just said I don't know what I'm doing. Now you say I do. What are you talking about? You are definitely playing fast and loose with the English language. I should know."

Maura Beth paused to review the situation and a grin

broke out. There were times these days when she was certain she had lost control of her facial muscles. "Oh, so I did. Well, that's not important now. What I wanted to say was that you've got to stop pretending you know what I'm going through and mimicking me all the time. Because you don't, you know."

Jeremy appeared to understand immediately, nodding with a smile. "You think I'm pretending? You think I'm making it all up? You think I don't have these twinges and pains at the same time you do? I guess you know you weren't supposed to have all these cravings so soon, according to Dr. Lively. That was supposed to come later, if I recall. And yet here they are, big as life."

"I appreciate all the reading you've done and the effort you've been making, but it's unnecessary. No two pregnancies are alike, you know."

Jeremy nodded and took a deep breath. His attitude at the moment was truly good-natured and patient. "But it's not an effort. I'm not faking it. I've read up on everything at the library, and I think I'm on solid ground. Some husbands do take their wives' pregnancies to heart. Their empathy is real and physiological. I think that's a very good thing considering that some men can't be bothered and are even worse contributors once the baby arrives. They live in another century, and they wouldn't go within ten miles of a diaper change."

Maura Beth reflected thoughtfully, drumming her fingers on the kitchen table. She couldn't very well fault him for using her new, state-of-the-art library on the shores of Lake Cherico, as she continually thought of it when she was daydreaming at her desk. After all, with considerable effort she had fought for and won it from the lucrative City Hall coffers, long hidden from public scrutiny by the scheming Councilman Durden Sparks. Three months earlier, the library that bore his name and those of the other major benefactors—Mamie and Marydell Crumpton, along with Nora Duddney—had opened on the Fourth of July to a boisterous and colorful fireworks celebration, a country music concert by Waddell Mack, a bevy of food booths that would crown the Queen of the Cookbooks, and day-long guided tours of Cherico's sparkling new facility. That Jeremy had become one of her best patrons since the opening was a feather in her cap. He had taken advantage of everything except the children's story hour, although that certainly loomed large in his future. In fact, he had told her how much he was looking forward to the day when he could take his child to hear one of Miriam Goodcastle's creative sessions. How could she be mad at him for that?

But she also thought he had gone a bit overboard of late. That first round of morning sickness, for example, even if it had come earlier than expected. After she had lost her breakfast that morning, she had stood in the bathroom doorway and confronted him firmly. "Don't you dare go in there and stick your finger down your throat to show your solidarity."

"I wasn't going to do anything of the sort," he had told her, somewhat taken aback by her ferocity. "I was just going to see if anything needed to be tidied up. Just call me Mr. Clean."

"I've already taken care of that."

"I could have done it for you."

"Thanks," she had told him, "but I'm pregnant—not helpless. I still know where to find the bleach and the paper towels. I've always been the type of person who cleaned up her own messes."

Jeremy took his time, not wishing to make things worse. He was totally willing to bite his tongue at every turn, if that's what it took. "There's this article I read online a few weeks ago, and I thought it made a great deal of sense. I mean, this is new territory for me, too."

Maura Beth cocked her head smartly and folded her arms expectantly. She was both genuinely interested and hoping to trip him up. Wasn't that a caution? Or was that just the nature of her condition? "Yes?"

"No, really. It was meant to be funny, but it made sense."

"I'm waiting."

"It was called 'How to Be a Pregnant Man,' and it listed all the things a husband could do to be more supportive of his wife during the entire nine months. Even up to the moment she went into labor."

Maura Beth screwed up her lips, having her response at the ready. "Was this written by a man?"

"Yes."

"Was he a doctor?"

"I can't recall, but I don't think so. I think he was just a father."

"Was he also a stand-up comedian?"

Jeremy smirked but said nothing. He had read from more than one source that learning to listen carefully was an enormous part of tending to a pregnant woman. She needed to be taken seriously at all times.

"Go on, then. Tell me some of the supportive things that were listed. This should be good."

Jeremy's eyes shifted from side to side, searching for accuracy and hoping for the best. "Well, one that really stood out was never to take any pain felt by a pregnant woman lightly. It said something like, 'For God's sake, never shrug or complain that no one could possibly have that many twinges or stabs or things like that in one morning or afternoon.' It also said that once the baby kicks, the man had an obligation to kneel before the domestic altar and treat his wife prayerfully. Now those were the exact words. I didn't even think it was over the top."

"Really now? A man wrote that?"

"Yes."

Maura Beth had to admit she was pleased and showed it with a bright smile as she patted her hair smugly. "I like the idea of you worshiping me. I've always thought men should worship women, and they don't even have to be pregnant for that to happen. Go on. Tell me some more."

"It said something to the effect that any thoughtful husband should rush out at any time of day or night and fetch whatever it was his wife was craving. And it even suggested he could indulge with her to show he didn't think she was off her rocker. And I've done just that. I'm off to The Cherico Market at the drop of a hat. You know how I hate Vienna sausages. Nasty little fingers swimming in a sea of sodium. But eating pistachio ice cream out of the gallon with two spoons was a dream come true. That was like a children's birthday party gone wild."

Maura Beth's giggle was lengthy and a bit on the strange side, as if it were coming from some sort of windup children's toy. "Yes, we did finish off the entire thing, didn't we?"

"Not only that, but I've gained a little weight, too. Three pounds, to be exact. The article said not to go overboard, but if a husband put on a pound or two, the wife wouldn't feel so defensive about ballooning up. That it was important to make her feel beautiful all the way to the end."

"Even while she's screaming?"

"I don't know about that. We haven't gotten there yet. I'm not sure screaming is ever a beautiful thing to behold. But I certainly wouldn't tell you to be quiet, if that means anything. But you know I'll be there with you in the delivery room, and if the doctor tells you to push, then I'll tell you to push, too. Whatever it takes."

All Maura Beth could manage was, "Hmmm." It was impossible to tell what was actually behind that short utterance, so Jeremy proceeded with caution—something the article had also emphasized.

"Was that a note of approval, Maurie?"

"I don't know yet. I haven't really ballooned up that much. I sort of hate that word. But I certainly know it's coming. My mother showed me a picture of herself when she was nine months along with me. She reminded me of one of those old Volkswagen buses from the sixties with peace signs scrawled all over them."

Jeremy laughed and made the peace sign with his fingers. "Funny."

Maura Beth gestured quickly. "I know. She was out to *here*. But she also told me that I was worth all her body went through. I mean, I came out with fuzzy red hair and later there were my freckles, and neither of my parents knew where on earth I came from, but they finally realized that I was who I was and that I was never going to change just to please them. But that's my real problem these days. I can't seem to stop getting way ahead of myself."

Jeremy decided it was time for a hug, so he rose from his chair, leaned down, and did just that, giving the gesture everything he had. "There ya go," he told her, drawing back with a smile. "That's all you need to know."

Maura Beth thought for a while. She needed to believe in at least a smidgen of simplicity in her life at a time when everything was becoming more and more complicated. Despite the heated conversation they were having, Jeremy's touch had been reassuring and grounded her somewhat.

"That's a good point. My mother and I were pretty much at each other's throats until just before you and I said our marriage vows on your aunt Connie's fishing lodge deck. If we have a daughter, I hope it doesn't take us that long to resolve the mother-daughter thing. So much time and energy are wasted, and there's no reason on earth it has to be that way."

Which brought them to another juncture again. They had gone back and forth about whether to pursue the gender reveal. At the moment, they were in we-don't-want-to-know mode, but they weren't firmly committed. Dr. Lively had offered to let them know at any time. All they had to do was ask.

"What if it's a boy?" Jeremy said, resuming his seat as he raced ahead. "How does that go down?"

"I would hope it doesn't take you forever to become best pals with him," she answered. "And that means throwing baseballs and footballs with him if it turns out he doesn't want to become an English teacher and has any sort of athletic ability. I know how much you hate football because the headmaster in Nashville would never let you take a bus to Oxford or some other literary shrine, while the football team traveled all over the place for road games. Money was no consideration for that. But you at least have to consider the possibility that a son of ours may not be interested in the same things you are. I've always cottoned to the idea that whoever it is will ultimately have come through us, not from us. Very Kahlil Gibran of me, I realize, but I know you understand and agree with the philosophy."

"Yeah, I do. *Que sera, sera.* So do we want to revisit the advance notice thing about the gender? We could get it next time you go in. But I've decided to let you be the one to ask. I'm okay with not knowing until whoever pops out."

Maura Beth managed to laugh, but she didn't really feel like laughing. "You make me sound like I'm a jack-in-the-box."

Jeremy laughed, too. He had learned to adapt to her mood swings quickly. Then he snapped his fingers. "That could be the new title—*Jack-in-the-Box.*"

"The new title of what?"

"The novel I've been writing, of course. I've decided just now that I don't like the old title anymore."

Maura Beth stopped short of rolling her eyes. "*Buns in the Oven,* right? I didn't say anything when you came up with that a while back, but I thought it was on the corny side. Anyway, how much have you written now?"

He was counting with the sideways movement of his eyes, looking down at his hands as if he were holding the book that he hoped would eventually be published. "I'm up to twenty-six pages at the moment. It was thirty-four at one time, but I went through recently and edited the heck out of the manuscript. The whole thing feels like it's been written in my own blood, by the way."

She nodded without conviction. She had become deadened to his frequent literary progress reports. Yes, she recognized that he had a "baby on the way," too. But the path to eventual delivery was far less evident for him. He kept telling her that he had a novel inside simmering—that had been a frequent subject of discussion during their courtship—but his sudden decision to base it on her pregnancy and that of his sister, Elise, did not interest her too much anymore. It wasn't that she didn't want to be supportive of him. She wanted him to succeed, of course. It was more that he often seemed to be wandering in the desert where the right words were concerned. He hadn't actually called it writer's block, but he had come close.

"I'm think I'm having trouble making pregnancy sound appealing," he had told her at one point.

She had barely managed to disguise her frown. "Why are you taking that approach? It is what it is. I think you should concentrate on the reality of it all. Sometimes it's messy, and messy isn't very appealing."

"You mean graphic, don't you?"

"I suppose."

That particular conversation had ended in shrugs from both of them, though they both knew the topic of his novel was far from over. The end of the first trimester showdown, however, contained a resolution of sorts.

"I'll soft-pedal my depictions of you from here on out, if that's what you want," Jeremy said at last. "You'll be front and center without any competition the rest of the way, Maurie."

Maura Beth finished off her lemonade, puckering slightly. She hadn't put in enough sugar this time around, which was peculiar considering that her craving for anything sweet was growing exponentially. Really, now, did the baby require that much extra energy and vitamin C? "I didn't really mean to make such a big deal out of this, sweetheart," she answered. "I can't explain why I say or do anything anymore. Except that I'm pregnant."

Jeremy got up from his chair again and moved behind her, placing his hands gently on her shoulders. Then he leaned down and kissed her cheek softly. Still facing forward, she reached up with her right hand and placed it atop his. The quiet moment needed nothing further, no words needed to be spoken, even though Jeremy knew that he had not seen the last of such showdowns with the woman he loved who was carrying their child. After all, their showdown hadn't really been a quarrel. There was a playfulness, a give-and-take quality about it that was satisfying to both of them, and that meant their marriage was on solid footing.

Maura Beth had kept her "mirror" sessions from Jeremy so far. In fact, no one knew about them; and they would never know, unless she changed her mind. Sometimes, she came home from the library for her lunch hour and indulged them after she had consumed her calories according to the instructions cheerfully but carefully given by Dr. Lively. Originally, she had stepped before the full-length mirror in their bedroom to monitor her weight gain without her clothes on. She would effortlessly step out of whatever she was wearing to work that day and examine herself nude from every angle—front, side, and from the rear—with the aid of a strategically placed hand mirror. Perhaps she was being obsessive, but it was her body, and she wanted to monitor the experience in every way possible. It was the ultimate rite of passage, and she didn't intend to miss an ounce of it.

But it did not take long for her to use these secret sessions for something more. It had surprised her when the conjectures started bubbling up from somewhere inside. Did other women think such things about themselves and their future children? She wondered as the questions filled her brain, offering no easy answers.

If I have a son, will he be a male version of me?

If I have a daughter, will she be a female version of Jeremy?

Will I understand what I would have been like as a male?

Will Jeremy understand what he would have been like as a female?

What if it's not so clear? What if whoever it is, is a blend?

What if I have a daughter, and she is like me?

How do I deal with another me? Do I want another me in the world? Isn't one enough?

What if she is so different that I can't understand who she is, the way my mother couldn't understand who I was practically until I got married?

What if there is a health issue connected with our child?

Would I be strong enough to face it?

How would our lives be changed by such a stark reality?

What a crapshoot this game of genes was! It would take a long time to find out what was what, in any case. In the meantime there would be lots of hopes and dreams invested in and pinned on whoever came along. Vicariously? Or realistically? Was that even remotely fair to the child? Should parents ever live through their children? Many seemed to do so with mixed results.

Cara Lynn Mayhew, the ultimate, stylish New Orleans socialite, had wanted her only redheaded, freckle-faced, public librarian daughter to return to the Crescent City for the high-church wedding and sacred social club reception of the year. She was militant about it, calling long-distance at least twice a week and hoping to wear her daughter down. But Maura Beth had refused to give in to her mother's lobbying, insisting on remaining with her Cherry Cola Book Club friends in Cherico and having a much simpler ceremony on the deck of Connie and Douglas McShay's fishing lodge. It had come off beautifully with a memorable Lake Cherico sunset as their background and altar painted in the sky.

What if her own daughter turned out to be just such a rebel with a mind of her own? Would Maura Beth be wise enough to respect the differences between mother and daughter? Would she have learned from the lifelong conflict with her own mother? Or would she somehow turn into her mother after years of hit-and-miss parenting had changed her focus and made her forget the challenges of her own life?

These mirror sessions were close to being terrifying to Maura Beth, perhaps because she kept them to herself. Did she dare share such fears with Jeremy? Maybe that was the thing to do, particularly if she discovered that he was having similar doubts about himself and his ability to be a good father. It seemed reasonable that men would go through such phases, but she had no way of knowing without asking.

During her last mirror session—which reflected a weight gain of four pounds when she stood on the bathroom scales—something flashed into her head. Maybe she and Jeremy could indulge such sessions together. They would stand side by side—not necessarily naked, of course, although they certainly could for the sheer fun of it—but next to each other much as they had as bride and groom. They would then trot out their fears one by one and, by exposing them, render them completely powerless to drive them crazy.

Or maybe that was too structured and extreme. Couldn't they compare notes just as well over dinner or before going to bed or even taking a ride in the countryside in Jeremy's yellow Warbler?

Maybe she should just wait until later in the pregnancy. Perhaps Dr. Lively would reassure her about certain things, and her hormones would calm down. She chuckled out loud at that one, as if she were staring at her own distorted reflection in a fun-house mirror. She didn't believe for a second that her hormones would be calming down anytime soon. She knew they would get worse, and it would be harder on both Jeremy and herself as the baby grew, siphoning off more of her nutrients and changing her body even more drastically.

More to the point—and despite everyone's unfailing good wishes and her own native optimism—what had she gotten herself into?

2

Buyer's Remorse

Elise Marian McShay had been from the beginning as much of a challenge for her parents, Paul and Susan McShay of Brentwood, Tennessee, as Maura Beth had been to William and Cara Lynn Mayhew of New Orleans, Louisiana. Both little girls had refused to fit the mold of "conventional" females. With Maura Beth the first clue had been her freckles and red hair. Then the obsession with being a librarian had come later. But with Elise—Leesie as she was known to her brother, Jeremy—it had been more of a behavioral thing from the start.

At a somewhat tender age, Elise had firmly rejected dolls of any kind, though her mother kept trying to interest her for her birthdays and at Christmastime. Whether they were rag dolls or the more realistic type with carefully sewn hair, synthetic skin, and sweet, wide-eyed faces, Elise would toss them aside and say with a pouty expression, "I want what Jeremy got."

For years Jeremy was fascinated with model cars, both the kits and the finished products, which he would race on his bedroom floor while supplying the engine sounds for that boyhood version of realism. Not quite *varoom, varoom*—more like *rrrummmm, rrrummmm*. One Christmas, Santa Claus had even brought him his own "filling station," complete with service bays and miniature cars to place inside. Unbeknownst to him, his parents had stayed up all night assembling it, tossing back a few spiked eggnogs for courage to get the job done.

Finally, Paul and Susan had given in to their daughter's complaints, and Elise received her own fleet of model cars. Ironically, she lost interest in them shortly thereafter and began coveting Jeremy's new obsession—a bicycle. She had expressed no interest in getting one before, but once she realized the freedom it afforded her brother, she wanted one, too.

"I like how fast Jer can go," she had told her parents. "He goes as fast as the wind. He looks like he could ride forever. Why can't I have a bike? And I want a boy's bike just like Jeremy has. I don't want a girl's bike."

So they had given her a boy's bike, and she and Jeremy had ridden them together along the sidewalks of Brentwood and in the safer, quieter streets and cul-de-sacs of their well-heeled neighborhood. That had been Elise's most satisfying period growing up. During that time, she had a sense of equality with her brother because of the bike riding they had done in tandem. While they were in motion, there was no difference between them. Boy and girl had no meaning. They were just exalted creatures with their faces to the wind, and there was nothing they could not accomplish in life.

But inevitably, things had changed again. Jeremy became obsessed with the chemistry set his parents had given him the Christmas he turned twelve. He had seen some program on local television that featured a mad scientist as the main character, and he couldn't get it out of his head. Doctor Dry Ice, the wild-wigged, ghoulishly made-up actor had named himself, and Jeremy thought he was the coolest thing ever.

"I'm going to blow up some things with this," Jeremy had told his sister with a wicked gleam in his eye. "It's going to be fun. Wait and see."

Elise had witnessed his chemical mini-explosions enviously, wanting to create a little smoke and chaos of her own. So Paul and Susan had given their daughter her own set for her birthday; then brother and sister had given their all to seeing who could make the biggest mess out in the garage. That turned out to be a standoff. Both had been ordered by their mother to clean up everything in an equally annoyed tone of voice.

"You two are like twin tornadoes," Susan had told them while wagging a finger. "I don't know which one of you is worse. Why your father and I gave you those things is beyond me."

It had pleased Elise to hear that description of herself as equally damaging, but at some point it occurred to her that she was always trailing her brother, and she could definitely put her finger on the reasons. He always seemed to get the fun, "boy" things to play with. She got the impression that she was an afterthought. By the time she had graduated high school, her view of the world was that girls and women came second in everything. In ballroom dance class it was the boys who were allowed to ask the girls to be their partners. It was never the other way around. From that she gleaned that what boys and men wanted came first, and that girls and women were always trying to catch up with them and show that they were "just as worthy." They were the ones who had to wait to be chosen. Boys had to wait for nothing. They only had to ask. Girls had to speak up loudly to get what they wanted, and sometimes even that didn't work.

Later on, a stocky girl with thick glasses named Rita Carkeet from a small town in rural Kentucky had moved to Brentwood their sophomore year in high school, and Elise had been absolutely floored by something Rita had confided to her at the lunch table one day.

"There aren't any strict rules here in Brentwood," Rita said between bites of her peanut butter and jelly sandwich.

Elise had perked up, putting down the ham and cheese on rye that her mother had packed for her. "What do you mean? The teachers hand out demerits right and left from what I've seen."

"No, I meant that you can go up any stairwell you want here. At Mansfield High back in Kentucky, there was a stairwell for the boys and a separate one for the girls, and they were strictly monitored. You could get detention for disobeying."

"You're kidding."

"Nope, and sometimes if you had a class at the bottom of the boys' stairs but you were on the second floor, you had to walk all the way across the second floor and go down the girls' stairs and then all the way across the first floor to get to it. The boys had to do the same thing."

Elise sat back, shaking her head in amazement. "But why?"

Rita shrugged. "I don't know. I guess to keep us apart for a short time."

"But didn't you have coed classes?"

"Yep, we did."

"What nonsense! I don't see the point."

"That's why I like the fact that you can walk up and down any stairs you want here," Rita concluded. "Brentwood is cool."

Thus was born the militant feminist and Professor of Women Studies at the University of Evansville that Elise had studied to become. Who had never tired of confronting her extended family with criticism of their conventional choices—particularly their marriages with children—wherever she turned. Husbands and wives raising the nuclear family were

considered the ideal by everyone. But there were other ways
to live life, she had told them all at family gatherings, and they
had not appreciated hearing that. They had smiled and nodded politely, but it was quite evident that they had resented
Elise's radical posturing.

Then came the epic confrontation with her mother, Susan, one summer when Elise had uncharacteristically visited
from Evansville. The two of them were having spinach salads
and garlic toast at a fashionable restaurant in the Cool Springs
Galleria, where Susan ran her "empty-nest" crafts boutique.
Anyone observing the two of them from a nearby table could
not have failed to notice the contrast.

Where Susan was impeccably coiffed, dressed, made-up,
and accessorized, all of which flattered her still-attractive,
middle-aged face and figure, Elise was strictly unadorned in
jeans, her long blond hair parted down the middle in retro,
hippie fashion, and her features fresh-scrubbed and simple
with no trace of cosmetic enhancement. They were from two
different eras, both in appearance and in thinking.

It was Susan who unleashed the fury from somewhere
deep within her daughter's psyche by saying absolutely the
wrong thing at the wrong time between bites of spinach
leaves and feta cheese.

"Will you be totally honest with me, darling?" Susan began. "I think we're both mature enough to appreciate the
truth now. Are you . . . well, is all this interest in Women's
Studies because you are . . . well, I'll just come out and say
it. Are you gay? Is that why you never bring home any men
to meet us? I know you had your crushes on certain boys in
high school, but nothing ever seemed to come of it. We had
to force you to go to the prom with that nice Ellis boy. Could
you just level with your mother for once?"

Elise had dropped her fork noisily into her salad bowl and

sat there staring at her mother for an uncomfortable minute or so. Then she delivered what she considered to be the speech of the ages.

"As a matter of fact, Mom, I'm not gay. But what if I were? So, you think my lifelong devotion to women's issues is because I am sexually attracted to other women? That's what you've been thinking all this time? Do you not understand anything about what I've been trying to accomplish? My mission at the university is to help women understand that they don't have to take a backseat to men and what men want. They have a right to their own lives apart from men. And so what if some women are attracted to other women? I get the impression that you would be horrified if that turned out to be the case with me, your own daughter. Oh my, how would you explain it to all your friends in Brentwood? What a social mess that would be, wouldn't it? Well, don't worry. You'll never have to do that. I'm not sexually attracted to women, but I don't need a man in my life to make it complete, either. I really thought you understood that after all this time, but apparently I was mistaken."

Susan had gathered herself as best she could, taking a sip of her Chardonnay for good measure and managing a polite smile. "I certainly didn't mean to offend you, sweetheart. And, no, if it turned out that you were interested in women that way, I would accept it. Your father and I have known for a long time that you were your own woman. Give us a little credit. You do remember the party we gave you when you nailed down your teaching position at the university, don't you? We were very proud of you. But you just don't talk to us very much about anything anymore. You leave us guessing about everything important in your life."

Elise had allowed herself to calm down a bit. The big payoff was that it felt good getting all those words off her chest.

"Okay, maybe I overreacted a little going on and on like I did. I just want you to understand that I have no intention of ever giving up my mission in life."

"No, I would never ask you to do that. I just wanted you to level with me, that's all. There are some things a mother needs to know as the years go by. I don't think I was out of line to put any misconceptions to bed."

Mother and daughter had left it at that, calling an uneasy truce.

Yet after she had entered her thirties, and somewhat surprisingly, Elise found her priorities shifting somewhat. Teaching young women how to think and redefining what it meant to be female was immensely gratifying, to be sure. But they were young women who entered her life briefly, exiting upon graduation as they learned how to invent themselves and venture forth on their own. What if her influence could extend beyond the period of matriculation? What if, despite her protestations about marriage and children, she boldly undertook at least part of that proposition? A child of her own might afford her that opportunity. If she had a daughter, she could bring her up to be the perfect, dynamic, well-adjusted female in the twentieth-first century; and if she had a son, he could become the ideal man, respectful of women and treating them as equals. Both would be major accomplishments in this day and age.

Beyond that, however, there was the issue of loneliness. Some people could handle it, whereas others could not bear it. Elise had examined her heart and emerged with the idea that she neither required nor feared it. Under those circumstances, bringing a child into the world seemed not only reasonable but also inviting. She felt she was on solid ground and had given herself the go-ahead for her pregnancy.

So she decided that a part of herself would continue. She wanted her genes to enter the mix and continue to do laps in the pool. As for the origin of the other half of the person she would bring into the universe, did she really need the man behind the genes hanging around in her life? Clinging fast to her proclivities, she decided that all that was necessary was the fertilizing, not the patronizing a man might bring to the equation. To be sure, she was willing to concede that there might be a diamond in the rough out there, but she also was convinced that there were more than enough hard black lumps of coal for the taking, and that was hardly worth the risk.

So it was that she opted for the emotionless convenience of a sperm bank in Evansville, and now, like her sister-in-law in Cherico, she had a baby on the way and a lifelong adventure before her. She firmly believed that a woman could indeed have it all—a career and a family on her own terms. Why was that so difficult for some people to understand? She did not have to settle for the conventional and the socially acceptable to be happy.

And then, once she had settled into the upstairs guest room with the unparalleled view of the lake and the four-poster bed that her aunt Connie and uncle Doug had graciously provided her until the baby was born, the reality of being pregnant began to invade every cell of her being. It was chemical, hormonal, and emotional, but in any case, it wasn't what she thought it was going to be—at least not so far.

But she did not panic. Surely, her sister-in-law, Maura Beth, was experiencing the same thing. Didn't all women have these kinds of doubts? It was time to compare notes and get some reassurance. Yes, that would do the trick. They were both mothers in the making, and they would start commiserating with each other in earnest.

"Don't you two stay out here too much longer," Connie McShay said to her two favorite pregnant young women. "It's getting chilly, and we have that nice, warm fire waiting for you inside." In fact, a late-October killing frost had set the tone for comfort inside the lodge's sprawling, high-ceilinged great room, and Douglas had done his manly, husbandly thing and put in a generous supply of wood as a result.

"We won't," Maura Beth answered. "But you know how it is. We're thick as thieves these days."

They had all just finished up one of Connie's delicious dinners consisting of bell peppers stuffed with wild rice, baked squash casserole, and—with a nod to autumn—homemade pumpkin pie for dessert. Jeremy and his uncle Doug had retreated to comfortable chairs in front of the Tennessee sandstone fireplace to talk about the woeful world situation and lesser matters, while Maura Beth and Elise had insisted on venturing out onto the deck for a breath of the crisp air. At the moment they were leaning against the railing, enjoying the lights of the fishing camps on the other side of Lake Cherico—little jewels dancing on the surface of the dark water, they were.

"Yes," Connie told both of them as she stood in the deck doorway. "I imagine you two have some notes to compare as usual."

"That's exactly what we're doing to do, Aunt Connie," Elise said, turning around for a moment. "In fact, we can't wait."

"I wish I had had a gal pal to go through my pregnancy with my Lindy," Connie continued. "But I'm glad you two have each other. Enjoy."

After Connie had left, it was Elise who was the first to address her concerns. "I think I'm losing track of the person I used to be. Are you experiencing the same thing, by any chance?"

Maura Beth looked down at her belly. She was wearing her very first maternity outfit—a floral sheath—even though she still wasn't showing as much as Elise was. But she couldn't wait to show herself off to the world, despite still standing before the mirror and trying to figure everything out all at once. What a confounding but exhilarating experience this was turning out to be, nothing quite like she had imagined. If Jeremy couldn't write a book about it, maybe she could. Now that was a thought, but it seemed a bit bogus when she reflected just a little. Taking Jeremy's "pregnancy" away from him might be more than problematic at this point.

"What do you mean by losing, Elise? I think you're still very much you. You're still the same liberated woman who refused the bouquet at my wedding when she caught it by accident."

"But that's just surface stuff. What I mean is, I don't feel the same way I used to about important things."

"You mean politically?"

Elise looked up at the night sky, as if searching for inspiration. "Not exactly. I mean I don't seem to get worked up about issues the way I used to. The outrageous things certain politicians do would drive me up the wall, and I would go on and on about them during my lectures in class. My students loved my passion and fed off of it. Now, all I seem to do is lie around and eat things. I feel like Mae West in that movie where she says, 'Beulah, peel me a grape.' Almost the same way, I ask Aunt Connie to fix me the most outlandish concoctions in the kitchen, and she's such a sweetheart about it. She never complains, no matter what I order up. She brings them up the stairs to me on a tray. She won't even let me come down and eat at the table, although I tell her the exercise is good for me. But she won't hear of it. Can you imagine? At least I convinced them to let me pay them for room and board. They were going to let me stay for free, you know. Now that wasn't going to fly with someone who firmly believes women should always pay their own way."

Now it was Maura Beth's turn to laugh. "Hey, you're family. What did you expect? You're going to be treated like royalty because you're pregnant. Did you imagine you were in training for a marathon? Lean isn't going to cut it. You're going to go a few sizes up when all is said and done, and Connie is delighted to help you get there. She went a few sizes up years ago, as she's always happy to confess."

There was more subdued laughter between the two, more sisterly than anything else. "I understand that, but I have to level with you. I seem to have jumped ahead about three or four years in my mind to the time when I can interact with my child and teach her—or him—about the world. I want to get this gestation part over with quickly, but it's not going so fast. Or at least not fast enough for me."

Maura Beth drew back slightly, barely avoiding a confounding smirk. "It is what it is, Elise. It's not like having a cocktail or a big dinner that's out of your system in a matter of hours or overnight at the most. Didn't you consider that before you got pregnant? That's pretty much what happens when sperm and egg meet. They don't say good-bye to each other at the door and stop dating, you know."

Elise laughed at the image, but afterward, her sigh was quite prolonged. "But I just want to get to the important part—the part that really matters, which is when I get to see who it is I've brought into the world. Aren't you even the least bit curious about that, too?"

"Of course I am. Who wouldn't be? But I'm willing to be patient. It seems to me the part before we get to that is pretty important, too. I know that holding and touching and talking to your baby grounds the child from the very beginning. Maybe the early parts are a bit messy with the spitting up and the diaper changing and all that, but we have to go through them. Dr. Lively will be there to guide us, no matter what, and Jeremy has promised to do his fair share of it all."

Elise gave her sister-in-law an exasperated look. "You mean to tell me you haven't experienced any doubts at all about being pregnant and what the future holds? There are people out there who think that being pregnant automatically means you're happy. A blessed event, they call it. Maybe that's true in some cases, but it can't be universally true."

Maura Beth wasn't quite sure she wanted to go there but relented in the end. "Well, to be totally honest with you, I have had some doubts about all of this. I conduct these long sessions with myself before my full-length mirror in the bedroom. And no, I'm not being narcissistic. Jeremy doesn't know about them, and I'm not sure I'll ever tell him. He might think I've gone off the deep end. How will it all turn out? I ask myself over and over."

"Then you do understand what I'm talking about. I'm so relieved. For someone who's always been so self-assured, I find myself uncharacteristically uncertain. That's so unprofessorial of me."

Maura Beth reached out and took Elise's hand. "You know it's probably the hormones, don't you?"

Elise nodded, but there was reluctance in the gesture. "I guess. But I find myself waking up in the morning and thinking that it might be nice if men could get pregnant, too. Then they might understand women better. Do you think I'm being vengeful and unreasonable?"

Maura Beth squeezed Elise's hand emphatically for a second, as if the bond between them had just been cemented forever. "Not at all. I'll level with you and tell you that I've had to take Jeremy to task about mimicking all of my symptoms. Sometimes he wants to be a part of the pregnancy too much, but deep down, I really like him being so solicitous. He really means well, and I wouldn't like it the other way around where he thinks everything is up to me until the end." She paused, averting her eyes. "I hope you don't mind my asking, and I'm certainly not trying to start anything, but do you . . . well, do you miss not having a husband to share it all with?"

Elise offered up surprising but carefree laughter. It seemed to last much longer than it needed to, and Maura Beth wondered if she had struck some sort of nerve. "But you're wrong about that. I have Vittorio."

"Who is Vittorio?"

"My sperm bank donor."

Maura Beth's puzzlement produced a studied frown. "But you told me before that your donor was anonymous. Did you find out who he was somehow? Have you been snooping around, doing detective work like some of these people do when they find out they're adopted?"

"No, nothing like that. The donors are anonymous, but you're allowed to determine things like ethnicity, any health issues, and even whether they're college-educated before you choose their swimmers. Did I not mention that mine turned out to be Italian American with a degree? I could have had a Scandinavian if I'd wanted, of course. But I'm already blond. I decided to go in a different direction and try for a little different look in the genetic crapshoot."

Maura Beth shook her head, fascinated but saying nothing.

"Well, anyway, I decided to name him Vittorio. Very international, don't you think? It just seemed to fit. And I have to say that Vittorio does not meddle at all, especially when I have one of my frequent mood swings. He's gotten very good at staying out of my way, and that's just fine with me. I don't think a real husband would be anywhere near as cooperative at that as he is."

Maura Beth was grateful for the whimsy and the humor and decided to forge ahead. "Then you don't have buyer's remorse about this after all? Since you've come this far, this is one you don't want to take back."

Elise's tone was resolute. "It's funny. The phrase 'buyer's remorse' has occurred to me now and then. But I took the one-year sabbatical from teaching to do this, and I'm not one to take things lightly. I don't back out once I've committed, as you well know. Maybe I've been overthinking this too much."

Maura Beth was silent for a while, finally emerging from her thoughts with a fist pump. "I've just had another of my brilliant ideas. What Cherico needs is a support group for pregnant women like ourselves. And guess where it's going to meet?"

"The library, of course."

"Right. In our new mini-auditorium where we crowned the Queen of the Cookbooks this past summer. There's more than enough room there, and we have the stage with the audio equipment and everything. Of course, I designed everything way better than I knew. I gave our architect all the input, and he came through beautifully."

Elise's excitement clearly registered in her voice. "I think that's a terrific idea. I always encourage my students to support one another outside of class and get involved with other women in the various relevant organizations on campus. I tell them to always be expecting great things from their lives and to act upon that impulse. Run with it right away."

This time, Maura Beth snapped her fingers, looking and sounding supremely confident. "That's it!"

"What's it?"

"That will be the name of our support group—Expecting Great Things. We'll invite anyone who is pregnant or has been pregnant to come and share their insights and concerns. We can have visits from doctors and nurses and other health-care professionals, too, and it'll be fun organizing the whole thing. It'll be like a mini Cherry Cola Book Club. Of course,

I can see Jeremy pitching right in and doing more than his fair share. He wants to help out in the worst way, and this will give him an outlet, too. Otherwise, I think he'll end up driving me crazy."

Elise laughed and patted Maura Beth on the shoulder. "I don't have to worry about Vittorio, though. I picture him as busy right now on a model shoot in Rome for one of those cologne ads. He's probably posing on a motorcycle with a beautiful woman holding on to him for dear life as his passenger. Then later, he'll probably take her back to his apartment and have sex with her."

Maura Beth couldn't resist. "For someone who claims she doesn't need a man in her life, you certainly do spend a lot of time fantasizing about it. Or am I reading you wrong?"

"In this case, fantasy is so much better than reality. There's no harm in it. So, when do you want to get started on this?"

"Right away. Tomorrow I'll set the wheels in motion. You can come to my office, and we'll spend the day brainstorming. It'll be so much fun, and we'll turn all our doubts into something constructive. And I'll go to my Cherry Cola Book Club for my first recruits. Becca Brachle just gave birth not long ago—nine months to be exact—and her little Markie is my godson. I'm sure she'd be willing to share her experiences with us. I know Aunt Connie would pitch in about being pregnant with her Lindy, too. This is going to be fun, even if we have to play it by ear at first."

As if on cue, Connie stuck her head out the deck door, smiling in that pleasant, matronly way of hers. "Now you two have been out here long enough, and the wind is picking up off the lake. I don't want either of you catching a chill. Which reminds me, have either of you gotten your flu shots yet?"

"Ah, the voice of reason. That's your nurse's training kicking in, isn't it, Aunt Connie?" Elise said.

"Guilty. Once a nurse, always a nurse," came the good-natured reply. "Particularly in the ICU. Looking after people is my thing, but I'm really enjoying tending to family this time around."

"You've done that beautifully for me so far," Elise said. "You wait on me hand and foot to the point I'm a bit embarrassed by it all. Come on, Maura Beth. She's right. It is getting right nippy, and we've done good work out here tonight."

"Yes," Maura Beth added as they headed in with a snap to their step. "We have some exciting news to share with you, Connie. Let's join the men by the fire and see what everyone thinks about my latest brainstorm."

3

Beginnings

A few weeks later, the first meeting of Expecting Great Things was well under way in the library's mini-auditorium with a crowd of sixteen or so in attendance, and Maura Beth was congratulating herself mentally once again as she sat back in her seat on the front row. If there was one thing she knew how to do, it was to get the word out about her favorite project of the moment. In a supremely successful effort, she had managed to entice many of The Cherry Cola Book Club core members to attend—both female and male, as it happened— to share their most amusing experiences regarding the hallowed state of pregnancy.

These were to be all about beginnings and the hopes and dreams that accompanied them. Everyone was to keep it lighthearted as the perfect way to ease into becoming an effective support group. Weightier issues would be dealt with later on, including informational visits from healthcare professionals. For now, there were to be no graphic horror stories about lengthy, difficult deliveries, or, God forbid—tragedies such as miscarriages. Those dark episodes might be an unfortunate reality for a few, but they weren't particularly helpful or inspiring. Nice and easy was going to get the job done. The idea was to make the monthly gatherings of Expecting Great Things as welcoming as the potluck reviews of The Cherry Cola Book Club itself, even if some of those had gone astray here and there over the past couple of years.

At the moment, Connie McShay was holding forth at the podium, getting into the gist of her most amusing experience, her good-natured energy clearly evident.

"There was this family-owned market that I went to in Nashville for our groceries," she was saying. "It was called Betty and Bob's, and they had all these homemade deli items that Douglas and I really enjoyed, like German potato salad and overstuffed corned beef sandwiches with Dijon mustard. The Kuhns were a wonderful German couple. I don't mean they were recent immigrants, though—they just specialized in that kind of food. Betty and I particularly became good friends, and I loved the way she pitched in with everything, even performing cashier duties from time to time when someone was out sick. It was that kind of 'backbone of the country' place. I think what really made us click was our figures. We both were and still are somewhat Rubenesque, if you will. And not a bit ashamed of it, either. I've always taken comfort in the knowledge that women with our curves were once much in demand as models. I find myself thinking all the time what fun it would have been to have been born in that century and been captured for posterity on canvas as a museum piece."

Connie briefly stepped from behind the podium and modeled the loose-fitting, brightly colored garment she was wearing, turning this way and that to show off her pleasingly plump bulges to good advantage. "It seems I've always been watching my waistline and hips, but I can also tell you that Douglas has always liked me this way. Never any complaints from the mister. Even though I have to admit I envy him his manly metabolism. I don't think he's gained an ounce she we got married thirty-eight years ago. Plus, he gets to show off his graying temples while I'm a slave to my color touch-ups at the salon." She paused to point to her husband sitting in the front row next to Maura Beth and Jeremy. "There he is, just as pretty and preening as big as you please."

"There's always been lots of you to love," Douglas said, waving at his wife affectionately and then blowing her a kiss. "I wouldn't have it any other way. And if you ever decided to go gray and give up your coloring, I would support you one hundred percent."

Connie resumed her spot behind the podium and cleared her throat while the group laughed politely and briefly whispered among themselves. "Thank you, sweetheart. You know I'd do the same for you if you ever went bald."

"Sixty-two and still not receding, though," Douglas said, pointing to his thick, dark hairline.

"At any rate," Connie continued, nodding diplomatically, "it seems that Betty and I were always zigging and zagging on the subject of pregnancy. We never did get it right. The first time the zigging happened, Betty was checking out my groceries, and all of a sudden she stops in the middle of ringing things up and says to me, 'When are you expecting, sweetie?' Of course, I realized immediately we were in an awkward 'oops' moment, but I decided to level with her. 'I'm not,' I told her, trying not to sound upset with her in any way. 'Douglas and I are trying—but nothing yet,' I went on. I had, of course, put on some extra weight. So what else was new? Then, Betty went all pink in the face and was at a total loss for words hemming and hawing the way she did, so I put her at ease. 'I promise you'll be the first of my friends to know when it does happens,' I told her.

"Then I zagged with her because I knew she and Bob were trying, too. That was just one of those things that came out as we shared confidences over time. Just idle conversations at the checkout counter, but you do learn a few things if you take the time to listen. 'Ooh,' I said to her later on, 'is it my imagination, or do you have some good news to share with me?' 'Nope,' she said. 'I've just gained ten pounds over the holidays. Too much eggnog and my mother-in-law's wicked rum fruitcake and such.' We were always guessing wrong, and it got to be a thing with us. Finally, I thought of a way we could both stay out of trouble. 'Have you lost weight?' would be our standard greeting until the real announcement came along for either of us. We'd laugh and laugh about that all the time, but I got there first, giving birth to our Lindy."

"Our daughter was worth waiting for, too," Douglas added quickly. "And Lindy's given us our only grandchild, Melissa."

"Lindy takes after her father. Tall and slim and can eat anything she wants. Isn't that always how it goes?"

Then Connie turned her attention to Maura Beth and Elise, nodding in their general direction. "As for those of you who don't know how it will all turn out yet, just be patient and enjoy the journey. I don't have to tell you that your lives will never be the same, but you have no idea what that will mean to you until whoever it is arrives and takes that first breath out of water. You'll both gasp at the sight of each other, and that's the teary-eyed game changer that will never leave you."

Everyone was a bit surprised when both Justin "Stout Fella" and Becca Brachle took the stage together next. They had all assumed that Becca would be the one talking about her Markie, who was a couple of months away from his first birthday now, and it was she who did speak first.

"First of all, I'd like to say that I can fully appreciate Connie's anecdote, but every pregnancy is different," she began, pointing to her friend and fellow Cherry Cola Book Club member. "I didn't gain all that much weight with Markie, but then I've always had trouble keeping weight on. I call it The Eternal Cheerleader Syndrome. It's Stout Fella standing here beside me that's fought the battle of the bulge after his college quarterbacking duties were over and done with. Of course, I didn't help him all those years *The Becca Broccoli Show* was on the radio. I filled him up with comfort food right and left, and he loved every one of the recipes I trotted out on my cooking show that all of you are still probably using."

The tall, big-boned Justin looked a bit sheepish at first but gathered himself. "She's telling y'all the truth. When you work out in the weight room and expend all that energy on the field, you don't have to worry about pushing away from the table. Actually, that training table really gives you a distorted view of things. You think you can eat that way forever. Then, I was a sucker for my wife's wonderful cooking. But selling real estate the way I do now all over Cherico is kinda sedentary compared to the demands of my playing career. So I can understand our good friend Connie McShay's struggle. I'll never know what it's like to be pregnant, but I'm here to tell you something you may not know. Especially you men. I want you to follow along closely."

Justin hesitated as he quickly surveyed his wife from head to toe. "This cute, little, blond wife of mine who got her figure back right away never looked more beautiful than when she was carrying our Markie. She didn't have much of that morning sickness, did you, baby?"

Becca shook her head and shrugged. "Nope, and I can't say why. I was told to expect it."

"What she did have was a major case of glowing, though," Justin continued. "Now I see all those puzzled looks out there, but I'll explain. I don't mean like something out of a science fiction movie or a rerun of *The Twilight Zone*. There were just lots of times when her face seemed to have this kinda inner glow to it. The way I figured, it was more that something wonderful was going on inside her, and she was showing it off to the world without even trying."

"That's so sweet of you to say, Justin. You're making me blush," Becca said, gingerly touching the tips of her fingers to her face as if testing it for color.

"But that's the thing. It wasn't like a blush, folks. It was definitely more a glow she had, particularly in the mornings. It got to where I couldn't wait to wake up so I could see it all over again."

"Sometimes he even woke me up early just to see it, folks," Becca added with a pleasant smile. "Even before the alarm went off. I don't see how I could have looked all that appetizing after having my sleep disturbed and a great dream possibly cut short. Cranky and glowing just don't seem to belong in the same sentence, but Justin still swears by it."

Maura Beth spoke up from her seat. "Did you ever ask your obstetrician about that glowing thing?"

"No, I didn't think to do that," Becca told her. "When Justin first told me about it, I immediately went to the bathroom mirror to figure out what he was talking about. But I didn't see what he was seeing no matter how long I stared or no matter how many different ways I turned. I even tried different levels of lighting. We have one of those knobs on the wall that controls that, you know. I looked like I was auditioning for a play or was on one of those model shoots. Finally, I just attributed it to a proud father being in love and left it at that."

Maura Beth turned to Jeremy during the outburst of "Awws!" that filled the room. "Have you experienced that with me?"

"The glowing thing?"

"Of course."

Jeremy thought for a moment, looking very unsure of

himself. "Not exactly, though I think you're the most beautiful thing in the world no matter what. But I do like to talk to the baby bump now that it's finally showing up. We're solidly in the second trimester now. It's really moving along."

"You should hear him sometime," Maura Beth said to the group. "I could swear he's going to launch into a reading of *A Tale of Two Cities* one of these days and then give the baby a homework assignment to boot."

"A little Dickens never hurt anyone."

Maura Beth shook her head, but there was an affectionate smile on her face. "English teachers! You have to be in love with one to really understand them."

"Same goes for librarians," Jeremy said. "They don't at all fit that old stereotype about spinsters wearing glasses with their hair pulled back severely in a bun. Not my redheaded Maurie with all her curls and that feisty spirit of hers."

"Well, for what it's worth, I talked to the bump, too," Justin added. "And I read this article while waiting for getting my teeth cleaned at the dentist's that said listening to music was also a good thing for the baby inside. I stopped short of singing to my son, though. I don't have any kind of voice to speak of, even though I try when I'm soapin' myself up in the shower."

"No, he can't really sing a note. Take my word for it," Becca said. "Plus, he really has a thing for country music like the kind that Waddell Mack sang at the Fourth of July concert a few months ago when the library opened. Now I ask you, can jangly, twangy notes be all that soothing for a fetus? Can 'she done him wrong' songs be the ticket for a future father-son relationship?"

"Hey, now, the kid's gotta find out about girls and women and broken hearts sometime."

The auditorium broke out in generous laughter. Then Justin said, "I just wanted to contribute something here tonight from the father's point of view. Some of us men are all in on raising a child. As far as I'm concerned, it's way better than selling every last house and plot of land in Cherico. Coming from me, that's sayin' a lot. After all, I had a heart attack not all that long ago worrying myself to death about my next big deal. It changed my priorities but good. It was a huge wakeup call, and I'm here to say that my next big deal is our son, Markie, and that's that."

Maura Beth and Elise decided to step up together next since they had been spending so much time sharing their experiences. They had even begun to think of themselves as a couple of sorts.

"We're almost like sisters these days," Maura Beth said, taking the mike first. "You have no idea how reassuring it is to know that all the crazy things you're doing and saying aren't that unusual."

"Tell us about some of the crazy things," Voncille Nettles Linwood said. "I missed that boat, you know."

Maura Beth and Elise exchanged amused glances. "You go first, sister-in-law dear," Elise said.

"Well, I seem to be very sensitive to light now. I'm always shading my eyes whether I'm inside the house or outdoors. My obstetrician, Dr. Lively, says it's nothing to worry about, but if this keeps up too much longer, I think I'm well on my way to crow's feet as I hit thirty," Maura Beth explained, pointing to her temples.

"Won't make a bit of difference to me," Jeremy added. "You'll still be beautiful in my book."

"With me, it's music—of any kind," Elise said. "It seems too loud all of a sudden, particularly when I'm driving around with the car radio on. Is it my imagination, or am I worried that I'm somehow offending the baby? There are times when I could swear I hear the baby shouting, 'For God's sake, change that channel!' You see how crazy that sounds?"

There was a polite wave of laughter. Then Jeremy said, "Tell them about some of your cravings, Maurie."

Maura Beth started counting on her fingers and then looked up with an impish grin. "I've gotten worse in the second trimester. There's no rhyme or reason to what I ask Jeremy to go out and get me at The Cherico Market. Cocktail onions, hummus, ripe bananas nearly about to go black, grapes, and prunes. And I don't mean I crave the prunes for the reasons you're probably thinking. I just seem to like them on everything these days—cereal, ice cream, you name it."

"I've wandered into Candyland big-time," Elise said. "Anything sweet will do, but I particularly like jawbreakers, jelly beans, red hots, and any kind of hard candy that I can suck on all day. Even licorice, which I used to despise. Now I can't seem to get enough of that root beer taste, and I get a huge kick out of looking at my black tongue in the mirror. I feel like a five-year-old at times."

"That must be a wonderful feeling," Miss Voncille said, "and I love the idea of giving in to the old sweet tooth. But if I could change the subject for a minute, I was thinking that maybe our next meeting might be in one of the smaller rooms. This auditorium is very nice, and it was perfect when we crowned the Queen of the Cookbooks back in July, but it seems too big for a group this size. It feels too formal having us step up on the stage and look down on everyone. Maybe next time we could all be at eye level with one another. What do you think?"

Maura Beth considered for a few seconds and then nodded. "You know, I think you might be right about that. I didn't know how many people would show up the first time, so I thought big in case we got an overflow reaction to my publicity. But maybe the boardroom would be perfect for the next meeting. We could certainly fit everyone here tonight around that long table for our discussions. How about a show of hands from you, folks?"

There were no dissenters, and Maura Beth made a mental note to reserve the boardroom for the next gathering.

After Maura Beth and Elise had exhausted all their second trimester anecdotes, the group was treated to a surprise when Periwinkle and Parker Place asked to step up to the podium. As the recently married owner and pastry chef, respectively, of The Twinkle—Cherico's most popular restaurant—they embodied success in everything they touched. From Periwinkle's sophisticated appetizers and entrées to Parker's luscious sweets, they had cornered the "dining out" market in their small town of five thousand.

Furthermore, their panel van driven by the responsible Barry Bevins delivered everything from tomato aspic to Parker's grasshopper pie within a fifteen-mile radius of Cherico itself to those who just couldn't get out on any particular day or night in person to enjoy the subdued lighting, soft music, and star mobiles dangling from the ceiling that had become the restaurant's memorable trademarks.

It was the folksy, earnest Periwinkle Violet Kohlmeyer Lattimore Place—without her customary wad of chewing gum—who spoke up first. "I suppose you're all wonderin' what Parker and I have to say tonight here at this first meeting of Expecting Great Things. Other than we're always glad to socialize with our best friends and customers, and we're still trying to get over this wonderful new library that Maura Beth has built for us. You've really outdone yourself this time, girl."

"I never get tired of compliments like that," Maura Beth said. "Please keep them coming, all of you."

Periwinkle smiled and then gave Parker a furtive glance,

after which he leaned in and said to her almost in a whisper, "Go ahead. Tell them. You can do it. We rehearsed it long enough."

Periwinkle lifted her chin proudly after his encouraging words. "Well, my Mama Kohlmeyer over in Corinth doesn't even know this yet, and frankly, I don't know how she's going to react when I tell her. You're the first to hear the news. You're our guinea pigs. Parker and I thought it over a long time, and it wasn't an easy decision. We went back and forth about it quite a lot. Should we or shouldn't we? Well, I should stop beating around the bush and just tell you that we've been trying for some time now to get pregnant. I don't mind revealing that I'm forty-two years old—a few of you ladies out there already knew that—and Parker is fifty-six, so we're not exactly spring chickens. But the good news is that we're going to be parents. So when Maura Beth called me up and told me about the support group she was planning, I nearly dropped the phone in the bowl of eggs I was beating to make a frittata for our breakfast. She must have been reading my mind, I thought to myself. That's exactly what Cherico needed; then I realized that the first meeting would be the perfect opportunity to let our good friends know about this all at once. And then we could keep coming back for more support throughout the pregnancy. Frankly, it was a dream come true."

It took a while for all the "Congratulations!" and other words of approval to die down, but when they did, Parker took up where his wife had left off.

"I only wish my dear mother, Ardenia, could have lived to see this. As you all know, she died last year unexpectedly but was a devoted member of The Cherry Cola Book Club until the end. She loved the food and the companionship, especially since she couldn't even use the library when she was a little girl growing up. Like just about every mother I've ever known, she wanted me to settle down and give her some grandchildren more than anything in the world. She was always on me for that the older I got, and I wasn't trying to be obstinate about it. Honest, I wasn't. I just hadn't found the right woman until I came to work for Peri at The Twinkle, and then being around each other as much as we were, we just clicked while we were whipping up food to sell to people. I guess we just found the right recipe."

"I think life works out best when you don't press too hard," Periwinkle said with a smile in her voice. "Just keep your eyes and ears open and let it all fall into place. Call it a blessing, call it whatever you want. It will happen when it happens."

"Even if it seems to take forever," Parker added. "Things weren't easy for my mother growing up during the time of segregation and Jim Crow—and I even got in on the tail end of it—but she did live long enough to see things get turned around. I'll never forget that morning she gave me a big hug and sent me off to school that first year of integration to Miss Voncille Nettles's homeroom at Cherico High." He paused to point out his favorite high school teacher sitting next to her husband, Locke Linwood. "I found only acceptance there, but my mother and I had no way of knowing that before the fact. It was a tense time for me."

"You were an apt pupil regardless," Miss Voncille said, giving him a perky little salute. "I never tire of telling you that."

"With a little help from you, I was; and here you are today still supporting people with your genealogical research and attending this meeting." He paused again and collected himself. "The fact that Peri and I live in a world here in the millennium where a mixed marriage such as ours isn't such a big deal anymore pretty much shows how far we've come. So we look forward to future meetings of Expecting Great Things because we both really are expecting great things out of this pregnancy. For us, it will be a brave new world. Any pregnancy is, for that matter. I think we need to embrace the wonder of it all and enjoy every minute."

Parker's little speech set off a wave of polite applause; then Periwinkle took her turn again. "Looks like we've got the book club baby express headin' our way full steam ahead. The beauty part is we can bounce our various experiences off of one another and be all the wiser for it. We don't ever need to feel alone in this, and I think that's a wonderful service to offer the general public."

"Well said," Maura Beth added. "I think Expecting Great Things is off to a great start, and I can't wait to see what lies ahead for all of us."

4

Ill-Fitting Genes

Elise could sense something of significance was in the air. After four months of living in the lodge with her generous relatives, she could always tell by the way her aunt Connie became even more solicitous than usual. Not the ordinary "what do you want to eat for supper this evening?" kind of solicitous. But the other kind, full of thinly veiled small talk about the importance of family, how much it meant to everyone to stay connected and that sort of touchy-feely thing. Tonight was no exception as the two of them sat on the sofa enjoying the warmth of the late-October fire in the great room, while Douglas had decided to retire early. Or, Elise speculated, had her aunt asked him for a little alone time with her by the fire? She leaned strongly toward the latter, Douglas being the gentleman and good husband that he was.

"I thought that was just a lovely meeting this evening at the library," Connie was saying, her hands folded properly in her lap. That was another clue that something akin to a lecture was on the way—the overly composed demeanor. "Maura Beth certainly has a knack for bringing people together, doesn't she? It felt like one big, happy family in that auditorium, just like The Cherry Cola Book Club always does. Creating something like that in such a short time is nothing to sneeze at. It's really a gift when you think about it. I know I've said it before to you, but there's nothing more important than family."

Elise turned to her aunt and smiled pleasantly, reasonably certain of where the conversation was headed. "Yes, I was very comfortable with everything that took place. It all made me feel more connected to . . . well, I don't know what. But I did feel better about my pregnancy. I felt the support from everyone there, and that was supposed to be the purpose of the meeting in the first place. I was particularly surprised by the input from the men. It wasn't what I expected."

"Take my word for it. All men are not chauvinists. For instance, your uncle Doug isn't."

"I didn't mean to imply that. I've always loved Uncle Doug. He's always given me the best advice."

"And he loves you. We both do."

A brief, awkward period between the two of them followed. Only the logs on the fire that Douglas had so carefully chopped for the season offered up their crisp, crackling noises to break the silence.

Then, as Elise had surmised, suddenly there it was, and she steeled herself for the onslaught. "Yes, everyone pitched in tonight, but there's something I have to tell you," Connie said. "You can't put this off indefinitely, you know. Part of our agreement to let you stay here with us until the baby was born was that you let your parents in on your pregnancy. Susan and Paul have a right to know, and not in a last-minute phone call from me once you're out of the delivery room. You just can't exclude them this way. That's the sort of thing they may not be able to forgive in the end, and I know that's the last thing you want. It's the last thing any of us want."

Elise looked and sounded resigned. "I know that, Aunt

Connie, but I can't seem to gather up the courage to call them. You don't know how many times I've picked up my cell intending to follow through. I've been so critical of everyone else when it comes to the subject of marriage and children, though. I've busted up more than one family gathering at Christmas or on the Fourth of July. I can even recall a time or two when people practically ran out of the room covering their ears when I got on my soapbox the way I sometimes do. I never pulled my punches, and now here I am trying for a family on my own terms. Do I have the right to ask people to understand?"

Connie patted her niece's hand gently. "Yes, I think you do. All that lecturing you did is in the past. Everyone understands that you're a strong woman with strong beliefs, even if they aren't conventional. You tell me all the time how you encourage your female students to stand up for themselves and do the right thing. Take some of your own advice. You've chosen this route to motherhood, and nothing is ever going to be the same. But I've said it before and I'll say it again: You can't keep your parents out of the loop. I can't tell you how much Douglas and I enjoy spoiling Melissa when she comes to visit us here in 'Cherry Cola,' as she calls it."

Connie paused and briefly chuckled, eyes cast to the ceiling. "That's how the book club got its name, you know. Melissa couldn't pronounce Cherico. Anyway, she's our only grandchild, and we consider her one of the biggest perks of growing older. Now, let me guess. Are you by any chance afraid your parents might turn their backs on this child of yours because none of us will ever know who the father is? Do you think they won't ever approve of your 'single mother' status? Is that what this stubbornness of yours is all about?"

At last they were getting down to it, and Elise couldn't hold back. "Well, isn't that a possibility? I've never taken their advice about anything, and I couldn't wait to break out on my own and escape from their privileged life in Brentwood."

Connie stopped smiling and stared her niece down. "You can call it what you like, sweetie, but it's a life that paid for your extensive education and ultimately enabled you to obtain tenure at the University of Evansville. Your father was a well-respected professor of psychology at Vanderbilt all those years, and your mother is a savvy businesswoman. Things don't happen in a vacuum, you know."

"I realize that much, and I don't want you to think that I'm ungrateful," Elise said, somewhat sobered by the facts that had just been presented to her. "But getting back to what you mentioned before, isn't it a possibility that my parents will have trouble accepting my child? I wouldn't blame them, actually."

"I really can't see that happening. How could they embrace Jeremy's child and not yours? The two will still be cousins, no matter what. That would be downright cruel of them to make any distinction, and that's not who they are. Think about this long and hard. Half of the genes in Jeremy's baby will come from Maura Beth—someone who is not a McShay. And half of the genes in your child won't be from a McShay, either. Good heavens, I'm not even a McShay, I married one. We're all half of one thing and half of another, for that matter. If you're going to get really technical about it and if you go back far enough, we're all eventually related. That puts all the rest of it to bed, really."

Elise's surprise registered in a riff of laughter. "Now that halfway sounds like something out of the Bible, Aunt Connie. You know, the 'so-and-so begat so-and-so' prose that goes on and on and on for pages until you're practically cross-eyed. I never in my wildest dreams thought you'd go there."

"Well, try this on for size. Time is of the essence. I've

invited your parents down for Thanksgiving, and they've accepted. We need to get this out in the open once and for all, and I think you've got to trust your parents' judgment. I don't see them going off the deep end because you've chosen a different route to parenthood than most people. It's not like you were careless, or this was something you didn't want and some no-good rascal looking for a good time walked out on you. You're letting your imagination get the best of you. Give Susan and Paul some credit for being adult about this when they see you're obviously pregnant."

Elise did not respond for a while, letting the fire temporarily mesmerize her. She was glad for the warmth, and it was somehow reassuring. "I know you're probably right, of course. Maybe what we ought to do is have you give me a pep talk just before they walk in the door, and if I start showing signs of wimping out and falling apart at any point, you step in and rescue me."

Now it was Connie's turn to laugh. "For Heaven's sake, sweetie, you're not a stray at a shelter. You don't feel that way about yourself, do you?"

"Of course not."

Connie pointed to her niece's baby bump with a delighted expression on her face. "I know it must seem like it, but this isn't going to last forever. You literally won't be able to keep this inside too much longer."

"You do have a way with words, Aunt Connie. No one should ever get on your wrong side."

Connie offered her hand, and the two of them shook on it. "Well, maybe I can help you find the right words when the time comes. We could work up an act and do a bit of rehearsing right up until Turkey Day."

"You make it sound like we're in vaudeville or something. Connie and Leesie. It has a nice ring to it."

"Well, why not? You could be the straight man—or woman in this case. And I could keep the howlers coming. Now that doesn't sound so bad, does it?"

"I suppose not. Maybe it won't be so hard if I pretend that we're both in a play. I do have a flair for the dramatic."

"Sweetie, the longer you live, the more you'll feel that way about life. We all have our roles, and there are always people watching. What you hope for is a little honest applause every now and then."

Periwinkle couldn't remember when she had ever been so nervous about anything, even though her visits to her mother in Corinth were always a trial. Life with her Mama Kohlmeyer in general had always been a standoff. Perhaps that was why Periwinkle and Maura Beth had become such good friends from the very beginning. Both had never been the daughters their mothers had expected. With her red hair, freckles, and library director ambitions, Maura Beth had both puzzled and disappointed Cara Lynn Mayhew and her New Orleans socialite pedigree.

In a different way Mama Kohlmeyer and her daughter, Periwinkle, had done battle over the years. While Periwinkle had been the quintessential tomboy from a very early age, her mother was the ultimate girlie-girl growing up, prone to playing with makeup, her Easy-Bake oven, and trying on dresses and shoes later in life when she went shopping up in Memphis. Periwinkle wanted none of that. She would rather have played baseball in the backyard with the neighborhood boys, where she outran and outpitched them—much to their chagrin. She had saddled them with the onus of "losing to a girl," and that was a hard thing to forgive.

"Sometimes it almost feels like I have a son," Mama Kohlmeyer had once told her daughter in a fit of rage. They had been arguing over what kind of clothes a lady should wear in public, and the jeans that Periwinkle was fond of trotting out were beyond the pale to her mother's way of thinking. Periwinkle had never forgotten the remark about her being a son. The truth was that they were just two different types of women—they had never been a good fit nor comfortable companions—and clothes were the very least of it.

Things had not improved between the two of them when Periwinkle had married manipulative Harlan Lattimore at her tender age of twenty. "Mark my words, Periwinkle Violet, that man is just no good. His reputation spreads far and wide. Even all the way over here to Corinth. He's just one a' those pretend-cowboys with his boots and hat and line dancin', and he'll do you wrong as soon as your back is turned."

The fact that Mama Kohlmeyer had sized up Harlan perfectly from the beginning had only made things worse between mother and daughter. Harlan had indeed cheated frequently, had even built a room in the back of his Marina Bar and Grill on the lake to "entertain" his busty young conquests. The ensuing divorce had been particularly nasty, and then years later, Harlan had tried to win Periwinkle back when her Twinkle, Twinkle Café had taken off, leaving him in the dust and in the red. She had eventually seen through his financially motivated, second marriage proposal, and he had returned to his hometown of Jefferson, Texas, with his tail between his legs. From Periwinkle's point of view, it was strictly good riddance.

Still later, when Periwinkle had announced her intention to marry Mr. Parker Place and then had actually done the deed without fanfare in the Cherico African Methodist Episcopal Church instead of her mother's Baptist church in Corinth, Mama Kohlmeyer's icy behavior had reached arctic proportions. She had refused to attend the wedding, and the rift between them seemed close to irreparable.

Why then was Periwinkle even bothering on her day off

to drive to her mother's house in Corinth to tell her about
the pregnancy? Maybe the more recent news that they were
going to have a little girl would soften the blow. As she drove
along the winding back road from Cherico, she almost felt
she was sneaking up on the inevitable confrontation. She had
passed only two cars so far. There would be almost no wit-
nesses along the way to her masochistic mission. And without
her Parker by her side to boot. He had wanted to come and be
her sturdy backup, but Periwinkle had nixed the idea vigorously no matter how passionately he argued in favor of it.

"I just don't want to expose you to her right now, Parker.
Not until she's had a change of heart. It seems I've been letting her down all my life."

"Have you ever thought it might be the other way around,
Peri?" Parker had told her with some conviction. "That she
might be the one who's letting you down? Don't be so hard
on yourself."

Periwinkle had conceded his point but stood her ground.
So she was making the journey alone while Parker held down
the fort at The Twinkle, and it felt like the audition of her life.
But what was she hoping to accomplish? Did she think acceptance could possibly be ripe for the taking? It seemed unlikely
considering her history with her mother.

As the turnoff to the country road leading to her mother's
house came into view, she began to toss around various ap-
proaches in her head.

First: "I know how you feel about my marriage, Mama,
but maybe you'll feel different when I tell you you're gonna
become the grandmother of our little girl." Periwinkle shook
her head. No, it sounded accusatory, as if she wanted to pick
a fight. They had both had enough of those over the years.

Next: "I have some wonderful news for you today. Can
you guess?" This time, Periwinkle frowned outright. This

was no time for twenty questions. This was a very adult subject—not a child's game.

Another try, complete with a wide-eyed expression on her face as she glanced at the rearview mirror. "News flash: Parker and I are gonna have a little baby girl." Was that too direct? That almost sounded like she was one of those glib, smooth-talking, TV anchorwomen with the smile that wouldn't quit and hair that wouldn't move.

Then it occurred to her that she had no business being remotely apologetic about her pregnancy. So what if some people had antiquated views on the subject of mixed marriages and the children who might result from them? This was the millennium, and the world was changing fast. She had to at least try to get her mother to embrace her approaching grandmother role. If she and Parker and their child were to be shut out over the long haul, then so be it. Better to find out now. Because she simply could not leave things the way they were.

Mama Kohlmeyer's living room in her little house with the screened porch just outside of Corinth looked exactly the same as it had when Periwinkle was growing up. The only thing that ever got changed was the blue and purple hydrangeas in the tall vases on the end tables, and even they would never have been switched out were it possible for flowers to remain fresh in water forever. Otherwise, the long blue sofa with the plastic cover, the comfortable chair with the blue and white afghan, and the turquoise throw rug on the highly polished wood floor had become iconic fixtures of the cozy, little household that Mama and the late Papa Rex Kohlmeyer had called home from the first month of their marriage.

Remaining predictably the same, too, was Mama Kohlmeyer. She never left the house without being perfectly coiffed and attired. Curlers, flip-flops, and ill-fitting housecoats covering up everything beneath were anathema to her, and her opinions were rigid and frequently unforgiving of everything from politics to religion. There were never two sides to anything for her, and she had made it clear to Periwinkle that her husband, Parker, was not welcome in her home. The very notion was unthinkable.

"You're on your own. Why on God's green earth did you have to fall for a . . . umm . . . a black man?" Mama Kohlmeyer had said when her daughter had first broken the news of their engagement.

Periwinkle fully realized the impact of the pause in her mother's question. There had been times over the years when coarser words had emerged from her mouth regarding racial issues, and Periwinkle felt guilty that she had never called her mother on it. Not that it would have made any difference in the outcome.

Things had deteriorated further when Periwinkle had answered with a question, desperate for the resolution she knew would likely never come. "For that matter, why did you fall in love with Papa Rex? Who knows why these things happen? For the most part, they just do."

"Don't you dare compare your father to this short-order cook you're playing around with!" came the reply. Mama Kohlmeyer's nostrils were flaring as her lips curled up in ugly fashion.

"He's a very talented pastry chef, Mama, not a short-order cook. You do that just to annoy me, don't you?" was all Periwinkle could think to say. "And we're not playing around. We're serious about each other. I'd think you would realize that by now, considering that we're getting married."

Mama Kohlmeyer's eyes were moving around like pinballs at the mercy of flippers gone wild. "That's your mistake, then."

Would there be more of the same this time around?

* * *

Periwinkle did not have long to wait for her answer, once the two of them were settled in on the living room sofa. "So, what's so all-fired important that you couldn't tell me over the phone?" Mama Kohlmeyer said. "I don't like secrets, as you well know. They're the work of the Devil."

Periwinkle steadied herself, placing both hands on the sofa's plastic cover, recoiling slightly at the artificial feel of it. "That's why I wanted to tell you this in person, Mama. I felt it deserved more than just a phone call. I went to the doctor recently and—"

Mama Kohlmeyer looked alarmed as she interrupted. "Are you gonna die of some terminal disease? Is that it? How much time do you have left? This isn't one of those three-month deals, is it? Please don't be puttin' me through that."

Happy for a way to some levity, Periwinkle was unable to repress a hearty chuckle. "Oh, for heaven's sake, Mama, it's nothing like that. I'm happy to say that I couldn't be in better health."

"Then get on with it and stop scarin' me to death."

Periwinkle struggled to get the revelation out amid the pauses and throat-clearings, but finally she managed. "I'm having a baby. Parker and I are gonna have a little girl." It was perhaps the most difficult sentence she had ever uttered in her life.

The right side of her mother's face hitched up dramatically, as if she were having a stroke. Then a couple of facial tics appeared, followed by a simple but devastating response. "Are you gonna keep it?"

Periwinkle could hardly believe what she was hearing and said nothing. It was the last thing she had expected, whatever else she had imagined.

Mama Kohlmeyer persisted, her voice dripping with impatient cruelty. "Well, are you?"

Recovering her senses, Periwinkle dove right in. "Mama, you're the last person in the world I would ever have thought would bring up abortion. Not with the way you never miss a Sunday in church."

"I didn't say the word *abortion*. That was your interpretation, my girl. You could always give it up for adoption, you know. That's what I meant, and that's what I think you should do. If more people thought about adoption, this would be a much better world to live in."

"And why should I give up my child? And it's Parker's child, too, remember? Why should he give up his child? What you're suggesting is cruel and unnecessary. I can't even begin to imagine where your heart is."

Mama Kohlmeyer looked uncomfortable, wiggling in her seat while drawing herself up. "You can stop with the insults. I'm just being practical is all. Why should you take all that on?"

"All *what* on?"

Now there was another level of scorn in her mother's voice. "Do I have to spell it out for you? You grew up here in the South just like I did. Why would you want to take on having a Negro child to raise? You know what they go through and all. They just don't . . . well, they don't fit in. They're not the same as everybody else. It's always been that way for as far back as I can remember. I didn't make up the history of this country. It wasn't me who did all those things to those people. Wouldn't it be better to have the child raised by two black people?"

"Instead of her parents?"

"Yes."

"This is all a matter of color, then."

"It's not just that. It's all the rest. They have different music and different people they vote for, and they talk different, too. All this rap music is just so low-class. You aren't cut out for that sorta life. Plus, here you are, a menopausal woman trying to have a baby. You're too old, and they say you run the risk of the bad genes getting in the older you are when you get pregnant. Have you even thought about that for a minute? Prob'ly not."

"For your information, I am not going through menopause. True, I am working on forty-two, which some a' those Hollywood stars consider prime time for a baby bump these days. But I'm showing no signs of menopause whatsoever. My obstetrician assures me of that."

Mama Kohlmeyer pursed her lips. "So now you're copying all those women on the front pages of those tabloids they sell at the supermarket? I'd thought you were raised better than that."

"Now you know that's not true. I'm even sorry I brought that up."

Mama Kohlmeyer had her nose in the air, making a point of avoiding her daughter's gaze. "Whatever, Periwinkle Violet. That little girl is gonna have problems. You might as well admit it. Maybe you'd have had problems if you'd had any children by that scoundrel Harlan Lattimore, too, but they wouldn't be the kind this child a' yours will have."

Periwinkle had come this far. She decided not to back down now, folding her arms defiantly. "Go on, then. Tell me more. I'm not sure what you're about to say, Mama, but I'm pretty sure I'll disagree with it."

"Oh, really, Miss Know-It-All? You just need to look at this with a decent head on your shoulders. You know as well as I do what they'll call this child behind her back in school and on the playground. It's the human nature of it all. Why, some'll smile to her face but stick their tongue out as she walks away. She'll be in for some heartbreak, that's for sure. It'll be like the child is not yours at all. She'll be his, that Mr. Place you've up and married like there were no consequences to it all. They'll only see the black part of your baby. Your part won't even count, whatever she looks like."

Periwinkle expelled the air from her lungs forcefully to keep from exploding. When she had gathered herself, she said as calmly as possible, "It sounds to me like you won't acknowledge this little baby as your grandchild, Mama, and that you won't have anything to do with her. Despite what you've been saying, she'll have some a' your genes. Do I have that down right?"

There was only awkward silence as Mama Kohlmeyer faced forward, her fingers contracted into fists.

"You could at least have the decency to answer my question, Mama," Periwinkle said finally. "I want to know where I stand with you right now. Let's don't beat around the bush."

"It's a lot to ask of me. I am who I am, and I can't help it. I'm sixty-six years old and too far along in life to change my ways. You might try to see it from my point of view. The fact is, I'll never understand you as long as I live. You've never done things by the book. It's always been your way or nobody's. But this, this decision you've made to marry a black man and have his child, this one takes the cake. You act like I'm supposed to accept it as if everybody else in the world thinks it's nothing. You know that's not gonna happen. You'll be judged by people, and so will your child. Is that what you want to be a part of the rest of your life? It's like you won't even be white anymore. You'll be giving that up for this man and his baby by marrying out of your own kind."

It took every bit of Periwinkle's resolve to avoid screaming, but somehow she managed, biting her lip and saying nothing.

"The God's honest truth is, Periwinkle Violet, you've never been a practical person, even if you have made a success of The Twinkle over there in Cherico. I'll give you that much, but this new thing you've undertaken, well, the outcome may not be as pretty and everybody may not be shakin' your hand like you've done somethin' great. By the way, is that husband of yours taking over the restaurant for you now that you're pregnant, I hope? If you're gonna insist on going through with this, you shouldn't be standing on your feet and slaving over hot stoves all day and night."

"What an image! But, yes, I'm still working," Periwinkle told her. "Dr. Jacobs told me I could go right on working up until about four weeks from delivery. He just said don't overdo it and have some common sense about things. For the record, Parker is doing more now—not at my request but at his. That's the kind of man he is. He's very responsible, and you would realize that if you gave yourself a chance to get to know him. The way I see it, the only reason you're not doing that is because he's black, and that's a horrible thing to do to me. To us."

Mama Kohlmeyer briefly looked away and muttered something under her breath.

"What was that, Mama?"

"I have no more to say, period. Fact is, most people just aren't gonna approve of what you're doin'."

Somehow, Periwinkle found just the right words, suppressing her pent-up anger. "Some people may see it that way, yes, but you have the opportunity not to be one of those people who judge and shake their heads and talk about us behind our back. If what you say is true, you'd be one less person in the world for me and my child to worry about. Don't you think you should give your little granddaughter that much of a head start?"

"You would find a way to bring up one of those big government programs, wouldn't you?"

This time, Periwinkle was unable to avoid her disgust. "You are so damned good at deflecting, aren't you? You always just change the subject when something doesn't suit you."

"That's my privilege as a tax-payin' American. And by the way, you could have told me this over the phone and avoided all of this if you think I'm so all-fired wrong about everything."

Periwinkle rose from the sofa abruptly, the waves of tension radiating from her. "Yes, I could have, and I should have, now that we've had this conversation. I went back and forth about the wisdom of my even coming over to see you while I was driving over here. Believe me, you have no idea how wound up it got me. I prob'ly need to have my head examined."

"You said it, I didn't."

"At least you're consistent about everything, Mama."

"I do what I think is right. You've known that about me for a long time, Periwinkle Violet."

Periwinkle briskly headed for the door, turning at the last minute with narrowed eyes. "Then I take it you won't want me to post any cute Facebook pictures when the time comes."

"Ha! I don't believe in Facebook. It's one of those communist plots where the Russians are tryin' to break into everybody's computer and get all their information so they can open credit card accounts in their name. I read about it in the paper just the other day, and then our pastor warned about how evil the Internet was. All this is sneaky stuff."

"Then it must be true. Good-bye, Mama. You know how to get in touch with me in case you change your mind."

Periwinkle left in the proverbial huff. Too soon, in fact, to witness Mama Kohlmeyer rising from her seat and halfheartedly uttering the one word under her breath: "Wait . . ."

But Periwinkle had already slammed the kitchen door

behind her, and Mama Kohlmeyer was left standing there, frozen in place and feeling vaguely guilty. But the moment passed quickly. Why should she feel guilty about who she was and her view of the world? It was her daughter who was sticking her tongue out at everybody and expecting them to approve. What was the world coming to?

5

The Free Sample Sisters

It all started when Maura Beth had set out on her own one Wednesday to do the grocery shopping for that week. Jeremy had taken it on without complaints since they'd gotten the news about her pregnancy, but he had a series of faculty meetings out at the high school that would keep him long after school hours, and their pantry and fridge needed considerable restocking. Jeremy had even made a list for her so she wouldn't forget anything.

Maura Beth had no sooner effortlessly parted The Cherico Market's sliding glass doors and also yanked a cart out from the long, interlocking tangle of metal with some effort when the amiable, pudgy James Hannigan, immediately walked over to her and gently put his arm on her shoulder.

"So glad to see you today, Miz McShay," the store's long-time owner and Cherry Cola Book Club member said. "We're starting something brand-new on Wednesdays, and I'm telling all of my wonderful customers about it as soon as they all come in. I think you're just gonna love it, especially considering I bet you like to nibble a lot these days."

Maura Beth could not deny the truth of that and said,

"Tell me something I don't know, Mr. Hannigan. I just can't stop. Sometimes I feel like I could eat everything under the sun and then some, and I could swear I hear this baby of mine whispering in my inner ear all the time, 'More, more, more. Gimme some more, Mama.' And, of course, I talk right back, assuring my little one that more nourishment is indeed on the way."

The two of them laughed, and Mr. Hannigan said, "That's too funny. I don't know why I've never done it before, but we're gonna have free samples of various food items every Wednesday from here on. It'll give you a chance to have a little taste of a few things maybe you haven't tried before. Seems like this is the ideal time for you to do it, too."

Maura Beth ran her tongue across her lips and gently rubbed her protruding belly. "Sounds yummy. Like what, for instance? I've discovered these last few months that there's nothing I won't eat."

"Well, let's see. I don't want to forget anything." He closed one eye in an effort to be thorough. "We have samples of pepper jack cheese in the dairy section, white and red grapes in the produce section, broken-off cookie pieces on the goodies aisle—I believe that they're a new brand of dark chocolate chip we're carrying—and mini slices of carved turkey and turkey bacon crumbles from the deli. Now, how does that sound to you? Delicious, I hope?"

Maura Beth gave a barely perceptible little shiver and then drew in her breath. "Like heaven on earth to a pregnant woman entering her third trimester. Just point me in the right direction and I promise to sample everything you're offering up today. If it all goes well, I could bust my budget for you."

"I wouldn't want you to do that, but the produce is to your right, of course. She's down there at the end by the melons with all the grapes in little paper cups. She's the sister of one of our best stock clerks. Sweet little thing by the name of Cindy Pearson, and I'm trying her out, along with a few of her friends. I'm sure she'll take care of you in style."

"Even if I want too many grapes? I might go crazy you know. I do that all the time at home. Jeremy gives me the most incredulous stares when I go on one of my eating binges on the spur of the moment."

Mr. Hannigan shrugged her off. "She'll see you're expecting. I wouldn't worry about it."

On that particular Wednesday, Maura Beth had indeed liked everything she sampled at all the stations, and as a result, she added a block of pepper jack cheese, a large bunch of white grapes, a package of carved turkey slices, and a box of dark chocolate chip cookies to the considerable list Jeremy had prepared for her. Furthermore, once she had gotten all the groceries home, she had sat down at the kitchen table and kept right on sampling. Who would have guessed that bites of turkey would pair so well with white grapes, and that pepper jack cheese slices would provide the perfect savory companion for each and every dark chocolate chip cookie she gobbled down? It was an unlikely feast—a study in yin and yang—but one she did not quit until she had devoured nearly half of the extra items she had bought after such a delightful afternoon of sampling. Did it get any better than that?

That was when Maura Beth decided to let Elise and Periwinkle in on the deal. She called each of them up and told them about the Wednesday sampling and what a satisfied piggie she had made of herself with no regrets whatsoever. To her way of thinking, three little satisfied piggies were better than one—and would be much more fun an experience to share.

"Let's circle the next Wednesday," she told them, sounding like a schoolgirl getting ready to go shopping for a prom dress. "It will be our girls' afternoon out. Just us, our grocery carts, our baby bumps, and our appetites. I know Mr. Hannigan will be delighted to see us all. He's such a dear man, and he's always been there for me since I came to Cherico. I know I wouldn't have been able to keep the old library open and get the new one built without him making all those announcements over his PA system and letting me pin my petition pamphlets all over his bulletin board. The extra business will be one way I can pay him back. This will be impulse buying at its best."

Both Elise and Periwinkle thought the outing sounded like a lark, but Elise went one step further after a spontaneous inspiration. "Let's call ourselves The Free Sample Sisters. Our motto will be, 'Arise and nibble!' I'm big on the sociology of women sticking together, as you know. As a matter of fact, why don't we ask my aunt Connie to go along with us? We shouldn't restrict this to those of us who are pregnant. That would be very undemocratic of us. Besides, she's waited on me hand and foot, so why not do something fun for her?"

"I agree," Maura Beth said. "I'll even get in touch with Becca, Voncille, Nora Duddney, and some of the other ladies in the book club. We'll make memories we'll never forget."

"Should we let Mr. Hannigan know we're on the way?" Elise added. "He's probably never had a small army of pregnant women coming at him. I wonder if he's ever seen such a spectacle."

"Nah," Maura Beth told her. "Let's just surprise him. He's a darling man. He'll roll with the punches."

Although everyone Maura Beth contacted thought the debut of The Free Sample Sisters sounded like a blast, only Connie was able to accept the free-wheeling invitation to participate. Becca had to take Markie to the pediatrician that day for a checkup, Voncille was going out of town with husband Locke Linwood to visit a cousin of his in the Delta, and the others had appointments or commitments they simply could not cancel. Perhaps another Wednesday, they all said, but it was clear from their tone of voice that they all meant it. First, The Cherry Cola Book Club, and now, this new concept from Maura Beth to play around with.

So they were to be four in number when the next Wednesday finally rolled around at The Cherico Market—"The Free Sample Sisters and Their Mother Hen"—as Connie had designated herself jokingly in the interim. Pulling their cars up in the parking lot one after another, they walked through the doors with the soldierly look of women on a mission. They had agreed not to be too methodical about it all—they would set out in different directions around the store, more like they were on a scavenger hunt; but they would willingly share news of their sampling discoveries with one another as they merrily rolled along. It was highly doubtful that schoolgirls could have this much fun with so little planning.

Even though he had not been forewarned of their presence, Mr. Hannigan was quick to spot them near the bulletin board and approached them in his usual effortless, jovial mood.

"We've all come to sample to our heart's content," Maura Beth told him even before he could open his mouth. "Tell us what's on the menu today, and we promise to visit every station you have. And if we like what we sample, we'll probably buy a lot more of it. We're on a spree, and we've all told our checkbook registers to loosen up for the day."

Mr. Hannigan looked as if he'd just hit a slot jackpot, clasping his hands together excitedly. "What a fun group of lovely ladies you all are. Well, today we're sampling cheese mini-quiches and broccoli salad in the deli section. Then we have turkey bacon crumbles and turkey frankfurter nibbles on toothpicks over by the meat." He paused briefly and then chuckled wickedly. "And for those with a sweet tooth—and

I know y'all probably have 'em in a big way—we have fresh blueberries and fresh strawberries in produce and spoonfuls of Italian gelato over by the freezer section. Two kinds of gelato, in fact—salted caramel and chocolate mocha. Oh, and a new brand of rosemary crackers by the cookies and crackers. Should be perfect for all those canapés you ladies like to serve up at your parties and such. How does that sound to you?"

"Let us at it all," Maura Beth said. "And we'll try not to clean you out. We barely had our usual breakfasts this morning in honor of the occasion. We didn't want to spoil our appetites."

Mr. Hannigan's smile was easy as he wrinkled his nose and indicated the aisles with a sweep of his hand. "Don't worry about a thing, ladies. Please, all of you, just be my guests."

Then, as if a starting gun had been shot in the air, they were off to the races, pushing their carts with the sort of boundless energy that might be reserved for game-show participants with an eye on a time clock. This, despite carrying the extra weight of a blessed event.

"I simply can't start off sampling sweets even if I am pregnant and sometimes out of my mind some mornings," Elise said over her shoulder as she headed toward the middle of the store. "I think I'll try the crackers first and then move on from there. Seems like the natural order of things to me."

"Well, I'm not standing on ceremony. We make up our own rules here today. I think those mini-quiches sound perfectly divine," Connie said. "I'm off to the deli to get first dibs."

"I'll go with you," Maura Beth added. "They do sound like they'll hit the spot. Where are you headed, Periwinkle?"

"All that fresh fruit sounds good to me. Maybe that'll ruin my appetite, but to each her own. I've found out that nothing makes much sense anymore when it comes to eating. I just go with the flow, and Parker just shakes his head."

For the sheer fun of it, Mr. Hannigan decided to keep an eye on the proceedings as best he could, though it would turn out to be quite a task.

First, Maura Beth and Connie sidled up to the quiche station and helped themselves to two each of the dainty little pies, and Mr. Hannigan quickly stepped in to advise his string bean of a stock clerk, Marvin Upton. "They can have as many as they want, son. There's plenty more back in the deli."

"These are just heavenly," Connie said, licking her fingers. "I can't believe you've never offered these before. Where have you been hiding them?"

Mr. Hannigan looked supremely pleased with himself. "Up my sleeve, I guess."

"You run and go tell the others, Connie," Maura Beth said. "They've absolutely got to get in on this."

With Connie off to the races, Mr. Hannigan pointed to the broccoli salad station down the aisle. "You gotta try our souped-up broccoli concoction, Miz Maura Beth. Ask little Linda Eason over there to let you taste a coupla cups."

Maura Beth made short work of her samples and beamed at Linda. "You didn't by any chance make this, did you? If you did, I want the recipe this minute. What are these in here—golden raisins? And do I taste water chestnuts?"

"I'm not sure what all is in there," Linda told her. "I just serve it up. Somebody back in the deli department did it. I'm real glad you like it so much. Mr. Hannigan'll be pleased."

Then Elise and Periwinkle arrived, rubbing their hands together. "What's this about the quiche Connie keeps telling us?" Elise said.

"See if I'm exaggerating, ladies," Connie said. "Go over there and try one. You won't believe how light they are."

"And when you get back," Maura Beth added, "don't miss this broccoli salad."

The enthusiastic sampling continued, stopping short of a feeding frenzy.

"How were those rosemary crackers?" Maura Beth asked Elise at one point.

"They weren't half-bad," Elise told her. "But maybe just a tad bit too much rosemary for my tastes. When there's too much, it starts to taste soapy."

Maura Beth looked genuinely puzzled. "I never heard that one before, but then I've never been a big rosemary fan."

"Me neither," Periwinkle added. "Although I don't understand the soapy thing. Do you mean it tastes like hand soap or dishwashing soap?"

Elise shrugged. "Either one."

"Anyone for turkey bacon?" Connie said, bored with the rosemary/soap discussion. "I'm kinda curious to try it. Douglas says I'd better not ever bring home anything but the real thing. He insists turkey is strictly for Thanksgiving."

"Here's my advice to you, Aunt Connie," Elise said. "Just slip it in next to his scrambled eggs sometime. Maybe he won't even know the difference unless you tell him. So I say, on to the meat department!"

They all hung out there for quite a while, going back and forth between the cups of turkey bacon crumbles and the turkey frankfurter pieces on toothpicks. There was a hickory barbeque dipping sauce on hand for good measure, and all the happy raves attracted even more customers to the fold.

"I really think I can fool Douglas with these frankfurters," Connie said finally. "Except I wouldn't think of it as fooling him. I think these things are really tasty if you ask me."

"Parker knows his sweets, that's for sure. He kinda leaves the meat department up to me most of the time. But I bet if I cut up some of these frankfurters and put 'em in an omelet, he'd be asking me for the recipe," Periwinkle said.

Then they all decided to wrap up their yummy outing with the gelato flavors Mr. Hannigan had been touting for some time now. After he'd led them over to the station by the freezer compartment, Maura Beth and Elise tried several spoonfuls of the salted caramel, while Connie and Periwinkle chose the chocolate mocha. Then the couples switched.

"I'm taking a gallon of this salted caramel home," Maura Beth said. "It'll save me the trouble of sending Jeremy out in the middle of the night."

Elise backed her up. "I'm stocking Aunt Connie's freezer. Got enough room in there?"

"More than enough. But I think I'm going to go with the chocolate mocha," Connie said.

"I was gonna go that route, too," Periwinkle said. "But maybe there'd be too much caffeine in the mocha, ladies. Whaddaya think?"

Maura Beth looked slightly startled. "I forgot about that. Yeah, Periwinkle. Maybe you'd better stick with the salted caramel, too."

In the end everything was a hit except the rosemary crackers and the chocolate mocha gelato, but Mr. Hannigan considered this particular sampling to be very successful.

"I've got a great idea for you, Mr. Hannigan," Maura Beth said at the checkout counter. "You need to show up at our next Expecting Great Things meetings at the library next Friday. I'll give you the floor and you can tell all about your sampling sessions to the other pregnant women who show up. Some of them may not know about them yet, although it's not for lack of The Free Sample Sisters spreading the word around. That should do the trick."

"I wonder what Cherico would do without you, Miz Maura Beth," he told her.

Maura Beth gave him a reassuring pat on the back. "You

never have to wonder about that, Mr. Hannigan. I'm not going anywhere."

As it would turn out, The Free Sample Sisters did not restrict themselves to carefree Wednesday outings at The Cherico Market for their bonding once the third trimester had set up camp in earnest. Not only did they share their crazy, food-craving experiences over the phone and continue to frequent meetings of Expecting Great Things—including the one that James Hannigan attended—but they eventually decided they needed even more contact of the intensely personal sort. All three pregnant women discovered through their conversations with one another that they were now dealing with unexpected demons and needed to exorcise them as soon as possible.

For Elise, it was the upcoming confrontation about the source of her pregnancy with her parents—Paul and Susan McShay—who would be coming down from Brentwood for Thanksgiving at her aunt Connie and uncle Doug's lodge. She needed advice in the worst way on how to handle the situation, and she figured three pregnant brains would be better than one.

For Periwinkle, there was the devastating unpleasantness between herself and Mama Kohlmeyer regarding her marriage and her mixed-race baby. She had, in fact, not yet let her husband, Parker, know about her mother's racist rejection of their child, though he already knew that Mama Kohlmeyer had not approved of the marriage and had been unwilling to set foot in The Cherico African Methodist Episcopal Church for the ceremony. How much longer did she dare keep the rest from him; and was there any hope of changing her mother's mind?

As for Maura Beth, a recent but perhaps inevitable development had reared its annoying head: the baby name game. Cara Lynn Mayhew, ever the New Orleans socialite supreme, had entered the picture with effusive suggestions for both a boy and a girl grandchild. In her naïveté a few months earlier, Maura Beth had imagined she might be able to get away with honoring both sides of the family by using such first names as Cara and Susan for a female, and William and Paul for a male. But she had another jolting thought coming, at least from her mother.

"I would just love for you to consider something from my side of the family," Cara Lynn had begun during one of her marathon long-distance calls. "Of course, I suppose you could always use Mayhew from your father's side. He's probably expecting it since his name couldn't be carried on any other way. But, we have such lovely, distinguished choices from mine: *Healy, Abbott, Beresford,* and *Profilet,* for starters. Any of those would work for either a boy or a girl, don't you think? Using last names for first names works very well for many families."

Temporarily blindsided, Maura Beth tried to remain non-committal. "I hadn't really thought about it that much."

"Hadn't thought about it? What are you telling me, Maura Beth? You're in your seventh month. Don't you think it's about time you did? You don't want to make some hasty decision at the last second."

Echoes of the Cara Lynn Mayhew who had existed before mother and daughter had reconciled their differences at the eleventh hour of Maura Beth's wedding on the deck of Connie and Douglas McShay's fishing lodge were creeping into the conversation. The same Cara Lynn who had finally seen the light regarding her daughter's librarian career and devotion to the little town of Cherico, Mississippi, after much needless gnashing of teeth. Was she back with a vengeance now that a grandchild was on the horizon?

"Jeremy and I have tossed a few names around," Maura Beth told her. "We just haven't come up with anything definite. We don't want to be rushed into this, no matter what."

At which point Cara Lynn had switched tactics as she was quite skilled at doing. "Do you know yet whether it's going to be a boy or a girl?"

Maura Beth had told her that they did not.

Cara Lynn had sighed plaintively and kept the pressure on. "But why? That way, you could concentrate on names more easily, knowing the gender. I have a lot of other family names for you to consider besides the ones I just mentioned. Wouldn't you like to have a sense of history included in your child's name? I'm sure you know that's a very treasured and respected Southern tradition."

For some reason, Maura Beth had been unable to contain herself. Perhaps it was a matter of the hormones surging throughout her blood. "So would naming a girl Scarlett O'Hara McShay or a boy Rhett Butler McShay, but we're not going to do either one of those things."

That had ended the conversation on a sour note, even though Maura Beth knew the prominent issue of baby names was hardly over. She knew there would be other calls and that she could not solve the problem by being short and sarcastic with her mother. Perhaps The Free Sample Sisters could give one another some helpful insights as they all moved closer to their delivery dates. Some consideration was given at first to dealing with their dilemmas at the next Expecting Great Things meeting at the library; but in the end the idea was nixed for a more private setting—namely a quiet, little dinner at The Twinkle one Sunday evening in November underneath the star mobiles, soothing Diana Krall music, and soft blue lighting.

"What did you tell Parker about our getting together here on your night off? I told Jeremy he couldn't come along and do any note-taking for his novel, even though he was pretty insistent. I made it quite clear that it was just for us girls," Maura Beth said, once they were all seated around one of the larger tables and digging into the caprese salads that Periwinkle had whipped up for them.

"I told Parker pretty much the same—just a much-needed session of pregnant girl talk," Periwinkle said. "He knows we've all gotten right chummy, so he didn't bat an eyelash. But he did offer to help out if I needed it—he's been such a sweetheart about everything from my moods to my cravings. I told him no—to just let us girls handle it all from soup to nuts."

"Which we can certainly do," Elise added, as she speared a forkful of tomato and mozzarella.

"Well, who wants to go first?" Maura Beth asked after a generous sip of her lemon water.

Periwinkle put down her fork and raised her hand. "I would, if y'all don't mind. As I mentioned to y'all before, my mother is giving me complete and utter hell about this baby on the way, and I've been trying to keep it from Parker. How do you go about breaking something like that to your husband, though? That your own mother won't accept his child—well, it's our child, really. I've lost a lotta sleep over this, I tell you. I'm not the least bit naïve about the world we live in, of course. There are more than a few folks out there who'll feel the same way my mother does. But it hurts to know it's that close to home."

Elise swallowed a bite of basil and tomato and drew back with an indignant expression on her face. "I'm afraid you nailed it, Periwinkle. Sooner or later, everything gets close to home. I've told my students that they should just go out into the real world and call their own shots, and I've pretty much done that myself. But sometimes there's a price to pay."

"Mama Kohlmeyer says I'll be dragged down by all this—

that I'll find out what it's like to be black, and it won't be a pretty picture," Periwinkle said. "As if she'd know what that was like."

Elise's scowl became even more pronounced. "I don't mean to offend you, Periwinkle, but it seems your mother isn't very good at putting herself in your shoes. All my life I've heard that our grandmothers are supposed to be very understanding about what their daughters are going through since they've been there and done that themselves. They're supposed to be an enormous part of the support structure, not put up obstacle courses. They're the ones who are supposed to spoil your child the way you never can."

"Apparently, there are exceptions, depending upon who you marry," Periwinkle said, her voice tinged with bitterness.

"Or who you don't marry," Elise added, sounding no more enthusiastic. "I have to tell my parents that I've done this on my own without a man in sight, and there's a part of me that can't seem to find the right words when they come to Cherico for Thanksgiving. Looks like both you and I are keeping things from people, Periwinkle."

"That's what this session is for, ladies," Maura Beth said. "I've got my mother breathing down my throat on baby names, and I realize that doesn't seem half as serious as artificial insemination and racism, but maybe we can come away from this dinner with some suggestions that will make our lives easier."

Over Periwinkle's entrée of baked chicken with sun-dried tomatoes and roasted asparagus, there was a breakthrough of sorts. It was Elise who seized upon the concept first.

"We've all got to stop being afraid," she told the others. "It's unbecoming to women who've accomplished what we have. Maura Beth, you've built a wonderful, state-of-the-art library that was long overdue for this little town. Periwinkle, you're running Cherico's most successful restaurant, bar none. I love the mood you've set for us tonight. And I've got tenure at the University of Evansville teaching Women's Issues. Even more importantly, we've all chosen to bring new life into the world with all the unknowns and risks that are involved in that. Now, we've got people coming at us who don't seem to be on the same planet as we are half the time. Well, we've just got to stand our ground and stop being so timid. Here all these years I've been telling young women to take the world by the horns, and I'm not following through the way I should. I've got to face my parents once and for all and tell them that this is the way my life is going to be. If they accept what I've done, then maybe we'll all be one happy family. But if not, I'll just have to be strong enough to accept that, too, and go on my way without them."

Maura Beth was quick to pick up on the theme. "And Jeremy and I have just got to tell my parents—and his, if necessary—that we will name our children what we want. We can take their suggestions under consideration, but in the end, it'll be up to us. It's our lives, not theirs."

Periwinkle remained silent, and the others could see that she was still greatly troubled by her predicament.

"I guess your task is a whole lot harder," Elise said, turning toward her. "I can certainly empathize."

Finally, Periwinkle came to, managing a weak, little smile. Alone among the three, she had been toying with the delicious food she had prepared. "The first thing I have to do is level with Parker. I think what's been holding me back is that I'm so ashamed of my mother's attitude. Parker's dear mother, Ardenia, would have been a lot more accepting, I truly believe. I had just begun to get to know her before she died unexpectedly last year, but she'd been through enough growing up in the Jim Crow South that I'm sure she wouldn't have turned her back on our grandchild. There was no place in her heart for hate, even though she had every reason to harbor it. So I've been dragging my feet because of all that."

"You should absolutely trust Parker," Maura Beth said. "You shouldn't be going through any of this alone. Let him know how your mother feels and take it from there. If it means you'll both have to be that much stronger for each other, then you might as well start now—the sooner, the better."

A sense of relief spread across Periwinkle's face. "You're right. I'll tell him as soon as I get home. This can't wait another minute."

"Don't sound all sad and defeated when you tell him, either," Elise said. "We're not responsible for the way our parents feel about things. Sometimes, they're not even responsible for the way we as their children feel. At any point in time, anyone can make up their own mind. The three of us are getting into something that's totally unpredictable over the long haul. We've got to be brave and responsible and realize that the point of all this is not simply reproduction. It's a lifelong commitment." Elise paused with a wicked smirk in spite of herself. "I guess I sound like I'm lecturing one of my classes, don't I? Sometimes I can't help it. It's what I do for a living."

"Give yourself some credit," Maura Beth said. "Let's give ourselves credit. This is why we got together tonight, and I think we've given each other some courage and inspiration."

"Let's be sure and keep each other posted and tally up all our triumphs, shall we?" Elise added.

"Sounds good to me," Periwinkle said. "Meanwhile, anyone for dessert? It's one of Parker's grasshopper pies. I have a sneaking feeling our babies will want to lap up all that sugar. Or at least we can always blame it on them."

6

The XY Factor

Jeremy sat lost in thought with his lukewarm black coffee in the Cherico High School teachers' lounge. It was hardly an inviting space—too cramped, too few chairs, a couple of tacky flower prints on the institutional green walls that were reminiscent of a cheap motel. But it was all that was available to escape the constant pressure of trying to elevate the teaching of high school English to another level, one that his superiors up in Nashville and here in Cherico had never appreciated. He had yet to get approval for one of his proposed student excursions to the literary meccas of the South, whether it was Faulkner's Oxford, Capote's Monroeville, or Welty's Jackson. All were well within striking distance of Cherico. He had always been told that buses were never available for such a purpose, though they were always gassed up, vacuumed, and ready to go for the football team's many road trips throughout Mississippi and even up to the small towns of West Tennessee. Still, he continued to fight for his vision of "Living the Classics in the Real World." He firmly believed it would be a game changer for his students if it ever came to pass. According to his vision of the world, millennials needed some extra help, and he was determined to provide it.

Then there was the matter of the Great American Novel he had been attempting to write since his honeymoon in Key West—an exercise in distraction if ever there was one. He had changed the title at least five times as he siphoned off bits and pieces of his wife's pregnancy to blend in to the high concept of his work. Yet, it still wasn't gelling for him, and his frustration was growing exponentially as his Maurie entered her third trimester. Lately, he had gone back and forth about a fiction versus nonfiction approach to the project but had resolved nothing in the end.

"Yo, Jeremy!" a deep male voice boomed, bringing him out of his reverie with a start.

He looked up to see that his husky cohort, Alex Brandon— he of the receding hairline and angular features—had entered the room and was standing over him with a cup of coffee, snapping his fingers. "You looked like you were in another world there."

Jeremy saw no reason to play games with his American history–teaching friend. "Maybe I was. I don't feel I'm getting the job done these days, and I was trying to work out a way to make things better."

Alex sat down beside him and took a sip of his coffee. "What are you talking about, man? Your students love you. At least that's the buzz I hear all the time. Hey, and all the teenybopper girls swoon over you, they say. I wish I had your good looks and a wife like Maura Beth to come home to."

Jeremy just shrugged. "Stop. You're always running yourself down. Everybody has problems. For instance, I think I have the worst writer's block in the world right now. Wish there were some sort of literary laxative I could take for it."

Alex chuckled after sipping his coffee again. "You and

your images. I don't see why you're having so much trouble when you can come up with material like that." There was an awkward silence, even though Jeremy managed a smile and a nod in his friend's general direction.

"By the way, I've been meaning to talk to you about something for a while now," Alex continued. "Do you have a minute?"

"That's why I'm here in the lounge taking what little downtime I can. What's on your mind?"

Alex put his cup down on a nearby table littered with worn magazines and briskly rubbed his hands together. "Well, it's your sister you're always talking about. You've intrigued me with your descriptions of her. Or maybe I should say that I've let my imagination run wild about the possibilities. I've never met someone who actually went down to a sperm bank and withdrew a deposit, so to speak. Do you think maybe you could arrange to have me meet her?"

Jeremy looked taken aback. "You actually want to meet Leesie? You want me to set you up with her?"

"I wouldn't call it that exactly."

"Then exactly what would you call it? Are you writing a term paper just for the fun of it or something?"

Quizzical lines broke out across Alex's prominent forehead while he shook his head vigorously, saying nothing.

"Is it the curiosity factor? Because let me tell you, curiosity killed the cat. I hate to use a cliché like that, but in this case it fits."

Alex frowned and leaned in, patting Jeremy's knee. "Okay, pal. I took into account the part about her being a big-time feminist and all. But she still intrigues me. So, could you arrange for me to meet her or not?"

Jeremy took a moment, eyeing his friend skeptically. "Do you mind my asking—what's your end game in this? Please tell me you're not looking to make Leesie fall for you with all she's got on her plate. Take the hint. She didn't get pregnant the conventional way, and the reason is because she doesn't want a man in her life. Trust me on this one. When she accidentally caught Maurie's bouquet at our wedding last year, she threw it right back and demanded a do-over."

Alex glanced at the ceiling, obviously working on a mental picture. "That's kinda funny, now that I think about it."

"I suppose it is in a way. Classic Leesie, and I should know. But then it ceases to be the least bit funny when she comes at you and launches into one of her blistering, feminist diatribes. You don't want to be on the receiving end of one of those, believe me."

"Maybe not. But give me some credit. I'm no thin-skinned wimp. I've been through a rejection or two in my time and gotten up off the mat. So, will you at least let me meet her?"

Jeremy hesitated, pouting and frowning at the same time. "I'll talk it over with Maurie and see what she says about it. But frankly, I don't think the two of you would have much in common. I know my sister, and I don't want to ruin our friendship by putting you in harm's way."

"Good grief, man! You make it sound like she's a terrorist or something. I'm starting to think you're scared of her."

"No, not at all."

"You could've fooled me."

Exasperation was beginning to creep into Jeremy's voice. "Look, it's true that we've gone more than a few rounds about politics and religion over the years. But she can be terrifying at times. I know what I'm talking about. She didn't even want to come to my wedding at first because she doesn't believe in them. She insists they're all about men exploiting women and that particular line of thinking. Everything boils down to XX versus XY for her. In her universe, the former combination is basically good, the latter, not so much. She even teaches a course up there at the university called The XY Factor. Now,

I'm not going to come right out and say it should be called Man-Bashing 101, but there's no shortage of female students who sign up for her lectures semester after semester. It seems it was something she was born to do. Plus, she had no trouble at all getting tenure, so I have to conclude that she's pretty damned good at what she does. I may not agree with everything she believes and advocates, but my sister is a pretty formidable woman."

Alex seemed to be wavering a bit, backing away ever so slightly. "Well, I didn't know that part about the XY course. You kinda left that out before. So you say she didn't want to come to your wedding at first. But she obviously did because of that bit about throwing the bouquet back. What happened?"

Jeremy flashed back to that moment of genuine surprise when his sister had shown up at his doorstep the day before the wedding, driving all the way from Evansville after having previously and emphatically R.S.V.P.'ed in the negative.

"Actually, she broke down and did come after all. Without my knowledge, Maurie had written her a very convincing and welcoming letter that changed her mind about the whole thing. I think Leesie even allowed herself to have a good time in spite of herself. The two of them have been pretty tight ever since, especially now that they're both pregnant at the same time. After all, their children will be first cousins. There's even some little group they've formed that has them all shopping at The Cherico Market together every Wednesday—she and Maurie and Periwinkle Place. Something about sampling free goodies. That's why I think I'd better run this past Maurie first, if you have no objection."

"Go right ahead, and I hope she decides in my favor."

Jeremy was still looking at Alex as if his brain had slipped out through his ear and fallen on the floor. "You should be careful what you wish for, my friend. Let's just leave it at that for now. Except that I think you'd be way better off pouring your time and energy into that new Algebra I teacher with the long legs. No way you haven't noticed her. You can see all the boys turning their heads as she walks down the hall with that little wiggle of hers."

"Grace Ann Winston?"

"One and the same."

Alex shook his head slowly with his eyes narrowed and a look of disdain. "Call me crazy, but I know for a fact that she spends way too much time in the designated smoker's area next to the cafeteria loading dock. It just so happens I don't like dating ashtrays."

"Just single, pregnant feminists, I guess."

Alex raised his hand with an impish grin. "Please get that outta your head. I never said I wanted to date your sister. I only said I wanted to meet her. Is that too much to ask?"

"You definitely *are* crazy, and I'm not sure I can let you go there. Something tells me that Maurie will feel the same way. We just can't let you go into the lion's den without feeling plenty guilty ourselves."

"Don't you mean lioness?"

"I stand corrected. But it still makes me wonder what kind of XY chromosomes you have that make you want to pursue my sister in any fashion whatsoever. You've got to understand that there have been times when she has regarded men as pythons, if you want to continue with the animal analogies."

Alex seemed not the least bit perturbed by the snarky banter and said, "I just thought I'd put in a good word for myself for what it's worth. If it isn't meant to be, I'll accept that like a grown man. Let's don't beat this to death."

Jeremy's skeptical attitude remained in full force. "I think you're hiding something. I have no idea what it is, but this whole thing just doesn't compute. I'll find out what you're up to eventually, you know."

Alex did not answer, offering up only a male Mona Lisa smile.

Jeremy glanced at the clock on the wall, took a deep breath, and rose from his chair with a sense of urgency. "Well, I see it's nearly time for me to clear my brains for my fourth period protégés. Catch you later."

Maura Beth and Jeremy were sitting up in bed that evening revisiting Alex's dogged, if somewhat mysterious, interest in Elise. A flickering, gardenia-scented votive candle sat on the night table, a staple for inducing sleep that Maura Beth had discovered by trial and error. Earlier, they had thoroughly discussed Alex's request for an introduction over their dinner of pot roast with rice, biscuits, and green beans, some of which Jeremy had even lovingly pitched in to cook with aplomb. But the entire matter continued to confound them both.

"I keep coming back to the fact that Alex knows quite well what Elise's positions are on men and what a political creature she is," Maura Beth was saying as she fluffed up her pillows. These days, she practically had to sleep sitting up for comfort because of her increased girth and pressure on some of her internal organs. She had, in fact, grown mightily weary of peeing around the clock. "And yet he insists on entering the arena like some sort of crazed matador, according to the impression you've given me."

Jeremy gave her a sideways glance. "Elise as *el toro* instead of a lioness? I like that image. Of course, she's equally dangerous either way you look at it, even though there probably wouldn't be any harm in the two of them saying hello to each other. I just have a great deal of trouble seeing it going much beyond that."

"Even more than one sentence beyond," Maura Beth said, gently nudging her husband.

"I can see Elise giving him the cold shoulder. Polite, but still cold. I suggest we both stay out of it. That way no one can blame us if all hell should break loose—which it very well might."

Then she gave a delicate little gasp, briefly covering her mouth with her right hand. "Except . . ."

"Except what?"

"Well, if Alex is so all-fired set on meeting Elise, then I think it should be done out in the open where everyone can witness it for themselves. None of this 'quiet, little dinner party' stuff right here in our home that could easily back-fire, and there's no one but us to witness the 'he said, she said' part. I can just hear everyone around Cherico gossiping over their phones about that kind of aftermath—'What do you suppose Maura Beth and Jeremy were thinking bringing them together like that? Didn't they have anything better to do?' "

"Wow! You've practically written a little play with that explanation, and I sweat bullets turning out even one page of my novel."

She shot him a dubious glance. "Calm down. As I've told you many times before, your muse will eventually show up. So here's what we do instead. Next time you see Alex, all you have to do is invite him to an Expecting Great Things meeting at the library. That way, he'll get a pretty good idea of what he's up against. Just let him listen to Elise on her soap box for a few minutes and see how he holds up. I predict ma-jor skid marks on the floor."

"That's not half-bad," Jeremy said, nodding enthusiastically. "Don't know why I didn't think of it in the teachers' lounge today. Maybe it was the shock of Alex being so determined to take on my sister and somehow thinking it was a good thing. It completely caught me off guard. But the Expecting Great Things suggestion certainly lets us off the hook."

"That it does. We don't want to become known as the Matchmakers from Hell, however well-intentioned we might have been."

"Then that's settled."

But Maura Beth wasn't ready to turn off the lights quite yet. "Well, that may be on its way to being settled, but I need to tell you that Mama called me again at work today. I don't even have to guess why she's calling these days. More baby name pressure. She's done more genealogical research and come up with a dozen Old New Orleans names, as she calls them, from her side of the family that she wants us to consider seriously. Whereas your mother has been laying low in the weeds. Not so much as a peep out of her, and you're supposed to expect at least a peep or two out of your mother-in-law. Susan has no idea how much I truly appreciate that, and I can tell you that she's much more likely to win the cherished Grandmother Sweepstakes with that sane and sensible approach."

Jeremy's laugh had a wicked edge to it, and he even gave Maura Beth his best boyish wink. "Don't worry. Let's just see how calm Mom remains once Leesie tells her about my surprise niece or nephew over Aunt Connie's turkey and dressing at the lodge in a couple of weeks. Leesie did tell me that that's when she plans to drag it all out in the open. Aunt Connie's been on her pretty good about telling our parents what's going on down here."

"I know all about that. Elise, Periwinkle, and I discuss our various family issues all the time, and sometimes Connie even gets in on it. It's turning out to be the most wonderful therapy in the world for all of us."

Then Maura Beth's tone took on an undeniable earnestness as she took Jeremy's hand and gave it a gentle squeeze. "By the way, how do you really think your parents *will* take the news?"

Jeremy pressed the fingers of his right hand to his temple in a flamboyant gesture reminiscent of a magician and closed his eyes. "So glad you asked me. Let me concentrate. Now, then. A moment more and it should be at hand. Voilà! My psychic powers tell me that—" He broke off abruptly and stared her down, though with a suggestion of a smile.

"Seriously, you're asking me that? I have no clue how they'll take it. You'd think they would take it in stride with all their education and sophistication and be happy for her. But they've been at odds with Leesie about so many things for such a long time now. Or rather, she's been at odds with them, to be truthful about it. Politics, religion, the XX and XY gender warfare she likes to wage on the spur of the moment—you name it."

Maura Beth cocked her head with ever-widening eyes. "I've never seen your parents lose it with anyone. When I think of cultured and composed, I think of Paul and Susan McShay of Brentwood, Tennessee."

"They generally don't betray that image. But in this instance, they could also just up and tell Leesie to her face, 'Well, isn't that just like you, Elise? We knew you'd probably pull a stunt like this someday.' I'd like to think things wouldn't get nasty or out of control, and acceptance would be the outcome for the sake of family unity, but you never know. Leesie has a way of stressing people greatly, present pregnant company excepted."

"Don't ask me why Elise and I get along so well," Maura Beth said with the gentlest of sighs and a dismissive flick of the wrist. "Maybe it's because I reached out to her the way I did and convinced her to come to our wedding. I've never written such shining prose in my life, if I do say so myself. I was practically Maura Beth Shakespeare. At any rate, she really is like the sister I never had. I can tell her anything, although I don't tell her everything. She hasn't asked, of course, but if she did, I would never tell her squat about our sex life. That's strictly off-limits."

Jeremy wagged his brows as if he'd just heard an immature, bawdy joke. "Atta girl. Never go there. I hope you realize that I'd never volunteer any information, either. It's sacred to me. I've never been one of those locker room–type guys. I just tuned that stuff out when I was growing up, and I think some of the jocks in my school viewed me with suspicion because of that."

"How so?"

Jeremy's tone was complacent, and it was clear that he was comfortable with who he was as a man. "Mostly that I might be gay because I wasn't macho and wasn't making lewd comments about girls all the time. Some rumors eventually got back to me, but I didn't let all that nonsense bother me. Those guys were the ones who didn't have their heads on straight. It was just more of that XY-generated stuff that Leesie campaigns against all the time. She may have a point in some instances. I do have at least that much in common with Leesie in that I take women seriously and respect them."

"I can vouch for that," she said, smoothing a corner of the purple quilt that covered her on such a chilly autumn night. "You're a lover of the classics, and that's one of the main reasons I married you."

Jeremy moved closer to her, as it was far easier for him to accomplish the act of snuggling than it was for her; then he gave her a peck on the cheek. "Just call me your literate lover."

She returned his gentle kiss and said, "And I fully expect you to be the most literate father this country has ever produced."

He offered up a round of hearty laughter. "You do the breast-feeding while I read *David Copperfield* to our *cher enfant* out loud."

7

Scream Queens

With no little effort, Maura Beth had arranged for Ms. Beryl Craine to come to Cherico from Memphis for the early-evening, mid-November Expecting Great Things meeting at the library. As a Lamaze Certified Childbirth Educator, her mission was to introduce expectant mothers to the Six Healthy Birth Practices that constituted the core beliefs of Lamaze International, and she came highly recommended from several sources. That seemed straightforward and promising enough, and Maura Beth was certain the session would be particularly helpful to those who would be attending. It would be yet another feather in her cap since moving into her state-of-the-art facility overlooking Lake Cherico. Furthermore, the much-anticipated meeting was moved back into the mini-auditorium from the boardroom so that the pregnant women and their loved ones would have plenty of space to practice various techniques onstage. Certain Greater Chericoans were already raving about the ongoing Expecting Great Things program, which was unspooling without a hitch. What could possibly go wrong?

"If all of our mothers-to-be will come up with the fathers, family members, or loved ones, we will begin," Beryl announced after Maura Beth had introduced her to the gathering, and she had then given a brief explanation of Lamaze itself. She was a tall, slim woman with close-cropped brunette hair and a crisp, no-nonsense air, even though something about her smile was forced and reminiscent of a beauty pageant contestant getting ready to answer the "fishbowl" question.

"Very good," she continued, once all the pregnant women and their companions had made their way onto the stage. "Why don't we begin by introducing ourselves to one another so we'll feel more like a family?"

Maura Beth and Jeremy smiled pleasantly as they identified themselves.

"And we're the Places," Periwinkle said next. "He's Parker, and I'm Peri, and we run The Twinkle downtown, as most of you know."

Two more couples—Sandra and Christopher Barnes and Mandy and Jimmy Nixon followed suit.

Finally, "I'm Elise McShay. I'm a single mother-to-be." Her nose was in the air, and there was a touch of defiance in her voice.

Beryl seemed entirely unfazed and continued. "So you have no family member with you today?"

Elise quickly pointed to Jeremy with a chuckle that came off as forced. "Well, my brother is right over there, but he's here with his wife, who is my sister-in-law, of course. So that pretty much ties him up. Two women at once is a bit much to ask, don't you think?"

"I do. Would you like for me to stand in for you?" Beryl continued. "Or maybe we could ask for a volunteer from the audience? It would definitely be helpful to have someone encouraging you with the breathing techniques once we get started with that. I recommend it."

A male voice shouted, "I'll be happy to volunteer!"

Alex Brandon shot up from his seat and headed toward the stage while Elise looked on disapprovingly.

"Is this absolutely necessary?" Elise said.

Beryl wrinkled her nose and then expanded her smile further. "Why don't we just play along, shall we? I think it will make things go a lot smoother."

Alex introduced himself to everyone and held his hand out to Elise, who grasped it limply.

"Very good," Beryl said, drawing herself up to her full height. "Now. The first birth practice I'd like to emphasize is that we always want to let labor begin on its own. Once that starts, we do encourage bringing that special someone or friend along for that continuous support—"

But at that very moment, something inside Elise snapped, and her crusading academic nature burst forth. "Excuse me, but do you mind if I say a few words to the group, Ms. Craine?"

"Uh, well . . . of course not."

Suddenly, Elise turned and started addressing those still seated in the audience almost as if she were running for office. More than a few people from Brentwood to Evansville had observed that a soapbox was her favorite piece of furniture.

"Ladies and gentlemen, I had my reservations about coming here tonight in the first place, and already I can feel this is going south on me. In retrospect, I probably should have listened to my inner voice and stayed home. You see, Ms. Craine, I did some considerable research on Lamaze International, and I found a few things that were disturbing and controversial to me. I feel it's my duty to bring them up now so that the other women can judge for themselves."

Beryl's smile disappeared instantly, but she maintained her composure. "Disturbing? What could possibly be disturbing about helping mothers have an easier, more comfortable delivery? What's controversial about that? I'm not sure I understand exactly where you're coming from, Ms. . . . McShay, was it?"

"Yes, anyhow, Ms. Craine, to cut to the chase—are you aware of Sheila Kitzinger's criticisms of Dr. Fernand Lamaze's methods? Specifically, that he actually preferred to rank women's performances in childbirth? For one thing, he graded them based on their screams. Can you believe that? Do you think that's appropriate? I find it reprehensible. In my opinion, it makes a mockery of the whole experience. Far too many people believe that women are out-of-control, emotional creatures, and that only adds to the perception."

Beryl suddenly seemed to be grasping for words. "I'm . . . aware of what you're bringing up. But, well . . . those criticisms . . . well . . . they've been completely debunked, and you're taking them out of context anyway. At any rate, that was a long time ago—back in the fifties, I believe. Lamaze has stood the test of time. Many millions have benefited from it, and that's a matter of record."

Elise did not let up. "That may be, but the research I did also said that extremely intellectual women were often not good candidates for Lamaze because they asked too many questions and provoked their providers. As in 'how dare these women act so uppity?' In today's world, women are far too docile and do exactly what they're told without questioning. My life's work has been based on that premise, and not only that, but—"

"Leesie, this is not the time and place," Jeremy interrupted, as Maura Beth looked on uneasily.

"What do you mean this is not the time and place? We're going to be instructed in these Lamaze exercises, and the information I've gathered indicates that we could all end up competing as scream queens for best in show."

Then a full-fledged showdown between brother and sister broke out as it had many times over the years. "Leesie, please don't ruin this for everybody else. If you don't want to participate, no one's going to make you. You're absolutely right. You shouldn't have come in the first place with all this stuff backed up on you."

"Keep your male opinions to yourself, Jer."

"I can't believe you and your raging hormones are acting like this in front of all these people, Leesie."

"If I may say something," Beryl began, having gathered herself and trying earnestly to salvage the tense situation. "The purpose of Lamaze is to help our mothers relax and gain self-confidence, not to rile them and drive their blood pressure up. Feeling the way you do, I doubt you would get very much out of this meeting, Ms. McShay. I'm so sorry you feel as you do, but perhaps you'll give the others a chance to participate, and we can get on with this?"

"I suppose that's fair enough," Elise said after a pause, finally lowering her voice. The surge of adrenaline had come and gone that fast. "Please, continue with your . . . meeting." Then she turned to Maura Beth with downcast eyes. "Sorry. I really never should have come."

Maura Beth managed a conciliatory smile and a half-hearted wave of her hand. But perhaps the person whose jaw had dropped the most as a result of Elise's outburst was Alex Brandon, and he was left shaking his head as she headed for the exits as fast as her third trimester girth would allow.

Although the rest of Beryl Craine's presentation went off without incident and was well-received, it was Jeremy who came up with the spontaneous idea of inviting Alex over for dinner later that evening. He and Maura Beth had just gotten home from the library and shed their coats when he picked up the phone in the kitchen and reached out to his cohort.

"If you haven't already eaten, we'd love to have you. It's

just leftovers, but we're both pretty good cooks over here on Painter Street," Jeremy concluded.

In fact, Alex had not eaten anything since his forgettable lunch of chili, green peas, and a cardboard roll at the high school cafeteria and accepted gratefully.

"I think he's probably in shock, Maurie," Jeremy said after hanging up. "Bachelors need their nourishment, too, you know. Plus, I tried to warn him about Leesie, but I guess he just had to see for himself."

Maura Beth sounded both resigned and guilty. "Well, we both told him to drop by the library for the meeting. I feel responsible, too. But now that I've had a chance to think about it a little more, I think maybe Elise got a bad rap at the meeting. She's nothing if not highly researched, and I think she had a right to bring up the historical perspective on Lamaze. I, for one, had no idea any of that had gone on."

"Well, this is hardly something new. Leesie will store things up until suddenly everything just explodes on her. You never know where or when it will happen, but the best you can hope for is to stay out of the direct line of fire."

Maura Beth looked skeptical. "There was nothing dangerous about what she said at the library."

Jeremy's tone grew very somber. "Okay, I'll grant you that. But I really wonder if she has the temperament to be a mother. She's going to expect so much from this kid, and children shouldn't be approached like classroom experiments. Does that sound like a horrible thing to say about my own sister? But I really can't help believing she didn't think this whole pregnancy thing through all the way. Her big problem is she thinks too much in terms of the theoretical, not the practical."

Maura Beth moved to the freezer and retrieved a big plastic bag of frozen chicken gumbo she had put up during the summer, knowing there would be times ahead when she wouldn't feel like making meals from scratch. That, some rice, and some jalapeño cornbread would be on the menu for their last-minute company.

"Of course, I've gotten to know Elise a lot better since we invented The Free Sample Sisters, so I'm well aware of her moods. But I can't very well point my finger at her, since I move the needle on the preggers meter back and forth myself a good bit, as I don't have to tell you."

"Yeah, you do, sweetheart," he said, blowing her a kiss. "But you have to know it's all good with me."

She caught his kiss and said, "The truth is, your sister has confessed to me that she's had moments when she wonders if she can go through with the pregnancy. Then, she and I—and sometimes Periwinkle and Connie—will talk it all out, and Elise's doubts seem to disappear just like that. She's the ultimate chameleon among us very pregnant chameleons."

Jeremy busied himself setting the kitchen table and said, "I had no idea she'd been researching Lamaze that way. Or that she would go on the attack quite like that in such a public setting. Sometimes it's difficult to predict her triggers."

"Poor Alex," Maura Beth said, putting on a pot of boiling water for the gumbo. "We both saw his face when she started lecturing everybody. He even physically stepped away from her a tad bit like he'd forgotten to put the chain of garlic around his neck or something."

Jeremy managed a skeptical grin. "His face was no worse than the others as I looked around the stage and out in the auditorium. Everyone showed up expecting something soothing and constructive to happen, which they eventually got. But it was rough going there for a minute or two. I know I felt uncomfortable until Leesie got it all out of her system."

Maura Beth popped the slab of frozen jalapeño cornbread she had made earlier in the week into the oven and then sat down at the kitchen table, while a quizzical expression crept into her features. "So this is more like a 'take pity on Alex' dinner, am I reading you right?"

Jeremy pulled up a chair. "Not exactly. There's more to it than that. I have a few questions I'd like to ask him about his interest in my sister. Maybe now that he's seen her in action, he'll come clean with me."

"What do you mean?"

"I suspect he has an ulterior motive in all this. Perhaps a good, home-cooked meal will draw it out of him."

"Sounds like a plan. I'll serve up the food. You serve up the questions."

It did not take long for the dinner conversation to focus on what had happened at the library earlier. In fact, it was Alex who brought it up shortly after he had complimented Maura Beth on her gumbo and cornbread.

"I could eat this every day of the week," he told her with a grateful smile. "You're one lucky guy, Jeremy."

"Yeah, I know."

"You sure weren't exaggerating about your sister, though," Alex continued. "That was something else this evening."

Jeremy took a sip of his Chardonnay and quickly shifted gears. "Yes, it was, but if you want to know the truth, I still have the feeling you're holding something back regarding your interest in Leesie. Or am I just imagining things?"

Alex put down his spoon, wiped his mouth with his napkin, and cleared his throat.

"You're a pretty perceptive guy, Jeremy. I think that's one of the main reasons we've hit it off as much as we have at the high school. So maybe it's time I leveled with you. I teach history because it's the one subject that changes with each passing day. Math is math, English is English, and so on. They're pretty static. But give history a few weeks, months, or years, and a whole new chapter gets written about the world we live in. Things are always changing, and I want to keep up with them in a substantive way. I haven't confided in you before because I wanted to wait until I had everything organized, but I have a special project under way with one of my classes."

Jeremy sat back, looking puzzled. "Glad to hear it. But what does that have to do with my sister?"

"Here's the payoff. My advanced class in Social and Intellectual History of America is tackling the theme of changes in the nuclear family in the millennium. Their term papers are expected to include various aspects of sociological changes, and it just seemed to me that your sister would make the perfect guest speaker for my class. Obviously, she'd be concentrating on issues like single mothers and their choices. If you want to know the truth, I guess I was a little bit intimidated by her academic credentials and wondered if she'd even consider working with me on something like this."

Jeremy and Maura Beth made furtive eye contact, and he said, "Ah, the truth comes out at last. Well, I don't think you have much to worry about. This sounds like something right up Leesie's alley. You should have mentioned it to me right off the bat."

"I seriously thought about it, but what if you didn't approve? Teachers' lounge talk over coffee and doughnuts is generally pretty superficial to pass the time between classes, although we've dug a little deeper now and then. I wanted to proceed cautiously."

Jeremy made a whistling noise. "Nah, you don't need to step on eggshells around me. I'm just a thickheaded guy." He thought for a while and then became suddenly animated, as if a wave of energy had been poured atop his head and covered his entire body. "Hey, I just got this great idea. I've spent months tracking Maurie's pregnancy—Leesie's, too, for that matter. You should see all my note-taking. Maurie can vouch for the fact that I've gotten a little intense myself at times. At first, I wanted to see if I could get a novel out of it. But now I'm thinking I've been going at it the wrong way. Instead of trying to be a man making sense out of a woman's experiences, what if I wrote a book called *Fatherhood for Dummies* or something like that?"

Maura Beth's voice was full of patronizing affection. "Sweetheart, I think that's perfectly brilliant. You've gotten in my way so adorably more times than you can even imagine all these months. Writing a book telling fathers-to-be what not to do might turn out to be a bestseller. I say full speed ahead."

Jeremy worked at pretending to be hurt but couldn't pull it off. "Have I really been that much of a nuisance?"

She smiled at him sweetly. "As I said, you've been adorable about it all, and I even think Elise would be happy to help you organize things if you asked her. She's got the credentials."

"That's a great idea, Maurie. Maybe we could pool our resources."

"And I could talk up your classroom speaker idea to Elise the next time The Free Sample Sisters drop by The Cherico Market," Maura Beth told Alex. "She's always in her best mood when she's nibbling those freebies. We all are. We just revert to carefree little kids in the candy store, and we're pretty certain our babies don't object."

"That would be great. Maybe I could help you with your book, too, Jeremy," Alex said. "I've got a few anecdotes about a man's behavior during pregnancy I can pass along from my own family that my mom told me about my dad. Really funny but clumsy things he did when I was on the way."

Jeremy nodded enthusiastically. "Well, go ahead. Share something with us right now."

Alex laughed out loud. "Well, there's one that particularly stands out. It seems Dad had seen that rerun of *I Love Lucy* where Ricky and the Mertzes rehearse what all they're gonna do when Lucy announces it's time to go to the hospital for the big event. I guess everyone's seen it at one time or another since the show is still on TV somewhere. Anyway, Dad put together this checklist of things to do when the time came. Mom said he even had them printed out on a sheet—one through twelve. Things like making sure the car always had plenty of gas, a ziplock bag full of snacks for himself to munch on, a couple of his favorite magazines to read while he was waiting, and stuff like that. Mom said that most of the things on the list were about him, though. Not much about her. I mean, she could picture him out in the waiting room leisurely munching on Fritos and reading *Sports Illustrated* while she was busy pushing me out. I don't think Dad was real big on the 'coach in the delivery room' thing. It wasn't as big back then as it is now."

Jeremy looked intrigued. "So what happened when the time for the delivery came?"

"Well, when Mom gave him the word, it didn't fit his time frame. She said he obviously expected it to come conveniently for the both of them—maybe like while they were watching primetime TV, or after they'd gotten up in the morning, had breakfast, and had their eyes wide open and their wits about them. Instead, it came in the middle of the night. Dad freaked and suddenly couldn't find anything, including the car keys. They'd only been on a hook in the kitchen since they moved into the apartment. He was frantic, running around their apartment, rifling through drawers, his coat pockets—anywhere but the usual place. Just like in the *I Love Lucy* episode, everything fell apart. But it got worse than that. Mom pretty much had to take charge right in the middle of her contractions and calm him down. It wasn't too funny at the time, she said, but they both managed to laugh at it once they got me safely home. She said it just proved it was a good thing men couldn't get pregnant. They would plan everything down to the last detail like it was an *I Love Lucy* episode and then promptly make a spectacle of themselves like roosters with their heads cut off. That was her exact phrase."

"That's great stuff," Jeremy said. "What do you think, Maurie?"

"Put enough things like that together, and I think you've got a great book," she said, winking at Alex.

In bed later that night, Maura Beth was particularly restless—perhaps because her baby was restless, too. A kick here, a kick there—there was no rhyme or reason to it—just a little trooper exploring its warm, cozy universe. As a result, sleep was eluding her for not the first time during her pregnancy, but a wide-awake brain gave her plenty of time to work certain things out. It suddenly came to her very clearly that too much was up for grabs, and there was no need for that to be the case now. So she reached over and grabbed Jeremy's arm, vigorously shaking him out of his sleep, which had been accentuated with an intermittent gurgle.

"Whu-whut? Whuzz wrong?" he said, half mumbling. He sat up and caught the expression on her face by the light of the scented votive candle they had chosen to let burn all the way down. She did not appear to be upset. Instead, she looked positively inspired.

"No, nothing's wrong. It's not the baby or anything like that. I've just had an idea. I think you and I should go ahead and ask Dr. Lively about our baby's gender, and we should tell Elise she should go up to Memphis Children's Hospital and do the same thing."

Jeremy blinked a couple of times while clearing his brain. "Okay, that's fine with me. I told you I was going to leave it up to you anyway. But tell me why you want Leesie to ask?"

"I think it'll help her come down to earth about her pregnancy. If she can know for certain that her life will be with her little girl or her little boy, she can plan accordingly. There won't be any more guesswork. As things stand, she's still too caught up in her sociology and gender politics for her own good. That's not going to help her with the day-to-day tasks of taking care of a baby."

Jeremy was nodding enthusiastically. "Well, it's worth a shot. I agree that she's got her head in the clouds about what it means to bring a child into this world. Hey, going off on Lamaze the way she did still makes me worry about her. But what about us? Why did you decide we needed to know all of a sudden?"

Maura Beth sat up straighter and drew in her breath as her baby kicked once again.

"Well, our little darling is pretty active tonight for starters. It just reminds me that we're getting closer and closer to the due date in late January. But mainly I want to get Mama off my back with all this hounding about names. There's no way I'll end up pleasing her, so I'm going to call her after we see Dr. Lively and tell her that we've decided to do it our way, period. No more hemming and hawing over the phone just to try to keep the peace. She needs to know once and for all that we are not giving any of our children first names that were last popular in the nineteenth century and that actually used to be last names. They'll go through school hating us for it."

"You are one smart mama tonight, aren't you?" Jeremy said, leaning over and gently kissing her on the lips.

"Yes, I am, and there will be no more discussion about this. I'm serious," Maura Beth said, pulling back slightly. "So you and I need to make our own list tomorrow at the kitchen table after we have breakfast. Simple, respectable names for a boy and a girl. No boy names for a girl, and no girl names for a boy. Nothing cutesy or trendy or futuristic or androgynous, either. I'd like to get back to basics on this."

"Give me a high five," Jeremy said, and they executed it quickly. "For the record, I do not want a junior if it's a boy. I've always believed everybody should have a unique name. A sensible name that belongs to them and nobody else. There are no juniors, seconds, thirds, and fourths in my little corner of the world. The gene split makes that impossible."

"I agree."

"And I didn't want to say anything all this time, but I would have been pretty upset if you had caved in to your mother and saddled our child with a string of historical family names that are a trial to spell, remember, and pronounce. So we're on the same page. We'll get this done in the kitchen tomorrow."

Despite what had happened at the library, Maura Beth truly felt that she had won the day and took a deep, cleansing breath of gardenia-scented air. Maybe that would even calm the baby down long enough for her to drift off.

"Let's sleep on it and see what we can come up with," she said, sinking back onto her pillows with a hopeful smile.

8

Who's in the Oven?

The Reveal Party at their Lake Cherico lodge was Connie's idea, once she had found out that both Maura Beth and Elise would be going up to Memphis Children's Hospital to get the big news from Dr. Lively. She lost no time in spreading the word, chiefly to her fellow Cherry Cola Book Club friends.

"It's not going to be anything fancy," she had told them all over the phone. "Just a few side dishes, canapés, and cocktails, obviously something soft or juices for the pregnant mothers. One level below our Cherry Cola Book Club outings, but come help us celebrate."

Nearly everyone was on board with enthusiasm: Becca and Justin Brachle, Voncille and Locke Linwood, Periwinkle and Parker Place, library front desk clerks Renette Posey and Marydell Crumpton, and library benefactors, Mamie Crumpton and Nora Duddney. Newcomers such as Ana Estrella, who had won the Queen of the Cookbooks prize in July, then turned around and generously donated the money to the library for an ESL program, were excited to be coming as well.

"We seem to have become the staging area for all the major events in Maura Beth's adult life," Douglas said a half hour before their guests would start arriving. He and Connie were putting the finishing touches on the tempting buffet they had prepared for the gathering. "First, her wedding, and now this."

"She's very comfortable with us," Connie said, placing sprigs of parsley in strategic places. Although she had originally intended to offer something more casual to her guests, the hostess gene within her simply would not let her settle for such a thing. She had also baked two small, almond-flavored cakes—one with pink icing and one with blue icing—to cover all the bases.

"We see more of Maura Beth than we see of Lindy, actually," Douglas added.

"It's a compliment to us that she wanted her wedding out on our deck instead of down in New Orleans like her mother wanted her to do, but it was a ceremony she'll never forget," Connie continued. "Saying their vows as the sun went down over the lake was an unforgettable moment."

Douglas stepped back and framed the colorful spread on the dining room table with his hands. "Now that's a pretty picture if I do say so myself. We've outdone ourselves, Connie."

"Let it never be said that you and I don't know how to give parties and make people want to come back for more."

Douglas was nodding, but his expression turned thoughtful. "I'm still wondering how things will go with Paul and Susan a week from now, though. It could be a tense Thanksgiving if Elise doesn't handle herself well. We've both seen her in action when she insists on getting her way."

Connie shrugged and waved him off as she rearranged dishes of nuts on the table. It came to her suddenly that she hadn't distributed them equally, and that was something she could not allow from a presentation standpoint.

"Douglas, we're just going to have to trust her this time. She's got to grow up someday, and this is the perfect opportunity to show that she takes full responsibility for her decisions. Everything we do in life has a ripple effect, particularly where friends and relatives are concerned. All those years being an ICU nurse taught me how interrelated we all are. The experience can be joyful, or it can be painful, but we don't live in a vacuum. Elise has this notion that she can do everything by herself, but there's a practical limit to that."

Douglas gave his wife his best, affectionate stare and then took her in his arms and gave her a kiss. "You are such a wise woman, you know that?"

"I married you, didn't I?"

"Yes, and you did it knowing I was a billboard trial lawyer. I've always been grateful to you for overlooking that little item."

Connie eyed him skeptically. "Now, none of that. You helped lots of people during your practice, and you know it. Don't you dare paint yourself with such a broad brush. We both earned our retirement through hard work."

Connie chimed her spoon on her wineglass to get the attention of the chattering crowd thoroughly enjoying their food and drinks around the lodge's rustic great room. Everyone who had accepted her invitation had shown up as promised, so there was a full house just itching to offer their congratulations.

"Folks," she began. It took another chime or two to get everyone's full attention and the buzzing to die down; then she continued. "Folks, it's time for us to find out who's in the oven from our expecting couples. I know you've all been waiting patiently for this moment, so let's not put it off any longer. So, will Maura Beth, Jeremy, and Elise come forward and share their good news with us, please?"

The trio made their way to one end of the buffet table, and Connie said, "Who wants to go first?"

Elise made a half bow and gestured graciously. "Let them. I don't mind bringing up the rear."

"Maurie," Jeremy said. "You do the honors. You're doing all the work now."

Maura Beth took a quick breath and surveyed her friends with a smile. How fortunate she was to have found and made a life with them all in this off-the-beaten-path, little Cherico!

"We're thrilled to announce to all of you that Jeremy and I are going to be the proud parents of a boy."

The outburst of warm applause and coordinated cries of "Congratulations!" made Maura Beth blush for a moment, but with Jeremy by her side, she shook what seemed like a hundred hands and managed, "Thank you so much!" without a hitch to as many smiling faces.

"Have you decided on a name yet?" Becca Brachle wanted to know once the din had faded somewhat.

"We're still working on it," Maura Beth told her. "But we're getting close. We made a list the other day, and we've narrowed it down to two choices, and both involve our fathers."

"I think you're wise to go that way," Becca said. "Justin and I had both sides of the family lobbying ferociously for their favorite names. Have you been going through that?"

Maura Beth's sigh was full of frustration. "I certainly have—mostly from my mother. She's been beating the New Orleans drum since she found out we were pregnant. I would never tell her this to her face, but everything she's suggested to us is what I'd call a *bully* name."

"I think I have an idea what you're getting at, but, please, give me your version," Becca said.

"My version is that it's the kind of stuffy, formal name that causes kids to get bullied during recess at school or on the school bus or just about anywhere else. Either that or the other kids make up a crazy nickname that sticks, and it's even worse for the child. These days, bullying has become quite an issue, and I don't want to do anything to contribute to it for my son. Naming a child should take into consideration what daily life will be like for them."

"Got it," Becca said, giving her friend a wink. "I think our little Markie will be safe from teasing, though, don't you?"

"My godson will be just fine, and I can't wait for our sons to become friends as they grow up," Maura Beth added.

Then Connie chimed her spoon again. "Now, folks, let's not forget we have Elise's news to hear."

There was a polite hush as Elise drew herself up with a smile. "I'm happy to report that I'll be having a little girl. I'm going to name her Constance Celice, and I'm going to call her Celice." Then she turned to her aunt. "The Constance is for you, Aunt Connie, and Celice is out of thin air. Don't ask me where it came from. I'm just a law unto myself."

"Why . . . thank you. I think Celice is a beautiful name, sweetie," Connie said, embracing her niece as the same wave of "Congratulations!" erupted throughout the room.

"A boy and a girl for the McShay family," Jeremy said, warmly embracing his sister. "We all have a lot to look forward to."

Elise's smile faded slightly as she answered, "I hope so."

Elise found herself on the great room sofa, facing the warmth of a chilly November fireplace as Connie began another of their confidential talks. The last guest from the Reveal Party had left, and Douglas had made himself scarce once again for another session of "girl talk" between his wife and his niece.

"Elise, sweetie," she was saying, "I'm perfectly thrilled you've included me in naming your precious little daughter, but—"

"I knew there was going to be a *but,* Aunt Connie," Elise interrupted. "I can always tell when you've got something on your mind."

"I certainly don't want to rain on your parade, but it's just that I'm wondering how your mother will take this. I mean, honoring me over her the way you have. She's your own flesh and blood, and I'm just an in-law."

"I don't think of you that way at all."

"I understand that, but you do know what I mean, don't you?"

Elise took her aunt's hand, sitting perfectly still for a moment or two as she tried to find the right words. "Listen, I've grown so close to you and Uncle Doug over the last six months. This isn't a question of genes. You've taken me in and been so kind to me as I go through this . . . well, I guess you could call it an experiment."

Connie gently withdrew her hand, but the expression on her face exuded warmth and understanding. "Sweetie, this is not an experiment. It's a child, and you're bringing her into this world."

"I understand that. Maybe I put it the wrong way. But what's wrong with me honoring you by giving my daughter your name?"

Connie sat in thoughtful silence for a while. "I was just moving ahead a few days to Thanksgiving. You're going to be springing the news of your pregnancy on your parents, as well as the method you chose to get pregnant. That's certainly not business as usual, but fingers crossed that that'll go off well. Just give your mother a thought or two. Maybe you could name the child Susan Celice instead of Constance Celice? It might keep the peace in the family. Just my two cents, sweetie. Will you at least think about it?"

Elise took a while but eventually said, "You do realize

that at this point I'm closer to you than I am to Mom, don't you? Of course, it's not a contest, but okay, I'll think about what you said. You haven't given me any bad advice yet."

Then Connie said, "I'm gonna scooch on over just a tad bit and give you the biggest hug ever, and please just know that whatever you name your daughter, I'll be the best great aunt who ever lived."

"I'm not worried in the least about that."

The time had come at last. After they had gotten home from the Reveal Party, Maura Beth and Jeremy had sat down at the kitchen table and picked the winner for their son's name. The next step was for Maura Beth to call her mother, Cara Lynn, and do another reveal—this one, perhaps, much more important than the one trotted out at the party for her friends, who would support her no matter what. This one might very well have consequences that could last a lifetime.

Jeremy remained seated at the table as Maura Beth picked up the phone and waited for her mother to answer. "Just stay strong and keep a smile in your voice, Maurie," he told her, giving her a thumbs-up.

Moments later, the conversation began with typical small talk about everyone's health, the weather, and so on. There was a tenseness about it that always accompanies delaying getting to some difficult point.

"I have some wonderful news," Maura Beth said, finally. "We decided not to wait any longer, and we found out we're going to have a boy. You'll soon have a grandson to spoil."

Cara Lynn's reaction was warm and genuine. "I'm so thrilled, and Daddy will be, too. You had us on pins and needles all this time wondering what was going on. I assume everything is okay with the baby? There wasn't any sort of complication you were worried about, was there?"

"No, it was nothing like that. Everything's fine. Dr. Lively says things couldn't be better. Is Daddy there, too?"

"Wouldn't you know it? He had a deposition tonight of all nights," Cara Lynn said in disgust. "He's consulting on a case as a favor to a friend. But he'll be back any minute now."

Then came the carefully rehearsed part that Maura Beth dreaded. She could only hope that she would not forget any of the lines she and Jeremy had so carefully contrived. She had even written down several keywords on a piece of paper if her memory should fail her.

"I wanted you to know that Jeremy and I took all of your family name suggestions into serious consideration—every single one. You gave us quite a variety, but we decided to simplify, though."

"What do you mean by simplify?"

Maura Beth could sense the subtle change in her mother's tone. Not exactly imperious yet—but headed that way. "Instead of last names, we're going to go with first names. I think you'll be pleased, though. We're naming our son Paul William McShay. The Paul is for Jeremy's father, obviously, and William is for Daddy. But we're going to call our son Liam for a touch of originality. We're both very excited about it and hope you are, too."

There was an ominous silence on the other end of the phone. It was crazy the way a few seconds could stretch out to infinity.

"Well, what do you think?" Maura Beth said, swallowing hard.

More silence, and Maura Beth felt the first stirrings of panic. Was this going to explode in her face?

"Hello? Are you still there?"

"Yes, I'm here," Cara Lynn said finally.

"Then don't keep me in suspense like this."

"I don't like to rush into things."

It was all Maura Beth could do to hold her temper, but just when she thought she'd reached the tipping point, Cara Lynn came through.

"I've been thinking it over carefully, and my opinion is that your father will be very pleased that you've honored him this way. I had hoped you might choose one of my side of the family's names, but perhaps if you have a little girl later on you could make that decision."

That was enough to burst the emotional dam, despite the fact that the issue had not been put to bed completely. Their son had made it through the obstacle course. Perhaps a future daughter might not. "You've made me so happy tonight, Mama. I couldn't have hoped for a better response from you. I thought Daddy would like it, too," Maura Beth said, the relief clearly evident in her voice. "Do you like our idea of calling him Liam? Is it too outside the box?"

"I don't think so at all. It has a dignity to it," Cara Lynn said. "Yes, I think I like it very much. Maura Beth, you are the most surprising daughter any mother ever had. I learned when you got married up there in Cherico that you were always going to be your own woman to the very end. You and I finally reached an understanding. What I hope for now is a healthy baby so I can get busy being a grandmother. I've been looking forward to it for I don't know how long, and now the time is nearly here. So I think I need to go ahead and get myself in the right frame of mind."

"I'm blowing you a big kiss through the phone right this minute. I hope you can catch it."

Cara Lynn waited a few seconds and said, "Caught it. And here's one right back to you. I'll tell Daddy all the good news as soon as he gets home. Would you like for him to call you?"

"Very much."

"Then it's done."

"I love you, Mama."

"I love you, too, baby."

Maura Beth hung up the phone and smiled at Jeremy across the way. He had already gleaned the outcome of the call from her end of the conversation and looked supremely smug.

"So we did all that worrying for nothing, I gather?" he said.

Maura Beth laughed and pointed his way. "Well, the rehearsing was worth it. You noticed I didn't trip up."

"You did good, Maurie."

"Yeah, well, Mama will always keep us on our toes," she told him with a gleam in her eye. "You can take that to the bank."

9

One Big, Happy Family

By late November, the northern stretches of the Natchez Trace Parkway had lost much of their autumnal palette. No more the golden, red, and burnt orange leaves to delight the eye as they decorated the hardwood branches on either side of the road. Having fallen from the grace of the growing season, they now formed a carpet of color on the grass below, but even that was starting to fade as the nights grew colder and less forgiving. Brown was rapidly becoming the default hue. Still, there were always glimpses of deer and wild turkey, posing and strutting about at the edge of the woods to entertain sightseers traveling down from Nashville or up from Natchez; there was also the occasional historical exhibit that attracted parkway visitors no matter what the weather was like.

On the day before Thanksgiving, Paul and Susan McShay found themselves making the journey from Nashville to Cherico, keeping themselves occupied with small talk and occasional speculation.

"I still think it's not like Elise," Susan was saying to her husband at the wheel of their SUV.

They weren't able to do the limit of fifty miles per hour because of several cars in front of them obviously enjoying the scenery and in no hurry to get where they were going. No one ever took the parkway to make good time. It was foolish to even try. It just happened to be the most direct route from Nashville to Cherico.

"Taking a sabbatical to study small-town life in Cherico just doesn't sound like something she would do," Susan continued. "Connie swears that's all that's going on, but I think there's more to this than that. Frankly, I never thought Elise would take a sabbatical until she retired. She's so consumed with all those ideas of hers. She once told me she had so many young women to reach, and there was no point in taking any time off. She might miss that special one who would go on to make a huge difference in the world."

Paul, ever the retired Vanderbilt psychology professor who still cut quite a figure in his sweater vests, continued to be amused by his wife's ramblings on the subject. "You keep doubting everything, but you never seem to be able to come up with another explanation for why Elise is down there staying with my brother and Connie."

Susan gently patted her perfectly coiffed hair. She was always a study in fashionable attire and skillfully applied makeup, no matter the occasion. "Maybe I haven't. But if Elise thinks she's going to find a whole bunch of hippie feminists to interview down there in Cherico who agree with her about everything, she's sadly mistaken. Those two things don't go together in the small-town South. I'm not sure you can find anyone who fits that description in Brentwood. Everyone in our neighborhood embraces the success we've all enjoyed. Let's face it—Elise is stuck in 1969, and she wasn't even around then. She lives in her own little projection of the past."

"Connie never said she was down there to interview hippies or feminists. That's not the same as studying small-town life," Paul said.

"That's all well and good," Susan said, brushing him off with a sweep of her hand. "But I'm a mother, and I still think there's something fishy about Elise being down there. Of course, she never phones to tell us anything. We wouldn't even know she had moved in with Connie and Douglas if Connie hadn't called us up. I'm pretty good at reading people, and Connie sounded so strange when she explained everything. If you ask me, there was an element of hemming and hawing to it. And if Jeremy and Maura Beth can pick up a phone and say hello every once in a while, why can't Elise?"

Paul made a grunting noise that clearly indicated he was annoyed. "That's nothing new, so stop thinking about it. Concentrate on Jeremy and Maura Beth and our first grand-child on the way. The last thing we should do is get into a big fight with Elise about her career when we have other things to celebrate. We have to give her the benefit of the doubt."

"I suppose you're right. It's just that I keep wondering where we went wrong with her. What did we do to make her so mad at us?"

Paul gave a sigh of frustration as the cars in front of him continued to crawl along. There was no point in honking, and passing was dangerous, if not impossible, on the winding, two-lane parkway. They were pretty much stuck until they got to the exit for Cherico. "It's a good thing we got an early start. This funeral procession is going nowhere fast. As for as Elise is concerned, I don't necessarily think she's mad at us, but I also see no reason to continue all this speculation. We hardly ever get to see her, and that's apparently the way she wants it. Let's just be glad we're getting together with her and the rest of the family for Thanksgiving. What could be better than that?"

That brought a smile to Susan's voice at last. "Maura Beth and I get along so well. We speak every week about how she's doing. She never leaves out a detail. I can't wait to become a grandmother, and I'm sure Jeremy will be just as good a father as you've been."

"She and Jeremy are a good match," Paul added. "I've thought so from the beginning."

Susan leaned in, lowering her voice as if someone or some unseen force of nature might be listening in to disapprove. "I would never say this to Elise, of course, but sometimes I feel like Maura Beth acts like the one who's really our daughter. The daughter-in-law thing doesn't always work out, you know. Your mother and I never got along until the day she died, as you well know."

"Don't remind me," Paul said in a monotone. "I was always caught in the crossfire big-time."

Susan winced as all the unpleasant memories flooded in from the beginning of her marriage forward. "Anyway, I promise you, I'll do everything I can to stay on an even keel when we get to Connie's."

"Let's just enjoy all the delicious food," Paul said. "We don't have to speculate about that, and I'm sure everything will turn out all right if we just give it half a chance. Is it a deal?"

"Deal. But I'll call Connie on my cell and let her know we might be running a little late."

Down in Cherico at the lodge, Jeremy, Alex, and Elise were sitting in front of the fireplace discussing an outline for *Fatherhood for Dummies*—the title they had all agreed upon. A few minutes earlier, Connie had put a pot of fresh coffee for the men and hot cocoa for her niece on the coffee table, making herself scarce after lighting a couple of pumpkin spice candles on the window sills overlooking the lake.

Just the day before, Elise had practically jumped through the phone when Jeremy had called her up and told her about his fatherhood project. Then he had forged ahead from there.

"Would you like to get in on this with me? I know you could help me in so many different ways."

Elise didn't have to be asked twice, but there would be a price to pay in inviting her to the party. It was an understatement to say that she was dominating the discussion there on the sofa, while both Alex and Jeremy tried their best to take notes. It was as if the idea had been hers from the very beginning, an off-the-wall extension of her familiar curriculum interests.

"If we're going to do this right," she was saying to them at the moment, "we can't omit any common mistakes that men make. Jer, you need to ask Maura Beth to tell you everything you did that rubbed her the wrong way. Reassure her that you won't get your feelings hurt. You won't, will you?"

Jeremy drew himself up, looking as manly as possible. "Of course not. She and I have been pretty open with each other all along."

"That's going to be important," Elise said. "We want the book to be humorous, but we want it to come from the truth."

"I think we've got that covered." Jeremy wanted to say more but decided to bite his tongue. He was determined to make this collaboration between himself and his sister work, so he changed the subject somewhat.

"Have you heard anything more from that small press you queried in Denver about our book? What was the name of it?"

"Saterstrom Press," Elise said. "They've published a couple of supplementary texts by some of my cohorts at the U of Evansville. My query positioned our book as something that might fit well into a sociology course."

"I think it would," Alex said. "The entire discipline of sociology could use a little levity now and then."

"But if they do show any interest," Elise continued, "they'll want to see several sample chapters, so we need to get going on this. We have to have our strongest material right up front to entice them further."

Jeremy and Alex exchanged glances while sipping their coffee, and Jeremy said, "Leesie, I don't think we should rush through this. Can you squeeze all this into the rest of your sabbatical and still take care of your baby girl?"

Even before he had uttered the last word of his question, Jeremy knew he had said the wrong thing to his sister at the wrong time, and a slight wince crept into his face as he prepared for incoming shrapnel.

"Jer, I knew I could count on you to bring up the subject of what a woman can and cannot accomplish. No one ever sets a limit on what a man can handle. Men can have it all. It's been that way since the beginning of time." Elise folded her arms above her baby bump and affixed a pout to her face.

"I didn't mean it that way."

Alex intervened quickly, feeling slightly uncomfortable. "If I could say something here, Elise. It seems to me your brother is just taking into account the birth of your child. I'm sure he doesn't want to assume to rate your priorities. From my point of view, that's something that only you can determine."

Elise's face softened as she turned toward him. "That's absolutely right. I take full responsibility for my life. I always have."

"Then we'll agree that you'll work with us on the project as long as you want," Alex told her.

Elise eyed her brother intently. "Jer, you shouldn't have even brought up the issue. Alex has the right attitude." She gestured toward him graciously, and Alex gave her a grateful nod in return.

Steeling himself and swallowing hard, Jeremy said, "Enough said. Let's call a truce, shall we? We aren't going to be able to discuss this project rationally if we're at each other's throats all the time. I'm sure we all want this book to be the best it can be. I realize that what I'm about to say sounds like a pun, but can't we all be on the same page?"

Finally, there was much-needed, gentle laughter among the three of them, and Elise said, "Well, perhaps I've been coming on a little strong with you guys. It's just that I've had to fight for so many things in my career for so long. Someone always seems to be defining me."

"Well, you certainly don't have to fight with us," Jeremy told her emphatically. "Right, Alex?"

"Absolutely. I'm very interested in seeing what the three of us can cobble together and also what my class turns out this semester because of your unique input, Elise."

Elise gave him a pleasant glance. "That's a nice compliment, Alex. I appreciate it, and I'm working hard on my presentation."

Jeremy put down his coffee cup and looked his sister straight in the eye. "Leesie, if I were you, I'd be thinking of what you're going to say to Mom and Dad when they arrive in a few more hours. Believe me, we aren't your problem. Have you even given it a thought?"

"Of course I have. I'm simply going to tell them the truth. I've talked it over with Aunt Connie quite a bit now, and she thinks that's the best approach. What else is there to say, really? If they can't handle it, then so be it. It's not like we've all been a part of each other's lives since I graduated from college."

"I hope it turns out well, for your sake," Jeremy said. "I just want you to know that I'm here to support you, and so is Maurie. We really appreciate Aunt Connie inviting us over for Thanksgiving. Frankly, Maurie just wasn't up for cooking a huge meal, and neither was I."

Elise's tone suddenly brightened. That, of course, was the

privilege of a pregnant woman at any time. Ditto, her tone going to the dark side. "By the way, Alex, what are your plans for Thanksgiving?"

"I . . . I didn't have any actually."

"Then you must spend it here at the lodge with all of us. I'm sure Aunt Connie won't mind. She plans on fixing tons of food tomorrow. In fact, she's already started on her sweet potato casserole as we speak. One more place at the table won't be any trouble at all."

Alex's smile seemed almost shy and boyish. "Are you sure?"

"Don't worry about it. You must come."

"Then I will. Thanks. Mom and Dad are gone now, and I don't have any relatives living down here in Mississippi. I was just going to make do thawing out something in the freezer and watching some football in my apartment."

Elise continued to probe, while Jeremy looked on, somewhat bewildered. He had never seen his sister get so chummy so quickly with a member of the opposite sex. "You can watch football here on that flat-screen on the other side of the room. Dad and Uncle Doug will be doing that with their drinks for certain. Did you say where you were from, by the way? I can't recall."

"Missouri. Caruthersville. It's in the Bootheel. Somewhat Southern, we like to say. But with enough of its own characteristics to distinguish it."

"People say that about Evansville, Indiana, where I teach. Part Southern, part Midwest."

"I've never been there."

Jeremy sat back and listened with a smile. What was it about Alex that was bringing out the best in his sister? Maybe it was as simple as not having a history of arguing with her all the time as a sibling. Or was there possibly something else going on? Wouldn't that be a kick in the head?

Two hours later, Jeremy and Alex were in the midst of a final review of their collaborative notes, reading them out loud to Elise, whose role was to verify their accuracy. Or, as she was often wont to do, add observations of her own, pro or con. Fortunately, for the progress of the project, Elise was content to give her nod of approval to everything that had been discussed. She seemed to be particularly fond of Alex's reminiscences, and he seemed to be bursting with appreciative smiles. This first important session had been officially put to bed.

"If you'll excuse me, then," Jeremy said, rising from the sofa. "I've got to run to the men's room real quick."

It was just a minute or so later in Jeremy's absence that Susan and Paul burst through the front door without knocking, each one holding a bottle of Merlot. They had never stood on ceremony before and had no intention of doing so now. As a result, they were treated to the sight of their very pregnant daughter across the room wearing a red maternity tee and jeans while standing beside a man they had never seen before.

It was a nonplussed Susan who spoke first after a very audible gasp. "My goodness, Elise, just look at *you!* Tell me that's not a baby bump."

Elise turned toward the door, her expression as surprised as her mother's. "And hello to you, too, Mom . . . and Dad!"

Somehow, Susan found the words. "Never mind that. Is that really someone else on the way? We had no idea." Before Elise could reply, the awkward questions tumbled out one after another. "Is that your husband next to you? Why have you kept us in the dark all this time? You see, Paul, I told you something else was going on down here."

Alex went crimson in the face but said nothing.

"Shall I bring in the luggage?" Paul said, unable to think of anything else.

Susan shook her head emphatically. "That can wait."

"This isn't what it looks like," Elise told them. "Well, it is, and it isn't."

Then, as if in a well-rehearsed play, Jeremy entered from stage right while Connie entered from stage left, both freezing in their tracks.

"Welcome. We're so glad you're here," Connie managed, finally. "You said you thought you'd be running a little late."

Jeremy moved to his parents quickly with warm hugs. "Welcome to Cherico, Mom and Dad. We're all happy to see you."

"Good to see you, too, son," Paul said, but he was craning his neck, and his eyes were still trained on his daughter. "Where's your uncle Doug?"

"He's coming in now," Connie said, taking her turn at embracing her in-laws. "I just saw him at the boathouse through the kitchen window. He's been out on the lake on *The Verdict* all afternoon. I'm sure he hasn't caught a thing— he almost never does this time of year. He just likes to drift, unless the weather gets too iffy."

"Enough of the daily fishing report, Connie," Susan said, pointing toward her daughter all the while. "Will someone please explain what's going on here? You're all acting like this is business as usual."

Elise approached her parents slowly, almost as if she were in the midst of a walk down the aisle. Then she kissed them both on the cheek with a smile and gestured toward the fireplace sofa. "I think we should all sit down for this first. I have a lot to say to both of you."

"Thanks for the wine. Here, I'll take those bottles, and then I'll make a fresh pot of coffee for everyone," Connie said, heading toward the kitchen. "This may take a little while."

"You knew about this all along and said nothing, Connie?" Susan added. "Instead, you lied to us?"

"It's complicated," Connie said, turning at the door. "Let Elise explain everything to you."

"She wasn't the only one who knew," Jeremy said as Connie left the room. "Both Maurie and I knew."

Susan reluctantly headed for the sofa with Paul in tow. "By the way, where is Maura Beth?"

"At the library next door, of course," Jeremy said. "She'll be off in another thirty minutes or so. I'll text her that you're here. She's been counting the days until your arrival. You have no idea how much she's been looking forward to Thanksgiving. Just one big, happy family and all that, you know."

Elise's voice was full of pleading now. "If everyone will just take a seat. I'll be happy to explain everything."

Susan remained agitated as she found her spot on the sofa between her husband and her daughter. "Working on a book about small-town life, indeed."

"But she is helping me work on a book, Mom," Jeremy said, pulling up a chair. "She and I and Alex just finished up our first brainstorming session on a book about fatherhood a few minutes ago. It's sort of a humorous look at how men handle their wives' pregnancies and sociological changes."

"Who on earth is Alex?" Susan said.

"I am," Alex said, raising his hand and feeling like he was somehow confessing to a crime. "I'm Alex Brandon, and I teach history at Cherico High. That's how I became friends with your son and how I met your daughter. The three of us are working on various projects together."

"Mom, Dad . . . if you'll just let me explain. This is all about me and no one else," Elise said, the impatience growing in her voice.

Finally, everyone got settled in—except Alex, who chose to remain standing—and Elise had their full attention. "First, Mom and Dad, please don't blame Aunt Connie or Uncle Doug for this. Once they agreed to let me stay here until the baby was born, I can assure you that Aunt Connie has been on me constantly to level with you. She's insisted all along you had the right to know what I've chosen to do. It's strictly my fault that I've been putting if off the way I have."

This time, it was Paul who spoke up. "Better late than never."

"Yes, well, as you can see, I chose to get pregnant. But Alex over there had nothing to do with it. He's just a friend, and yes, the three of us really are working on a book together."

Alex managed a sheepish grin and waved his hand.

Elise took a breath that seemed to suck up all the air in the room and continued. "The truth is, I decided that I'd reached the stage in my life that I wanted more than teaching, as fulfilling as that is for me. I decided that I wanted to have a baby. But on my own terms. I didn't want a husband. I didn't want to get married, either. You've both known how I've felt about that for a long time now. I just wanted a shot at raising a child who would make this world a better place."

Tension was still gripping the room, and Elise allowed everyone time to digest what she had said so far before continuing. "So . . . I went to a sperm bank up in Evansville, chose a donor, and here I am in my third trimester expecting sometime in January. Now you know everything."

"You say you chose a donor. Do you know who the father is?" Paul said. There was no hostility in his tone. Instead, he came off like a professor asking a question of one of his former psychology students.

"No, that's not allowed. I just know that he is of Italian ancestry and is college educated. I was allowed to shop . . . so to speak."

Susan sounded far less comfortable with everything. "Just like at the supermarket. So we'll never know who the father is? You'll have this baby without this man's support? Ever?"

"Yes."

Susan and Paul seemed to be having a conversation without speaking. It was all there in the movement of their eyes. Then, Susan broke the silence. "I don't know what to say, Elise."

"You could say you're happy for me, Mom. You could say you hope my baby will be healthy. I'm sure you hope that for Maura Beth and Jeremy."

"Our babies will be first cousins, no matter what," Jeremy added, intently catching the gaze of his parents.

"Yes, they will," Paul said, easing the tension somewhat. "I know we'll be praying for two healthy grandchildren, right, Susan?"

"Uh . . . of course," she said, gathering herself at last.

Elise leaned in against her mother with the biggest smile she could manage. "Mom, I'm having a little girl, so you're getting one of each. A boy from Jeremy and Maura Beth, and a girl from me. And wait for the kicker. I'm going to name her Susan Constance Celice McShay after you and Aunt Connie. How about that? She'll have four names."

"How very family-minded of you," Susan said. "Would it be too much of me to ask what you're actually going to call her with all that to choose from?"

Now Elise was in her comfort zone. All the rehearsal she had done with her Aunt Connie would surely pay off, and everyone would be satisfied. Or at least she hoped that would be the outcome.

"If it's all right with you and Aunt Connie, I'd like to call her Celice. She'd officially have both your names to honor you, but I thought I'd like to give her something original to go by."

Susan's lips moved as she repeated the name in silence. "It's a pretty enough name. How did you come up with it?"

"I don't honestly know. I just like the way it sounds."

"Do you mind if I take a few minutes to get a few things off my chest?" Susan said to her daughter.

Paul gave his wife a look of consternation that contained everything they had discussed on the ride down. "Maybe it would be a good idea to sit with all this for a while."

But Susan actually gave him a wink in return. "No, I promise I'll be constructive about all this. Elise, I wouldn't be doing my duty as a mother if I didn't put in my two cents. Bringing you and your brother up was no walk in the park. You were both so competitive about everything, but you both also knew what you wanted out of life and went for it. How could we not be proud of both of you?"

"Thanks, Mom," Jeremy put in quickly.

"That's nice to hear," Elise added.

"That said," Susan continued, "I can't imagine my life without Paul. There were times when I didn't know the answers regarding you two, but he did. I got through those episodes because of him—and only because of him. He was my partner in everything we decided to do."

Paul chuckled and said, "Don't make me sound like a saint, sweetheart. I'm far from it."

"No, my point is that I can't imagine being a single mother. But that's what you've chosen for yourself, Elise. I have to admit I'm a bit shocked by your choice, although in a way I shouldn't be. You really have always been your own woman. I just think raising any child is a huge responsibility, and if you need help with it at any time, you shouldn't be afraid to ask for it. Your father and I have already missed two trimesters. Don't shut us out of the third."

"Was that a note of approval?" Elise said.

Susan glanced at her husband and son before answering. "I suppose it is. But . . . is there anything else I need to know about what's been going on down here? I think I'm owed that much."

"Just that life here on the lake has been so relaxing for me," Elise said. "Aunt Connie's a wonderful cook, and she helps me follow all of Dr. Lively's rules to the letter. He's my obstetrician, of course."

Susan made a breathy sound with her lips that betrayed her deflated mood. "I could have wished you would have told us about this first. We would have been happy to take care of you in Brentwood, you know."

"Would you have, Mom? I mean, really?"

Paul answered instead. "Of course we would. Maybe it would have been a bit of a shock at first just the way it is now. But family comes first."

"Even if it's not traditional?"

"That's really no one's business but yours," Paul said. "And ours, if you'll include us. Do you want to stay down here until the baby comes? You can have your old room back if you want it."

Elise shot her brother a wide-eyed glance and tilted her head. "What do you think, Jer?"

Jeremy's jaw dropped, but he recovered with a smile. "You actually want my opinion on something like this? Hey, I know better than to butt in too much."

"Good point. I know I've asked you to back off more than once."

Elise thought for a while longer and said, "If you wouldn't mind, Mom and Dad, I'd like to stay down here at the lodge. Maura Beth and I have practically become sisters sharing our pregnancies. So I think I'd like to be around for her baby's birth, and I'd like to have her around for mine. As Jer said, they're going to be first cousins, no matter what. Plus, I really do have this book project to work on with Jer and Alex, and it would be difficult to do that up in Brentwood. But now that you know about everything, both of you can visit anytime you want."

"Well, that settles that, then," Susan said, managing a weak smile.

Connie emerged from the kitchen with the coffeepot and more cups on a silver tray and headed toward the fireplace table. "Sorry it took me so long. How are things going?"

"I think we've survived the first shock wave nicely," Elise said. "You have to start somewhere."

"Maybe I should go out and bring the luggage in now," Paul added, rising from the sofa.

Jeremy got up from his chair at almost the same time. "Do you need any help with that, Dad?"

"Sure."

"Oh, I'd forgotten about that," Susan said.

Paul shrugged. "I hadn't."

And then the two men headed out the door.

There was, however, a decided element of escape about it with all the clipped dialogue in rapid sequence, and Connie noticed. "Fresh coffee, anyone?" she said, trying to inject a note of normalcy into a situation that was anything but.

"Yes, I'll take a cup, thank you. It was a long drive. We got behind a parade of slowpokes along the Trace and thought we'd never get here," Susan said, watching Connie pour. "Do you want one, Elise?"

Elise put her hand atop her protruding belly protectively, giving her mother an incredulous stare.

Susan instantly winced. "Oh . . . the caffeine. I didn't think. You've got to give me some time to get used to this."

Elise gently rubbed her mother's arm. "Take all the time you need. I realize I'm still a handful."

★　★　★

Maura Beth's entrance ten minutes later was a welcome balm for everyone, and the conversation focused on her quickly.

"You definitely wear your pregnancy well," Susan told her, after everyone had embraced. "Is this flannel you're wearing? I would never have thought of that for a maternity outfit."

"Yes, it's a popover, and I couldn't resist the plaid design. Isn't it cute? I know it makes me look like I'm going on a hayride and I'm a farmer's daughter, but it sure is comfortable. Some of my patrons have commented on how much they like it."

"I ordered several of them for her so she'd have lots of different looks at work," Jeremy said. "Well, at least she'd have different colors. I've learned that that's pretty important to women."

Maura Beth sent a smooching sound in his general direction. "Susan, your son has made it so easy for me. You raised a good man there."

"I've tried very hard not to go overboard," Jeremy said, winking. "Believe it or not, there've been a few times that Maurie has had to pull me back from being pregnant myself. It's going to be the basis for the humorous book I'm trying to write."

"I'm not the tiniest bit surprised. When my children choose to do anything in life, they go all out," Susan added, laughing, but she was looking only at Jeremy when she said the words.

"The best part is, Maura Beth and I really are like sisters now, as I told you," Elise said, stepping in and resting her hand on Maura Beth's shoulder. "We're always comparing notes from everything to heartburn to how often our babies kick. It helps, believe me."

"That's nice," Susan said. "Only other women truly understand what it's like to be pregnant. Are you due in January, too, Maura Beth?"

"Somewhere around there. Elise and I are about two weeks apart. And we have another friend, Periwinkle Place, who's not far behind. She's a member of The Cherry Cola Book Club, and she and her husband also run The Twinkle. That's our most popular restaurant."

Susan continued to pump Maura Beth. "Yes, I remember you got the idea for the club when you came up to Brentwood year before last, didn't you?"

"There was a little more to it than that, but pretty much. You and Paul are still big readers, I'm guessing."

Susan nodded. "We both love to read. We like to keep up with all the bestsellers and such."

"Then you absolutely must let me take you on a tour of my new library next door," Maura Beth said. "It's my legacy to this little town of Cherico that I've fallen in love with and never want to leave. Jeremy and I want to raise our children here."

"I'd love it," Susan added.

"We're not officially open on Thanksgiving, of course, but I've got the keys, and you're family."

"That sounds delightful, doesn't it, Paul?"

He nodded in agreement.

Maura Beth took a seat on the sofa and continued to describe the amenities her library offered as Susan sat beside her, seemingly mesmerized, asking question after question almost as if she were a reporter. In fact, the entire room was focused on Maura Beth and her enthusiasm for her hard-won achievement.

Throughout it all, Elise grinned politely, even though she was suddenly overcome with a feeling of being slightly out of place. As she quietly surveyed the room, she noted with some surprise that only Alex was not paying attention to Maura Beth. Instead, he was looking at her with the suggestion of a smile—one that gently lifted the corners of his mouth. One that was both sweet and respectful.

And even though a part of Elise wanted to smile back, another part of her simply would not allow it. She felt stuck and conflicted, and did not know how to make the feeling go away.

10

Early

Periwinkle and Parker Place were going all out for their Thanksgiving feast as only two accomplished chefs could, dividing up the assignments judiciously. Although Parker would be whipping up a pumpkin custard pie for dessert, as would be expected of a pastry baker, he would also be contributing a squash, onion, and crumbled Saltine casserole, while Periwinkle would be basting four game hens wrapped in bacon—two for each of them—and assembling an appetizer of caprese salad made with heirloom tomatoes, fresh mozzarella, and basil with a generous drizzle of homemade balsamic vinaigrette dressing. This was going to be the Thanksgiving to outdo all others for the two of them. Three, counting the little one on the way, who would be the ultimate beneficiary of all that delicious food.

At the moment their preparations were right on time for a one o'clock meal, so much so that they had bought themselves enough leeway to take a break and put their feet up on the living room sofa. Parker was sipping his glass of white Zinfandel, while Periwinkle was enjoying a cup of pure, unadulterated, if store-bought, egg nog.

"I'm not going to wait until Christmas this year," she was saying. "Our little girl needs her calcium, you know."

Parker gently patted his wife's significant baby bump and beamed at what he had helped create. "Which reminds me, I've decided to create an egg-nog cheesecake for our dessert menu at The Twinkle this year. I don't know why I haven't ever tried something like that before. I never did it up in Memphis all those years. Doesn't that sound irresistible?"

Periwinkle quickly raised her hand. "I volunteer to be your guinea pig, of course. By the time we get to the finished product, you'll be ready for one of those contests on the Food Network."

"I was hoping you would say something like that. And yes, I think I could go on television and win one of those things. We could always find something to do with the extra money."

"As if I haven't been your taster and sampler a hundred times before. After all, I'm your quality-control gal."

He leaned over and gave her a peck on the cheek. "You sure are—and a damned good one at that."

Periwinkle took another sip of her egg nog, but then her playful, satisfied expression disappeared, replaced by creases across her forehead and a drooping sadness at the corners of her eyes.

Parker noticed and said, "What's the matter?"

"Mama, of course."

Parker glanced up at the ceiling, shaking his head with his eyes closed. "Peri, please. We've been all over that. You can't let her get to you like this. Let her sulk and fester all by herself, but don't let it ruin our life together."

"I know. You're right." She paused and sighed. "It's just that I'd hoped for some family support for our baby girl. Who wouldn't want a grandmother in the picture, spoiling her right and left? Isn't that part of the American dream? With your mother gone and my mother acting like a complete horse's ass, it doesn't look like that's ever gonna happen for us."

"If your mother never comes around, we'll just have to live our lives without her. Besides, we have all our friends here in Cherico—all the book club members will be there for us—Maura Beth and Jeremy, Becca and Justin, Connie and Douglas, and all the rest of 'em. An alternative family is sure way better than none."

"You're right again, of course." But there was little conviction in Periwinkle's voice.

The two of them sipped quietly for a while as the tempting aromas from the kitchen filled their nostrils.

"Do you . . . do you think we should go ahead and make one more try?" Periwinkle said finally.

Parker put his wineglass down on the end table and gently took his wife's hand. "Listen to me, Peri. We can't set ourselves up for more rejection like that. She won't even speak to me, and you've gone over there to try to reason with her with terrible results. You came back in tears. I've never seen you so unhappy, and it made me mad as hell. We'll just have to wait for her to come around, if she ever does. She has to make the next move. Maybe when the baby is born, she'll see the light. But we can't live our lives expecting it, and we can't go to pieces if she doesn't."

"No, we definitely shouldn't do that. I guess the truth is, you can't have everything in life."

"I wonder if anyone ever does," Parker said, finishing off his wine. "Meanwhile, I'll go check on all the food. Burning things is strictly not in our DNA. You just stay here and relax a bit longer."

After Parker had said grace about thirty minutes later, the two of them began to dig into their sumptuous dinner with great relish, and the caprese salad disappeared in no time. Next up came the main course and side dish.

"You've outdone yourself with the squash casserole,

sweetie," Periwinkle said after swallowing a generous forkful. "Did you sneak a little bit of sugar into this by any chance?"

"Guilty. But just a little. The onions have a natural sweetness, of course. If you go overboard with too much sugar, you practically have a dessert, and I make enough of those as it is."

"I never thought of adding a crust of crumbled Saltines in all my years of cooking," she told him. "But you really need it to offset the sweetness." She took another forkful. "I think I'm addicted to your recipe."

"You could also use oyster crackers instead of Saltines, you know. But don't eat too fast, though, baby. You don't want another case of your famous indigestion now, do you?"

She waved him off. "Of course not. But I just can't help it. I think the baby must be addicted to your casserole, too. She's kicking up a storm right this minute. At this rate, I think she'll turn out to be a champion soccer player. No pun intended, but wouldn't that be a kick?"

Parker enjoyed a hearty laugh. "I betcha she'll be the best at whatever she wants to do."

The carefree banter continued as they both tackled the task of carving their game hens. There had been an ongoing but playful debate earlier in the week about the merits of a huge turkey with all its leftovers for lots of sandwiches versus the one-time consumption virtues of much-smaller poultry, and of course the game hens had won the argument this time around. No refrigerator-hogging carcass this season to maneuver around.

Then there was a sudden, sharp intake of breath from Periwinkle. She dropped her knife and fork on the plate with a resounding clatter, which acted as an alarm that immediately filled the room with anxiety.

"What is it?" Parker said, leaning forward.

Periwinkle said nothing as she put both hands over her belly and grimaced.

"Peri? Talk to me."

"Call an ambulance. I'm cramping, and I think my water just broke. We need to get to the hospital."

"Oh, God!" Parker said, rising from the table and then fumbling with his cell phone on the kitchen counter. "Don't come now, baby girl. Please, please, please. It's too soon, too soon!"

That same feeling of being on the outside looking in that Elise had experienced once Maura Beth had entered the lodge the evening before continued throughout Connie's delicious Thanksgiving dinner consisting of the traditional turkey with all the trimmings. Everyone was polite enough, and there was plenty of small talk to keep the table occupied as course after course was served up. But Elise realized that her artificial insemination pregnancy was definitely the elephant in the room that no one wanted to address any further. It was so much easier to question Jeremy and Maura Beth about their "normal" pregnancy, and Elise truly understood. They were the happy couple who everyone admired. Meanwhile, she was on her own by choice. It was apparently continuing to make her parents uneasy. There had been no further discussion of it the evening before, even though she had wanted to go into their room after dinner and sit down with them. Anything to banish the terrible tension. But she stayed in her own room with her doubts, and they had stayed in theirs. Nothing had changed.

It was with a great sense of relief to Elise, therefore, when Maura Beth brought her back into the conversation. "I've gained another pound over the last week," she told the gathering. "But this dinner is sure to add one or two more. What about you, Elise?"

"I'm holding steady," she said. "But I agree. Aunt Connie knows how to keep people fat and happy. Or is it fat and sassy?"

"I'll admit to either one," Connie said, surveying the table with a smile. Then the landline rang, and Connie rose from her chair. "I'll get it."

The others continued to chat while Connie took the call in the kitchen. When she returned a few minutes later, the shocked expression on her face and the shaking of her head told everyone that she had just received some bad news.

"What is it, honey?" Douglas said, putting down his fork.

"That was Parker Place at Cherico Memorial," she began, her voice unsteady. "The baby came early. Two months, in fact, Parker said. They had to do a C-section, and the baby's in the NICU. He says it'll be touch and go for a while. Preemies are never good news no matter how much technology you have at your disposal. I was assigned the NICU once or twice in Nashville, and I witnessed some heartbreaking things that I'll never forget."

"Is Periwinkle all right?" Maura Beth said.

"Parker says she's pretty doped up right now since she was just transferred from the recovery room, but she came through the C-section okay."

"Can she have visitors?"

"He said to give her a day or two. He'll keep us posted, and he wanted us to spread the word to everyone else."

"What a horrible Thanksgiving for them," Susan said. "I can't imagine."

"You can't take anything for granted with babies," Connie said. "We always assume they'll get here without any problems, and then there's the old adage about the right number of fingers and toes, but that's just not the case sometimes."

Maura Beth leaned back in her chair as far as she could, perhaps for comfort as much as anything else; then she focused on Susan and Paul. "Elise, Periwinkle, and I have truly bonded over the past several months. We've been going to the library and checking out every pregnancy book we can find.

Our favorites so far are *What to Expect When You're Expecting* and *The Happiest Baby on the Block*. Elise and I would be totally crushed if anything happens to Periwinkle's precious baby. I don't even want to think about it."

"Then let's don't. Positive thoughts only, please," Elise said.

"Yes, let's all give thanks for what we have and wish only the best for Parker and Periwinkle and their baby," Maura Beth added.

"How about a moment of silence around the table?" Connie suggested. And everyone followed through, bowing their heads before resuming their meal.

The next afternoon, Maura Beth, Jeremy, and Elise were the first to visit with the Places at Cherico Memorial. Parker had made the executive decision to close The Twinkle for the weekend, as he wanted to devote all his time to his wife and baby girl. Periwinkle had protested briefly, but he would have none of it. At the moment, Periwinkle was sitting up in bed looking composed with a presentable-enough smile, but it was difficult to tell if she truly was that much in control or if she just wanted to put on a game face for her friends.

"Have you seen the baby yet?" Maura Beth said after leaning down and kissing her best girlfriend on the cheek.

"We've both seen her just once," Periwinkle said. "She's so tiny, and there are all these wires connected to her. She looked like some kinda science experiment, and we had to go in with masks on. It scares me to death, and I'm not one to scare easily as y'all know. Just call me the original Annie as in 'get your gun.' But . . . isn't she lovely, Parker?"

"You're quoting Stevie Wonder now," he said. "I always hoped that song would come in handy for me one day. And now we have this little café au lait angel."

"Do you have a name for her yet?" Elise said.

"We thought we'd name her after Parker's mother—

Ardenia Bedloe Place," Periwinkle told them all. "Bedloe was Parker's original last name before he changed it, as y'all prob'ly remember. And then we thought we'd shorten Ardenia to Denia. I know I've never heard that name before. Whaddaya think?"

Elise beat Maura Beth to the punch. "I really like it very much. I'm naming my little girl Celice. Denia and Celice. I like them both. A little something different in the scheme of things."

Maura Beth raised and then waved her hand. "Don't forget that Jeremy and I are calling our little boy, Liam. So that's three that are off the beaten path for The Free Sample Sisters."

"I'd expect nothing less," Periwinkle said, brightening a bit.

Elise raised her index finger. "All for one, and one for all."

"Have the doctors told you how long the baby will be in the NICU?" Jeremy said, injecting a serious note.

"At least a week or two. Maybe longer than that. She really is the tiniest thing I've ever seen. The nurse said she was less than three pounds. She was supposed to stay with Peri a little longer before coming out, of course. Seems there's an issue with her lungs right now, but, of course, they're doing everything they can to help her breathe," Parker said.

"We wanted you to know that we got in touch with most of the original Cherry Cola Book Club members, and they all said they were going to visit you to keep your spirits up," Maura Beth said. "You know you can count on all of us. As a matter of fact, Voncille and Locke Linwood are waiting to see you next. They'll only allow so many in the room at a time, you know."

"The more the merrier," Periwinkle said, but her words sounded forced.

Parker did not sound particularly carefree either. "Let's not go overboard, Peri. Visitors within reason."

"Do you want me to tell Voncille and Locke you're not up to more visitors right now? They could come back later, if you want," Maura Beth said. "You're the important one here."

Parker echoed her concerns and exhaled. "Tell me the truth now, Peri. Are you really up to it?"

Periwinkle sat up straighter, her smile widening. "No, I'm fine. I'd love to see Miss Voncille and Locke. They're such an adorable couple, and I got such a kick out of the two of them finding love at their age, even if they did run off and elope. I would have loved being a part of their wedding."

"I would, too," Maura Beth said. "But true love waits for no one, whether you're seventeen or seventy."

Now there was a gleam in Periwinkle's eyes. "Or something in between like Parker and myself."

Voncille and Locke Linwood were standing on either side of Periwinkle's bed, solicitously smiling down at their good friend. "We won't take up too much of your time," Locke told her. "The nurse told us you needed your rest."

"She really does," Parker said, wagging a finger at his wife from the foot of the bed. "But it's hard to convince her of it. I don't think she realizes what she's been through. She thinks she's Superwoman."

Periwinkle shot him a disdainful look. "Well . . . I am. But it's not about me, Parker. It's all about our baby. She's all that counts now."

"But I'm sure you do want to be in tip-top shape when she comes home with us, don't you?"

"You do make a good point there. That does make sense," she said, softening her attitude and then taking a sip of her water through a straw.

"Anyway," Voncille said, "Locke had something he wanted to share with you. We're both sure it will make you feel better about the baby." She pointed to her husband with a sweep of her hand. "You're on."

Locke stood up tall and cleared his throat, the very picture of the snowy-haired, Southern gentleman who people listened to and admired. "What I want you to know is that I went through what you're going through with my first wife, Pamela, may she rest in peace. Our son, Locke Jr., was premature, too. It really threw us for a loop. Back then, the technology wasn't nearly as advanced as it is now, but our son came through with flying colors. It took a while, and we had to be patient. The days seemed like months to us, but we just kept on believing that everything would turn out all right. And it did, of course. We didn't have the same problem with our daughter, and we were thankful for that. But both Voncille and I are betting that your sweet, little baby will be home with you before you know it. If there's anything at all we can do to help you out now or later, just let us know. You can count on us."

"Thanks so much for the encouragement and for sharing that story with me. We're naming her after Parker's mother and calling her Denia," Periwinkle said, reaching out to grasp Locke's hand. Then she grabbed Voncille's hand on the other side, linking the three of them as the genuine friendship flowed through them. It reflected both the camaraderie of the book club and years of interacting with one another at The Twinkle. "That means a lot to me."

"You know, I think the smartest thing any of us did was to join The Cherry Cola Book Club. Maura Beth is really a genius," Parker said. "Peri and I were a little behind the curve at first, but we couldn't stay away once we attended that first meeting and ate that delicious food and saw what a fun time everyone was having. My mama couldn't get over it when she joined since she couldn't even use the library when she was growing up. If you were black, you couldn't get a library card.

Anyway, the club brought us all together in a way nothing else could have, and now we have a brand-new library and Cherico's got a brand-new spirit because of it all."

"Most of us were there when Justin Brachle had his heart attack year before last," Periwinkle added. "Becca's told me over and over how much our support meant to them at the time."

"Yep, I remember that terrible night, and how we all crowded into the waiting room hoping for some good news," Voncille said, a pall overtaking her. "And then we got it when we found out Justin had been stabilized just before they took him up to Nashville to fix him up good as new. Then he lost all that weight and has kept it off ever since. Becca's so proud of him. I think his biggest incentive has been hanging around for that precious little son of theirs."

"Yes, Markie's a cutie," Periwinkle said. "He's already being spoiled with Maura Beth as his godmother."

"Speaking of which," Parker began, "would you two consider being the godparents of our little Denia? Peri and I have been talking about it for a while now, and your dropping by to share that story with us seems like the perfect opportunity to ask you. So, do you need some time to think about it, or can you give us an answer now? We don't want to rush you."

Locke and Voncille exchanged surprised glances, but their smiles appeared quickly. "We don't need to think twice. We'd be more than honored," Voncille said. "Right, Locke?"

"Yes, we would. A child can't have too many people loving her."

Parker clasped his hands together, and Periwinkle applauded lightly. "Wonderful," Parker said. "We were pretty sure you'd be on board."

"Just let us know where and when, and we'll be there," Locke told them, puffing out his chest.

*   *   *

The remainder of Periwinkle's visiting hours were sprinkled with brief drop-ins from some of her many friends: Connie and Douglas McShay, Justin and Becca Brachle, and Marydell Crumpton from the book club, and Renette Posey and Emma Frost from the library. But Periwinkle decided to shut it all down an hour early.

"I've had enough for one day," she told Parker, making a playful slash-the-throat gesture with her index finger. "Tell the nurse that's it. And I also want you to go home and get some rest and decent food. You've been curled up on that sofa all night, and I'm worried about you."

"No, I'm not leaving you or Denia for a second," he said, the defiance clearly registering on his face and in his tone.

"Please," Periwinkle continued. "Just to please me? You know I'll call you if anything happens. But you'll make me feel a lot better if you'll take care of *yourself*. Is that too much to ask? Living off those vending machines out there is just not gonna cut it. And I know you haven't slept a wink. Every time I woke up, you'd be over there staring at me."

"I wasn't staring. I was just keeping an eye on you."

"I appreciate that, but I have an entire hospital staff at my disposal to do that."

Parker finally gave in. "All right, then. But you have to promise to let me know the second anything changes with you or the baby."

She raised her right hand. "Promise, and I cross my heart and hope to . . ."

She did not finish the sentence, making a thin line of her lips as she saw the pain creeping into Parker's face.

"I love you, sweetie," he told her, recovering and leaning down to give her a kiss.

"I love you, too."

Finally, he was gone, and Periwinkle lost no time in calling Maura Beth. In fact, she had not grown tired of her visitors. They had brightened her day and lifted her spirits, and she would gladly have received more until the end of visiting hours. But she had something on her mind that she just had to try, and there was no one else to turn to but her closest friend in Cherico.

Less than ten minutes later, Maura Beth stood at her bedside with a hopeful expression on her face. "You said you wanted me to do something for you?"

Periwinkle pointed to a chair against the wall. "Maybe you should pull that over and have a seat."

Maura Beth looked puzzled but quickly complied. "You sound as mysterious as you did over the phone."

"Sorry about that part. But you're the only one I really feel comfortable with about this."

"We've been able to tell each other anything since I came to Cherico over eight years ago, and there you were at The Twinkle to welcome me. I don't know how I would have stuck it out at the library with Councilman Sparks breathing down my neck all the time without you," Maura Beth said with a smile in her voice.

"Best friends forever."

"So tell me what you want me to do. I'm about to die of curiosity."

Periwinkle had another sip of her water and took a deep breath. "Well, it's my mother. As you know, she didn't attend our wedding, and she's never even spoken to Parker. I think I told you about how she reacted when I drove over to Corinth to let her know we were having a baby girl. It just tore me up real bad the way she rejected me. It was like talking to a brick wall."

"Yes, I was so sorry to hear about that. I know what it's like to have issues with your mother."

Periwinkle began to tear up. "Maura Beth, I just can't face her—either in person again or even over the phone. But something inside me keeps saying that I need to try again and let her know about her premature grandchild. I keep hoping that maybe that'll turn my mama around. Maybe she'll start pulling for my baby to come through. Do you think I'm crazy to hope for that?"

Maura Beth took Periwinkle's hand briefly. "No, I don't think you're crazy at all. And I think maybe you're right to exhaust everything before giving up on her. If I were in your position, I think I'd feel the same way."

Periwinkle took a Kleenex from the nearby table and blew her nose before answering. "Maybe this is asking too much, but this is where you come in. Would you call my mama for me and tell her what's happened? If you don't want to, I'll understand, and I guess I'll find the strength to tell her myself. But it'd sure help me out if you could do it. Parker would prob'ly have a fit if he found out I was still trying to bring her around. He thinks we oughta just go on with our lives and not worry about her, and he might be right. But what if there's this tiny little chance she has a change of heart?"

"That's the hardest thing in the world to change, you know. I mean, someone's heart. And it can break your heart to try," Maura Beth said.

"I expect you're right." There was an awkward pause. "But will you at least try for me?"

Maura Beth took Periwinkle's hand again and squeezed it gently. "Yes, I'll do the best I can for you."

"Thank you, girlfriend." Then Periwinkle exhaled. "Just don't say anything to Parker one way or the other. Maybe you better not say anything to Jeremy, either. If my mama comes around, I'll have to work on bringing her and Parker together. I just hope I have the chance to do it."

"Don't worry about me talking to Parker or Jeremy. This will be strictly between us." An impish grin spread across her face. "After all, we're not only members of The Cherry Cola

Book Club, we're two of the three Free Sample Sisters, and that means everything."

"Well put."

Maura Beth held her hand out. "Just give me your mother's number, and I'll call her tomorrow when I get to the library. What I think I'll do is look out over the lake from my desk and let that calm me enough to follow through for you. A big body of water always does that for me. There's something reassuring about the way the sun hits the surface all through the day when there are no clouds. Yeah, I'll admit I sometimes get distracted, but it's the best kind of distraction. It gets me so energized that I think I can accomplish anything I want."

Periwinkle's laugh seemed almost carefree. "That was damned near poetic, Maura Beth. Like something out of a novel. I guess that's what you get for living with an English teacher."

The time had come for Maura Beth to make that all-important call to Mama Kohlmeyer in Corinth. But she had been putting it off since she had settled in behind her desk just after nine o'clock the next morning. The patrons and staff kept giving her excuses to postpone her promise to Periwinkle. First, front desk clerk Renette Posey came to the door with a complaint from an older man who had been unable to get access to any of the computer terminals from the minute he arrived.

"He says he needs to Google something right away and that it's an emergency," Renette told her boss in that sweet, teenaged way of hers.

"Did he tell you what the emergency was?"

Renette's expression went all full of dubious creases. "Something about thinking he has a contagious disease because of his symptoms. He says he's been coughing up a lung—his exact words now—all night and day. He's hacked a coupla times in front of me for sure. If he does have something contagious, he hasn't done any of us any favors by coming here and spreading his germs."

"You're absolutely right. Let's get him out of here quickly. You tell him firmly but politely to go to the emergency room at Cherico Memorial. We don't practice medicine here."

A few minutes later, Miriam Goodcastle, the energetic, recently hired children's librarian, popped in with a request to buy some supplies for one of her imaginative story hours, and Maura Beth was happy to spend more time than was necessary listening to Miriam's plans to stage a *Frozen* extravaganza.

"It'll go perfectly with the colder weather we're having now," Miriam said. "All the little girls and their mothers have been just beside themselves since I put up all those posters. I'm expecting a record crowd."

Shortly after approving Miriam's requisition, however, Maura Beth realized she needed to stop dawdling and pick up the phone to do her duty, off-putting as it was. In all the years she had been best friends with Periwinkle, she had only met Mama Kohlmeyer once, and that was briefly when the woman had driven over from Corinth to have dinner at The Twinkle courtesy of her daughter. Only a few words had been exchanged as Maura Beth had been sitting at a nearby table and Periwinkle had introduced them. While Maura Beth had attempted to keep the conversation friendly and alive, Mama Kohlmeyer had cut it short with an inexplicable frostiness that the woman made no effort to conceal. And now here she was being asked to convey some traumatic news to that same woman who was virtually a stranger and wasn't even on friendly terms with her own daughter.

Nonetheless, she finally picked up the phone and dialed, her heart surprising her with the way it was racing. Then, after three rings, came the "Hello?" from Mama Kohlmeyer.

Maura Beth took a deep, cleansing breath for good measure and then politely identified herself.

"Yes?" Mama Kohlmeyer said. It was astounding how much indifference could be crammed into one little word.

"I'll get right to the point. I'm sorry to be the bearer of bad news," Maura Beth began, the words coming out more easily than she thought they would, "but your daughter asked me to call and let you know that your granddaughter was born prematurely two days ago. It was a C-section, and Periwinkle is doing fine. Your granddaughter is in the NICU right now at Cherico Memorial. Periwinkle thought you'd want to know. The last report the doctors gave her was that the baby was holding her own for the time being. It might be a while longer before they know whether she can go home, though. Anyway, I promised Periwinkle I'd give you a call."

The silence at the other end lasted so long that Maura Beth thought the connection was lost.

"Hello?" Maura Beth said. "Are you still there, Miz Kohlmeyer?"

"Yes."

"I'm just the messenger here. Did you have anything you wanted me to tell Periwinkle?"

The tension flowing through the phone was nearly palpable as Mama Kohlmeyer finally said, "No, I don't have a message for my daughter. But I do have a question for you. Don't you go pulling any punches with me, either. I know you and Periwinkle Violet have been thick as thieves for a long time now, else why would she have you call instead of calling me herself? You tell me the truth—does my granddaughter look white?"

"What?"

"You heard what I said. Don't be playing innocent with me. I know you know. Does that baby look white?"

"No, I don't know. I . . . I haven't actually seen her. But I've been told she's a beautiful child. She couldn't be anything else, I'm quite sure."

Maura Beth's shock only grew as Mama Kohlmeyer said, "I'm reading between the lines, Miz McShay, and I can guess what you're not telling me. You might as well know that if that child doesn't look white and if she takes after *him,* I'll have nothing to do with her."

Maura Beth knew it wasn't her place to argue, but she did anyway. Her adrenaline was flowing, and she had to stand up for Periwinkle and Parker. "But that's your granddaughter we're talking about, Miz Kohlmeyer. Those are your genes."

"Don't you dare say that to me!"

"I don't mean to upset you, but facts are facts."

Mama Kohlmeyer's voice rose a decibel level. "This really is none of your business, Miz McShay. Who are you to talk to me like that? You should stick to running that library of yours. Now I've told you how I feel. I think we'd better end this conversation right now. Good-bye."

The suddenness of the dial tone had the effect of a thunderous cannon shot, and Maura Beth sat at her desk holding the receiver in her hand, completely unable to blink, unable to move a muscle. She couldn't seem to put it down. If she did, the call would truly be ended, and she would be left with the thankless task of repeating those words to her best friend. How could she possibly bring herself to do that?

Finally, she hung up the receiver and looked out over the lake again. This time there was no great wisdom waiting for her on the surface of the water. There was even a cloud bank blocking the sun to further prolong her sudden inaction. She only knew that she could not convey such blatant cruelty and further rejection to Periwinkle. Maybe it would be better to lie and say that Mama Kohlmeyer had hung up on her. Yes, that would be better and far less hurtful. In any case there seemed to be no possible reconciliation in the offing between mother and daughter.

Not when the mother was swimming in a pool of racism and did not care how many people she splashed or even drowned along the way.

11

Fallen

In the days that followed Thanksgiving, the outlook of The Free Sample Sisters seemed to be on the uptick. Elise had been buoyed by her parents' last-minute decision to stay at the lodge another night after everyone had received the unsettling news of Periwinkle's premature baby. The upside to a crisis was that it frequently brought out the best in people. The three of them had found the time to talk things out a bit more, and Susan and Paul had seemed to be warming to the idea of their daughter's unconventional decision.

"You'll just have to forgive us if we were a little taken aback at first," Susan had said as the three of them huddled on the sofa in front of one of Douglas's crackling fires. "Your father and I would love to have been in on this from the start. Honestly, I think we could have found a way to help you."

Elise knew she had to stop being difficult and tap into her seldom-used, gracious gene. "Well, you know me, Mom. I'm nothing if I'm not Helen Headstrong in that alternate universe I run around in where I'm always standing on my soapbox with my picket signs."

They had all laughed, and Paul had said, "You do know yourself very well. Just keep us posted from here on, and we'll look forward to coming down for Christmas. Your aunt Connie says she'll disown all of us if we don't show up for her annual gourmet feast."

And then Elise had closed the circle of good feeling. "I think I might, too, if you don't mind her."

Maura Beth had followed through on her decision to tell Periwinkle that her mother had hung up on that promised call, and that was the end of that. No words had passed between the two of them. The lie had surely prevented what would have been a punch to the gut, and it seemed that Periwinkle was willing to take Maura Beth's word as gospel and live with it.

"I'm not surprised, "Periwinkle had said. "The only time Parker tried to talk to her, she hung up on him."

"I'm so sorry. But it is what it is," Maura Beth had said, leaving it at that and feeling that Periwinkle would be satisfied.

It was far from an ideal situation, of course, but it was better than the raw ugliness of further exposing Mama Kohlmeyer for what she was. That, Maura Beth reasoned, was something that mother and daughter had to tackle eventually on their own in earnest, even if the outcome looked like it might be truly heartbreaking. For now, however, Periwinkle would be concentrating on her baby girl in that incubator, and that was all that mattered.

The collaboration among Elise, Jeremy, and Alex was gathering momentum day by day, and the initial tensions generated by Elise had largely dissipated as they had finally gotten one chapter under their belt. They were all gathered around the dining room table on this particular Sunday afternoon with their stacks of notes and laptops; meanwhile, Connie had lit a couple of gardenia-scented candles that she had placed on the window sills for background ambience, telling them that work was always easier with a heavenly aroma lingering. Then she had flitted away, wishing them well with a smile.

"I know I can go back and pull out a lot of those statistics and some of the interviews I did with single mothers from all backgrounds for my classroom appearance next week," Elise was saying. "If you want to know the truth, that's probably when I got the notion to try being a single mother myself deliberately. I certainly was in a position to pull it off financially. So I sat down at my office desk one day and said to myself, why not?"

"Brave new world," Alex said, giving her a deferential nod.

Elise looked at him with visible suspicion. "I'm assuming that's a compliment from you, sir."

"Yes, it is. All of my students are looking forward to hearing about the choice you made, particularly my female students."

"That's a good sign. We all need to be more and more open-minded as the millennium rolls on."

Alex raised his hand. "I'll take the widows."

"Guess that leaves me with the divorcées," Jeremy said. He gave his sister a quizzical glance. "Could we go back and get in touch with some of them again, or do we want to use these initial interviews and let it go at that? They have to be more than a few years old by now."

Elise answered quickly and authoritatively, as if she had just been asked a question by one of her students. "That's a good point. We might want to do another interview since their circumstances might have changed. For instance, if they've gotten remarried, their stories would be quite different now. Of course, we could end up with a patchwork quilt of a timeline, but we want to be accurate." She typed into her laptop at what seemed like lightning speed. For all intents and purposes, it had become her project, and the two men had decided to keep the peace by letting her lead.

"If they've gotten remarried," Alex said, "then we have another potential category that relates to changes in the nuclear family—the blended family. Were we going to try to include that in the book?"

Elise pointed her index finger at him emphatically. "Yes, I think we have to. We want to cover all bases. The blended thing is booming among the Boomers. Ha! I like the way that sounds. Maybe it ought to be a chapter title."

Alex picked up on her bright mood and stuck his nose in. "A lot of alliteration, though."

"Nah, we'll take out a *b,* and it'll fly."

"You should be in charge of chapter titles," Alex said, leaning in and coming off as somewhat flirtatious.

"I thought we were just going to use numbers for that," Jeremy said.

Elise caught his gaze playfully. "What could be the harm in spicing things up just a bit, Jer?"

"None, I suppose."

It was during a much-needed coffee break after thirty minutes of productive banter back and forth that Alex changed the subject. Elise's intensity and rapid-fire manner could be a bit overwhelming at times. "What's the latest on your Free Sample Sister and her baby, Elise?"

"I appreciate your asking about her. Periwinkle's been at home for a while now," she told him. "But the baby's still in the hospital. Making slow progress, though. You can't rush these things. The baby was so small to begin with. Now, every ounce she puts on makes such a difference." There was a pause that found Elise frowning. "I don't know if I could go through something like Periwinkle and Parker are going through. Especially Periwinkle. I mean, not knowing how it will turn out after carrying the baby for so long. To think that it all might be for naught."

"I'm sure the odds are against a premature birth for you, Leesie," Jeremy said. "Too coincidental. Besides, Aunt Connie says you're doing everything by the letter—when and what to eat, taking your supplements, doing your breathing exercises, and whatever else."

Elise looked a bit sheepish, which was something practically foreign to her temperament. "Considering I made a huge scene at that first Lamaze class at the library, I'd have to agree with you. At some point I think it finally dawned on me that everything didn't have to be a political statement. The next time I returned to Expecting Great Things, I behaved myself."

Jeremy's grin had a sarcastic shade to it. "Yes, Maurie and I were there, remember? You got with the program. It's just all about making the birth experience more comfortable, nothing else. Maurie and I practice whenever we can, and I think we're getting pretty darned good."

"I've always learned from my mistakes. Now, Aunt Connie coaches me all the time, and I really feel very comfortable about it all." Then she put down her coffee cup and rubbed her hands together vigorously. "Well, shall we get back to our work, gentlemen?"

It was after their collaboration session was finally over that Elise excused herself to go up to her room for a nap. "Doctor's orders," she had told them with a smile and then headed up, carefully holding on to the railing all the way.

Alex and Jeremy remained at the table, scanning their notes and checking files on their laptop screens. Then Alex looked up and said, "Do you mind if I ask you something, Jeremy?"

"Shoot."

Alex drummed his fingers on the table while screwing up his face. Whatever it was he had on his mind wasn't coming out so easily. "You're the only one I can tell this to, so I hope you'll keep it in strictest confidence."

Jeremy gave him a friendly wink. "You bet."

"Well, I don't know exactly how this happened, but . . . well, I think I've fallen in love with your sister. Do you have any advice for me?"

"You're kidding?"

"I assure you I'm not."

Jeremy took his time. This was a curve ball he hadn't expected from a colleague he had always thought of as well grounded. "I knew you were fascinated with Leesie's pregnancy choice and all that went into that, but I certainly didn't think it had gone any further than that."

"I'm afraid it has."

Jeremy continued to look and sound incredulous. "Please tell me you haven't said anything to Leesie about this."

"No, I don't think I'd have the nerve. As far as I can tell, this is strictly a one-sided crush."

Jeremy put his hands on the table and leaned forward, making solid eye contact in man-to-man fashion. "Listen to me and listen good, pal. I know my sister very well. Better than anyone else in the world does, probably. My parents can't handle her, but I can. I've had to since we were children growing up together. You're just setting yourself up for an unrequited fall. It's not that she doesn't like you—because I know for a fact she does. But strictly as a cohort, as an intellectual equal, not as the romantic lead in the movie of her life. She's never said or done anything to indicate to me she has room for that. Just for her career and that baby of hers on the way. She's determined to prove something to the world, and she's not going to stop until she does."

Alex sighed and shook his head. "I know you're right,

of course. But what can I do? I have the feelings I have, and I can't seem to stop them from getting stronger and stronger." He pointed dramatically to his heart. "They're right here, stuck in the middle of my chest, and they won't go away no matter what I do. I guess they just snuck up on me." He thought for a second, closing one eye. "Snuck? Is that a word? You're the English teacher."

Jeremy didn't seem particularly pleased with the remark. "It's probably sneaked, but who cares? Just what is it about Leesie that's turned you on so much? I know it can't be her figure right now. She's a hot mess most of the time, and she was like that before she got pregnant. That's only made it worse."

"That may be, but I just don't see her the way you do. For one thing, I don't have all that sibling history you do."

Jeremy drew back in astonishment. "If you're thinking you can have a relationship of any kind with her at this stage of her life, you're wasting your time. And I don't think you should say anything to her about his. It'll probably screw up our collaboration big-time, and we need all the help we can get. I'm giving you polite and fair warning for the last time. Don't take my sister on that way. You'll only be taking the fall of a lifetime, I can guarantee."

Alex managed an awkward little laugh. "Somehow I knew you'd say that. But I just had to get this off my chest."

"Well, now you've done that. I can't do anything about the feelings you have for her, but I can steer you in the right direction. And that's away from my sister. Keep her at arm's length as the apple of your eye. I know I'm an English teacher and that sounds trite as hell, and I'm downright embarrassed about spouting it, but right now, I can't think of anything more original, I'm so stunned."

"I guess I'm right in the middle of a hopeless cause, then," Alex said, shrugging, but he was able to keep a smile on his face. "Maybe it's the fact that she's such a loner. I was always kind of a loner myself—you know, not a jock, loved history and all the trivia that goes with it. We have that quality in common. I admire her spunk. Does that make any sense to you?"

"I guess so. But do you think you can keep on working with her under these circumstances?"

"Oh, sure. We've got this great book we want to get published, and I can't let my emotions destroy that opportunity. I know I can continue to be completely professional about this. Everything went smoothly enough this afternoon, didn't it? It even smelled liked gardenias the whole time."

"Yes, it did. Although sometimes you and I had to make the effort to keep things truly collaborative. Elise is her own whirlwind and tends to leave people behind. I sometimes wonder what it's like to be one of her students trying to keep up with her." Jeremy rapped his knuckles on the table twice. "Knock on wood you can live up to what you just said about playing it straight. I think it's very important you keep it platonic with Leesie if we're gonna produce a book on schedule. The last thing we need is a difficult romantic entanglement, although I really don't think it's possible."

"I completely agree." Then he stared down into his lap. "But it doesn't make it any easier to face the fact that I've fallen deeply."

It wasn't that Periwinkle lacked faith in the doctors and nurses at Cherico Memorial when they kept telling her that her baby daughter was making slow, steady progress but was nowhere near ready to come home. It was more that she couldn't get out of her head her mother's rejection of her marriage to Parker and the child who had resulted. It wasn't supposed to be like that between mother and daughter, and there were times when Parker caught her crying at the kitchen table or lying in bed to rest. But no matter how hard Parker tried to soothe her, it never seemed to completely shut down her fretting. She seemed to be intent on not allowing the wound to heal.

Then one night with the effects of the full moon streaming through the bedroom windows, Parker awoke to the sounds of her sobbing softly next to him well into the early-morning hours, and he knew he had to try again. He started by snuggling up against her and taking her hand.

"Peri, I understand how you feel about your mother, but you've got to let it go. It's robbing you of sleep and peace of mind. This can't go on."

"It's not just that. There's something else."

"Go on. Tell me."

She turned toward him, looking directly into his eyes. The moonlight had found its way into his pupils, as if a spell had been cast, making her think she could tell him anything without flinching. "I keep thinking we've done something wrong to deserve this."

"What are you talking about? Deserve what? Denia being a preemie? Where did you get that idea from?"

Her words came in spurts. "What I mean is . . . not everybody approves of us . . . and I heard . . . well, the front door to the restaurant was open once . . . and some man was passing by . . . and I heard him say that he'd never eat in a place run by a . . . well, you know, the N word."

Parker looked unperturbed. "So who cares what some redneck thinks of us? What are you trying to get at?"

"I know it sounds totally unreasonable, but I've had these crazy thoughts lately about us not fitting in and that somehow we've fallen from grace."

This time, Parker drew back, and the moonlight went out of his eyes. "You can't really think something like that, can you, Peri? This isn't the civil rights era anymore where there was a firebomb lurking around every corner or a Klansman burning a cross on someone's lawn. Hell, Mama lived through it from beginning to end, and you know how strong her faith was. She accepted us, and I know she would have cherished Denia. We are not being punished for being a nontraditional couple. I don't believe in a universe that works like that. Besides, we have some real friends in the members of The Cherry Cola Book Club. I know all of them think we're in the mainstream of life—running a business and trying for a family. Isn't that the American Dream?"

Sounding somewhat chastened, Periwinkle said, "Yes, I know you're right. What's wrong with my head these days? Maybe it's all the visits to the NICU, and Denia doesn't seem any better off. The nurses tell me she is, but I don't see it. I try to keep my chin up, and I tell Maura Beth and everyone else that it's going fine. But I can sense they think I'm not telling them the truth."

Parker moved closer again and kissed her on the forehead. "You're going way overboard with all this reading between the lines. Where's that feisty, spunky lady I fell in love with who built The Twinkle from the ground up and ran everybody else out of town, including your ex-husband."

Trying gamely to keep a smile on her face, Periwinkle said, "She got pregnant, that's what."

"Which is gonna make her the best mother of all time."

"Well, when you put it that way . . ."

He leaned over and kissed her on the lips, and she returned his ardor as they embraced. "Will you promise me to try to stop fretting over your mother? There is no way in hell we'll ever change the way she thinks. We, on the other hand, are good people playing by the rules, no matter what anyone else thinks."

Periwinkle sniffled a couple of times and cleared her throat. "One thing you have to understand is that this is maybe the first time in my life since my divorce from Harlan Lattimore that I haven't felt in control of things. He had me completely fooled and under his thumb all those years we were married. When he tried to propose marriage again, I saw through him and that he was mainly after all the money I've made off The Twinkle. But this not knowing with Denia—well, it makes me feel so helpless, and that's just not in my wheelhouse."

"I understand that," Parker told her. "But you need to stop beating yourself up. You're a strong woman, and I know in my heart that this situation with Denia is gonna go our way. She couldn't be our daughter and not be a fighter. You just wait and see if I'm not right."

The bewitching power of moonlight had returned to his eyes, and she took a deep breath. "I love the way you make sense of everything. I promise I'll try to do much better from here on out."

"That's my Peri," he said, giving her hand a squeeze. "Now let's get some sleep and dream about the day Denia comes home. The way I figure it, it'll be one helluva Christmas present."

12

A Timely Discussion

The mysterious element called time is an unpredictable little imp. It moves inconsistently according to the realities of every single person on the planet. While some would rather it roll along the plains of daily life like a tumbleweed, others would prefer that it slow to an imperceptible crawl like a glacier. Yet, perversely, it often seems to do the opposite of what is requested or fervently expected, and there is little that can be done about it.

For nearly everyone, however—at least in America—it adopts the tumbleweed effect between Thanksgiving and Christmas. Each day between the two zips by while a thousand more frantic errands and things to cross off lists pile up. There are never enough hours in the days. Suddenly, Thanksgiving comes and goes with its groaning tables of delicious foods and visiting relatives, and before anyone knows it, Christmas has arrived with its brightly colored lights and decorations, presents under the tree, carols, and church services. All of it takes place according to "tumbleweed time" before everything glaciers again in January at the beginning of another long, uphill climb of a year.

So it was that a great deal unfolded quickly during that

period in Cherico, Mississippi: Little Ardenia Bedloe Place continued her slow progress in the NICU, with incremental gains here and there. Each visit to the NICU at Cherico Memorial was still somewhat of a trial for her stressed-out parents instead of a devout prayer answered.

Sturdy, forthright Nurse Imogene Rodgers—she of the prominent bosom and heavy eyebrows—continued with her hand-holding and hopeful counsel, however. "There's always the chance she could be home with you by Christmas. We just need to put some more weight on her and make sure all her vital organs can function. We definitely don't want to risk anything by letting her go too soon. You just keep that in mind, and don't you despair."

When the news spread throughout The Cherry Cola Book Club that little Denia was still in a delicately balanced state, tidings of comfort appeared in abundance. Maura Beth even decided to call a special meeting of the club in the library's mini-auditorium. In fact, it was nearly a year to the day that she had done the same thing to lift the spirits of the town when everything seemed to be going south: Spurs 'R' Us had withdrawn its plans to locate a new plant in the industrial park, several businesses were just about to shut their doors for good and move away, and the sales tax base was dwindling so fast it could barely be grabbed and captured on the city's ledgers by Councilman Durden Sparks and his cronies.

But Maura Beth's special meeting had more than done the trick: Members had shared inspirational stories that celebrated life, illuminated and dignified grieving, suggested what the "big picture" was all about, and brought people together as never before. Not long after, country music singer Waddell Mack had been instrumental in turning around the Spurs 'R' Us CEO, Dillard Mills, and Cherico appeared headed for a new era of hope and prosperity. At least they would have well over three hundred new jobs to buoy that belief.

The format Maura Beth had chosen for this year's special meeting was a simple one and not altogether unlike the previous one: The core members were to get up on the stage and give Periwinkle and Parker a boost with their own particular good news. Perhaps this close-to-Christmas meeting would become an annual tradition as a result. And why not? Red, white, and green candles adorned two small tables at either end of the stage, and there was a large, red felt banner tacked above the proscenium with the words O COME ALL YE BOOK CLUB FAITHFUL in white block lettering. That was a timeless message, indeed.

At the moment, Maura Beth was leading off the parade at the podium. "We are confident that your little Denia will be with you before the year is out. One of Santa's helpers whispered it in my ear. He said they'd gotten your wish list up there at the North Pole, and they all thought it was the best they'd received in years. So, I think you're a cinch to get exactly what you want," she was saying, pointing to her friends seated in the front row.

"Thank you," Periwinkle said, blowing her a kiss while the others enjoyed the surge of good feeling. "We figured you'd have your finger on the pulse. Ever since you moved up here from New Orleans, you've had Cherico's best interests at heart."

"As for us, Jeremy and I have all the Lamaze exercises down, of course," she continued. "We should pass with flying colors when the time comes, but we'll take nothing for granted. All we want is healthy babies for ourselves and our friends, and my instincts tell me we're going to get them. The Free Sample Sisters absolutely will not fail in their mission to populate the world with their freeloading antics. No grocery store is safe from our tentacles."

Laughter erupted across the auditorium, but Maura Beth quickly interrupted it with a wave of her hand. "I think almost all of you know by now that Periwinkle, Elise, and myself made a habit of eating Mr. Hannigan out of his free samples every Wednesday at The Cherico Market for months, and that's how we came up with that name, right, girlfriends?"

"Guilty as charged," Periwinkle said, raising her hand.

"What she said," Elise added with a mischievous grin.

"Anyway, our little Liam's latest sonogram looks perfect, and we're thankful for that. He's still due the second or third week in January. He was a huge part of our discussion around the Thanksgiving table. Gosh, it seems like that was just yesterday and here it is almost Christmas."

"Isn't that the truth?" Connie said from her perch in the front row. "I don't know what it is about the holiday season, but it just whizzes by."

Jeremy spoke up. "Usually, when you anticipate something a lot, time slows down as if it's teasing you, and then afterward it reverts to the usual pace that you don't even pay attention to. But I truly believe that between Thanksgiving and Christmas, something magical happens."

"Magical and wonderful," Connie added, and there was pleasant buzzing throughout the room.

Maura Beth took the floor again. "Well, that was my little update and contribution before we adjourn to have some of all the goodies we brought to eat and drink. It wouldn't be a Cherry Cola Book Club meeting without that. I believe my sister-in-law, Elise, is next in line to add her thoughts."

It was safe to say that the reception for Elise was decidedly different from the one that Maura Beth had received. It was polite but not overly enthusiastic. Some in the audience still recalled the scene she had made at the Lamaze presentation during the first Expecting Great Things program, and they did not know what to expect. Still, it was always The Cherry Cola Book Club way to give everyone the benefit of the doubt and kindly reserve judgment.

"Hello, friends," Elise began, stepping up to the podium with the biggest smile she could manage and sporting her by-now trademark maternity knit pullover with blue jeans. "I know I'm not an official member of your club, but I've only heard wonderful things about it from Maura Beth and my brother, Jeremy. Every town should have a club like yours where you can support one another through thick and thin. I wanted to say that in the months I've been staying down here in Cherico with my aunt Connie and uncle Doug, I've come to appreciate what a community can do for the people who live within it."

She paused a little longer than was necessary, looking a bit puzzled and creating a sense of suspense. There were those in their seats who became ever so slightly uneasy, wondering if she would revert to the Elise they had witnessed during her Lamaze outburst. But thankfully, Elise's smile soon reappeared.

"Sorry. I didn't mean to make you think I'd lost my train of thought," she continued. "I was just changing it in my head. You see, I've been working on a book with my brother, Jeremy, and his friend Alex from the high school. We're taking a look at the changes in the nuclear family in the millennium. Changes of all kinds, you understand. And it suddenly flashed into my head, that your club here is a change. From everything I've heard, you're an alternative family for one another, and that's a very good thing. It occurred to me that Jeremy, Alex, and I ought to include a chapter about this very Cherry Cola Book Club. It might be an inspiration to other people around the country who're looking for a new kind of support group. The way I look at it, you're an all-purpose support group. Now, how many of those are around?"

Jeremy spoke up again. "Wow! I think you've definitely hit on something new, Leesie."

Alex, who was sitting next to him, said, "I think it would be a fantastic addition to our book."

Then Connie put in her two cents. "I agree with all that, but tell them about your baby, Elise. I think that's what we really came to hear."

Elise's smile widened, but there was a hint of embarrassment to it. "You're right. I almost forgot, didn't I? Well, Celice is on track just like Maura Beth's Liam. We both have due dates somewhere around the middle of January—maybe third week at the most. It's exciting that our children will be cousins, and we'll see that they get to know each other no matter where we all live. For the first time in my life, I'm seeing the importance of family in a brand-new light."

"As your aunt and Lamaze coach all rolled into one, I think that's a very wise and much-appreciated thing to say," Connie added.

When Elise had finished, Becca Brachle replaced her with more good tidings for the Places. "I don't have a doubt in the world that you'll soon have your baby with you all the time. Then all this worry and doubt will be forgotten as you focus on things like feedings and weight gains and trying to get enough sleep for yourself. But the big payoff will be that child of yours who will never again allow you to think of yourself as a single individual. You'll now have someone you've created who you're intimately connected to via the complex reality of DNA. Our little Markie's first year has been a revelation to me and Justin. How could anyone in the world be so enthralling and entertaining and continually surprising? Just when we think we've seen it all, he does something else to amaze us and stop us in our tracks. You'll soon have that to look forward to, and best of all, you'll have Maura Beth and Elise and myself—even though I'm almost a year ahead of you—to compare notes with. Oh, and one more thing, I'm so jealous that I wasn't pregnant at the same time the three of you were. I would love to have been one of The Free Sample Sisters with you. You don't think there'd be a limit to how many could join, do you?"

"No way, no how. And we would've loved to have had you with us nibbling all those quiches and munching those crackers and whatnot, girlfriend," Periwinkle said. "Hey, worry about calories? Not us."

"I'll tell you," Connie said, "I went with the three of them now and then, and I believe it was the most fun I've ever had for free. Although it really wasn't free because we all ended up buying lots of what we sampled, plus whatever else caught our fancy on the shelves. Mr. Hannigan swears by us."

Justin Brachle raised his big, ex-quarterback hand. "Can men do this free sample thing? Sounds like a good deal to me."

"Anyone can," Periwinkle said. "Fact is, Mr. Hannigan is kicking himself in the rear end that he never did it before now. I mean, it's been done maybe forever everywhere else in the universe, but he says he was just too conservative about marketing since he's just about the only game in town and doesn't have to worry about competition. Now, he's sold on sampling, and he's not just doing it on Wednesdays, he's upped it to Saturdays when more people have time off."

"I think maybe he'd go out of business if all you men gobbled up the freebies and then didn't follow up with actually buying groceries. That's where he makes it all up. I mean, you're not pregnant like we are, and you men never will be," Maura Beth added with a wink.

"That may be, but I'm a right hungry fella when I wanna

be," Justin said. "I'll just check out one of these freebie sessions, myself. Maybe I'll wander on down from the real estate office for lunch one day."

"I think we'd better go together. I'll need to keep an eye on you. I don't want you gaining all that weight back you lost after your heart attack," Becca said, stepping away from the podium and returning to her seat.

Justin bristled a bit. "Now I think I can pull away from the trough if I need to, honey." Then he gave her a wink to lighten the exchange.

"I was just kidding," Becca said. "But it does sound like something fun to do together."

Maura Beth couldn't keep from smirking, but afterward pointed in Periwinkle's direction with a flourish. "And now, I think our friend, Periwinkle Place, wanted to say something to all of you for coming here tonight. Will you step up and share your thoughts with us, sweetie?"

While Periwinkle headed toward the podium, all of her friends couldn't help but notice that she was still a bit fragile-looking. It was true that her frame had always been on the wiry side, but there was more to it than that now. More even than the recuperation from a C-section. All of them knew what an ongoing trial it had been for her and Parker to endure the daily reports from the NICU; that the visits were both reassuring and frightening, and would continue to be until little Denia was released to their loving care forever. Yet, there was always an air of confidence, a visible spunkiness about Periwinkle Violet Kohlmeyer Lattimore Place that never abandoned her, no matter the circumstances. And it showed the minute she opened her mouth to speak to her best friends.

"Aren't we full of our tall tales?"

There was an explosion of laughter, and it took a while to die down.

"Seriously, though," she continued, "we are the group to end all groups, aren't we? What Elise McShay said is true. We are a new kind of group. We don't limit ourselves to just one thing to lend our support. Whatever it is, we're there for one another. And, of course, I can't thank all of you enough for coming tonight. Parker and I live day-by-day with our situation, but we hear from you all the time. One of you will call us, and another will send an e-mail, and then we'll go out to the mailbox and open up a card that says, 'Thinking of You,' with a sweet little bird flying in the clouds on the inside, and it will just make our day. But it's even more than that. Parker's mother, Ardenia, is gone now, as all of you know, and I'm sorry to say I'm having trouble with my mother that I won't go into right now. So all of you really are our family, and you'll be our Denia's family. We're right proud to have you, too, so don't you ever stop doing all these nice things you do for us."

Several among the crowd called out, "We won't!"

"I know you won't. I also know this club started out just reviewing books over potluck dinners a couple of years ago. That was not only fun, it saved our library from being closed down by City Hall. But it soon became something else, and what it became is what we have here tonight. Good folks, good food, good . . . well, good everything life has to offer in the way of friendship. And that's about all Parker and I have to say to y'all tonight. We thank you, and we love you. Now, everyone turn to the person next to you and show 'em how you feel."

That triggered a truckload of encomiums and a healthy amount of hugging, cheek-pecking, and handshaking among most everyone, as if the Peace had just commenced in church. After considerable time had elapsed, Maura Beth finally managed to get everyone's attention.

"Folks, if no one has anything else to add to this timely

discussion, shall we all dig in to the comfort food everyone's brought tonight? Last time I looked it all over, I saw we've got a juicy baked ham, sweet potato casserole with marshmallows, Voncille Linwood's famous biscuits and jelly, a green bean casserole, and I know I'm forgetting a few dishes and need to apologize to a few people for that, but they're all over there for the sampling. And I believe there are more than a few Christmas cookies, candies, cakes, and pies, plus some eggnog to add to the menu this time around. What could be more in keeping with the holiday spirit?"

Was it Elise's sunny, upbeat speech that had encouraged Alex to do exactly what Jeremy had advised him not to do? Did her concluding emphasis on "family" signal a change in her attitude toward being a single mother and all that it encompassed? Or was he just indulging a pipe dream?

Whatever the case, something deep within kept urging him on. He just had to pursue this fascination, crush, obsession, or whatever else it was with Elise McShay. The opportunity arose when Elise broke away from the throng and sat down in a corner of the break room where the buffet table had been arranged, happily munching away on an impromptu little sandwich she had made of a small slice of ham, a smear of mustard, and a biscuit.

"You'll be having more than that before this is all over, I hope," Alex said, moving to her and standing in front of her with his own plate of ham slices and a generous helping of sweet potato casserole.

Elise swallowed her food and smiled. "You bet. I'm just getting started. The truth is, I'm not going to stop eating until I give birth. It's more or less doctor's orders, even if there are times I stretch that a little."

Emboldened by her cordial mood, Alex forged ahead. "I

really liked what you said about a new kind of support group back there. A new kind of family, too. We definitely should give The Cherry Cola Book Club its own chapter in our book. Who do you think should handle it?"

Elise put down her sandwich and thought for a second. "Well, I think Jeremy's best suited since he's the only one who's really been a member of it. I'm sure Maura Beth can give him lots of input, and that should be all we need."

"No doubt."

There was an awkward pause, and Elise gave him a quizzical glance.

"I get the feeling there's something else you wanted to say to me."

He pulled up a chair and sat down beside her, putting his plate on the floor. "You're right, I did have something on my mind. Sometimes I think you're one of those fortune-tellers. It's about the single mother thing."

"What about it? Did you want to have more input into that chapter of the book? If you think I'm doing too much on it, we could certainly discuss it—the three of us. I'll admit I'm new to a collaborative effort, but I'm learning. You two have taught me to be more flexible."

Again, he hesitated, clearly uncomfortable. "Glad to hear it, but no . . . this is not about the book. It's about real life."

"Okay."

"It's about your real life and my real life, actually."

"Go on."

Alex somehow found the courage to blurt it out, and get it over and done with once and for all. "Could you see yourself ever bringing up that daughter of yours with someone else in the picture?"

Elise's tone was totally matter-of-fact. "Of course I could. I told everyone I'd see that Celice got to spend lots of time with her cousin, Liam. And Aunt Connie and Uncle Doug, my parents, Maura Beth and my brother, and anyone else in the family who's interested. I was always a bit cavalier about the traditional concept of family, but now I see the good in it."

Alex managed a smile, but it quickly disappeared. "Yes, I understand all that, and I think that's terrific. What I meant was, could you see yourself bringing up your daughter with a husband in the picture?"

"Why would I want to do that? How would that ever happen?" Elise said, frowning. But there was incredulity more than anything else in her voice.

Alex looked down into his lap, avoiding her gaze. "Well, if someone asked you, that's how."

"Such as who?" she said, finishing the last of her biscuit with aplomb. It was as if the biscuit was truly more important than their conversation.

Alex did not understand how someone as perceptive and insightful as Elise could continue to avoid the obvious. Surely, she was not that oblivious. Or was she playing a game with him to let him down easy?

"Have I truly hidden my feelings for you that successfully?" he finally said. "Have I been that invisible?"

Elise looked dumbstruck. It took her a while to gather herself, but she finally caught his gaze. "Alex, I thought everything was strictly professional between us. It's been so much fun working on the book together. There's no denying that. We've spent a lot of time talking and laughing, and we've certainly gotten close that way. Are you sure what you're feeling is not just friendship for a colleague?"

He shook his head, closing his eyes briefly and saying nothing.

"Oh, Alex, dear Alex," she began. "You above all should know how I feel about what I'm doing. I'm incredibly grateful to you for giving me a platform for my positions and experiences by letting me speak to your class. My brother is just as grateful to you for your contributions to his fatherhood book. But you have to realize that that's as far as it goes with me."

The smile he found for her was not a bit labored. "A part of me knows that. The rational part, I guess. But there's another part of me—the emotional part of me—that wants more, that wants to know you more, and be a part of your life. I can't help it. It's something that has come upon me gradually until it's taken me over. That's the best way I can explain it."

She reached over and took his hand. "Honestly, I had no idea. I'll say it again—when we cut up and laugh during our brainstorming sessions the way we do, I just think we're clicking as professionals. And then Jeremy is always there, too, so I just think of the two of you as my book boys. I hope that doesn't sound too patronizing to you. I don't mean it that way."

"It doesn't."

"I don't know what else to say to you, then."

Alex thought over his next words carefully. If he could only find a way to keep the door cracked, he would find an altogether charming way to weasel his way in. "Then could I say something else?"

"Of course."

"I would just ask you to keep your options open. Once you have your baby, I know things will change for you. Of course I don't know from experience, but that's what Miz Brachle said in the auditorium before. Maybe you'll feel differently about your life at that point, and if you do, maybe you'd be willing to give me a thought."

Elise squeezed his hand for emphasis. "You know I respect these feelings you have for me, but I can't see myself changing my mind about being a single mother. This was my project from the beginning. My intent is to keep it that way. For the record, I can't see myself getting married to anyone. Or asking anyone to step into my life and share it that way. I hope you can understand."

"Yes, I do. But it wouldn't be right if I didn't let you know how I felt about you. By the way, your brother advised me not to say anything and to keep this under my hat. I've been going back and forth, but as you see, I didn't listen to him. I'm hardheaded that way."

Elise withdrew her hand and cupped her chin thoughtfully. "Jer knows me, he really does. But I'm tremendously flattered that you think so much of me. Most men have been threatened by me and don't even try to approach me. Or if they do, they soon tuck their tail between their legs and run off into the woods when I get into one of my feminist rants. I admit I'm bad about that. You may be one of the first who's stuck around long enough to open up to me the way you have. I asked you a while back if you thought I was some sort of curiosity because of my artificial insemination route to pregnancy, and you said no. I believed you then, and I certainly believe you now. Your honesty has to count for something, and I have to give you full credit for that."

Detecting the slightest crack in her armor, Alex spoke up with good humor. "Hey, don't throw me out with the baby's bathwater, then. Let's just keep working on the book with Jeremy, and you know I'll be around smiling and applauding when your little Celice makes her debut in the world. How does that sound?"

Elise offered her hand warmly. "I can certainly deal with that. Meanwhile, would you mind making me another one of these ham and biscuit sandwiches while I go on over and take a look at some of those veggie casseroles? Got to maintain my balanced diet, you know. As I said, I'm going to keep eating until I pop. Bad pun, I realize, but that's the truth of it."

"Be happy to oblige you," Alex said, picking up his plate and hers and walking toward the buffet table.

On the way there, he felt the faintest ray of hope regarding Elise and her agenda. Now his feelings were out in the open, and she was free to mull them over. He would keep on seeing her as they plowed through each chapter of the book right up until the Saterstrom Press deadline for the first draft. What good news that had been—further interest from a real publisher in their project! He knew without a doubt that he could keep up his professional demeanor easily enough, as he had promised Jeremy he would do. But now she would surely view him in a different light—one that had been doused by her relentless pursuit of her sociological goals. It wasn't the ideal romantic scenario—far from it. But under the circumstances, it was the best available, and at least he had made his case.

Besides, they said food brought people together. They might have different political or religious views, but there were very few people who could not break bread and forget those things at least for a while during a convivial meal. Elise had asked him to make her another ham and biscuit sandwich instead of making it herself. That was something, wasn't it? She could easily have made it herself. In fact, that was her modus operandi. She was the one who was always on her own. So, perhaps something subtle had kicked in and moved her beyond the professional colleague role.

As he stood at the buffet table spreading mustard on the bottom half of the biscuit he had split in half for her, he began to feel more and more confident that he was going to break through. Then, once he had completely assembled her sandwich, he paused to take himself to task mentally. He even managed to smirk about it. Was he on the verge of becoming a basket case with all this speculation in the midst of mustard-spreading and biscuit-splitting?

No matter. It was time to hand Elise her sandwich and let things unfold over the next month.

13

Sip 'N' See

There was one last tumbleweed effect after Christmas before the glacier effect of January set in. Although Ardenia Bedloe Place had not been able to make it home for Christmas due to a small setback with her lungs, Nurse Imogene Rodgers assured Periwinkle and Parker that New Year's Day was now the target for the long-awaited release to her eager parents.

"Just this one last week and I think she's home-free," she told them. "I know you've been waiting for what seems like ages for me to say that to you. But Dr. Dye seems pretty sure of himself, and I've worked with him long enough to know you can take his word."

Never had they wanted to get rid of the old year so fast once that was thankfully out of the bag. Each day seemed like a month, but they busied themselves making sure the nursery was ready with a few last-minute additions. They had already put in new wallpaper, which was pink with baby ducks adorning it, and there was a colorful mobile hanging over the crib, plus a baby monitor and a breast pump on the shelves, and everything else they had been advised to buy to welcome their little angel to her brand-new life.

The news spread throughout The Cherry Cola Book Club quickly, and it was Becca who reminded Periwinkle of a charming little event she had staged for Markie to introduce him to all her friends.

"Remember the sip 'n' see I hosted for all of you at my house?" she was saying over the phone. "It's easy as pie to stage, but I'll be glad to come over and help you if you want. You just need some wine, a bit of booze and mixers for the adults, and then the baby, of course, in all her glory."

Periwinkle was full of fond remembrance. "Ah, yes. That was so much fun. I sipped my wine and gazed down at your little Markie, and I recall thinking, Why haven't people thought of something like this before? Well, maybe they have in other towns, but I know I'd love to do it for everybody and Denia when the time comes."

"Then it's a done deal. Just let me know when you think your little Denia is ready, and we'll put our heads together."

Periwinkle put in one last word of caution. "But just let us get her home first so we can take a deep breath before we start planning her social calendar. She's not quite ready for the prom. We haven't picked out her dress yet."

Becca laughed heartily. "Your sense of humor has got to be the best in Cherico, if not the entire state of Mississippi. I've always loved the way you come out from the kitchen and visit with your customers at The Twinkle. Your food's not the only reason people keep coming back for more. You put on a one-woman show."

"I try."

"You succeed, too."

It was three weeks later and well into the New Year that Periwinkle sent out invitations to Denia's sip 'n' see. She and Parker were so relieved to have her out of the NICU at last, and things had been going so well once she was home that they decided it was way past time to show her off to their friends. Following Becca's suggestions, Periwinkle had laid out a generous bar on her lace-covered dining room table—all sorts of wine, liquors, and mixers, along with soft drinks, fruit punch, and water for the teetotalers. Then for all those who wanted to gnosh there were mini-quiches, bowls of nuts, spinach dip, and crackers. Of course, it wasn't about the food or the drinks or even the small talk with friends. It was all about taking a peek at the little one whose present and future life had been a question mark for so long. Thankfully, that was no longer a concern.

The event was to last one hour on a Sunday afternoon so as not to disrupt Denia's rigid schedule, and there weren't many latecomers. But there were plenty of *oohs* and *aahs* from the admiring guests as the time tumbled by fast.

"Isn't she the most precious thing you've ever seen?" Becca was saying, smiling down at the baby snuggled in her white bassinet with gray ribbons sewn around the bumper. The white blanket swaddling her set off her beautiful, café au lait skin, and wisps of curly brown hair adorned her tiny head. There was about her something of a golden aura, and everyone who saw her was mesmerized.

Becca nudged Justin, who was standing beside her, entreating him with her eyes and a nod of her head to make a comment as well.

"She sure is," he said, catching on quickly. "It takes me back less than a year ago. I was such a sucker for Markie the first time I laid my proud father eyes on him, so I know how you feel about your little Denia. She even looks like she's smirking at some kinda inside joke right this minute. That certainly is a unique smile, no matter what."

"Isn't that something? We noticed it as soon as we got her

home," Periwinkle added. "It was almost like she was saying to us, 'It's about time you got me outta that place with all those wires.'"

Everyone gathered around the bassinet laughed, and Connie said, "You'll get used to these adorable little tics and facial expressions. When we got Lindy home eons ago it seems like, I would even write all those things down in a journal and show them to Douglas every evening when he got home from work at the law office. I didn't want him to miss anything."

"She'd make me sit down with her and try to interpret them," Douglas added. "Can you imagine? Finally, she decided that some of them didn't mean much, if anything at all, and that she'd at least be willing to wait until Lindy learned to walk and talk before returning to that journal full-time. And believe me, she did just that. She practically wrote an epic novel."

Connie gave him a sideways glance and a playful punch on his bicep. "I did not. Besides, I didn't do anything any other first-time mother wouldn't do. Cut me some slack."

"I'll probably end up doing the same thing real soon," Periwinkle said. "I'm just thrilled to have the chance to do it at all, though. That's the main thing I don't wanna lose sight of."

"And we're thrilled for you," Maura Beth said, sipping on her bottled water with a twist of lime. "Of course, Jeremy and I can't wait to be in your position. It'll be any day now, according to Dr. Lively."

"Did you tell them what else Dr. Lively said?" Jeremy added, munching on a handful of cashews.

Periwinkle put her arm around Maura Beth's shoulder. "Well, I know you're definitely past due, girlfriend. What else do we need to know?"

"Definitely past due is the phrase. Two more days and

then Dr. Lively says he'll have to induce labor. Liam doesn't seem to want to come out and play. Elise is in the same boat with her baby."

Elise stepped up and entered the conversation as she was making short work of a mini-quiche. "I sure am. My Celice is hiding out in there probably doing some research for my next paper and doesn't want anyone to come looking for her before she's through. Induced labor is beginning to sound pretty good to me, and it looks like Dr. Lively might get two for the price of one. But I promise I won't complain. I'm ready to start being a mother. I've been ready for some time now."

"Parker and I know you'll keep us posted," Periwinkle said. Then she started surveying the room as she pulled out of the conversation abruptly. It was not the action of a gracious hostess merely keeping tabs on all her guests. There was genuine worry in her face and body language.

"Were you looking for someone?" Maura Beth said, tuning in on it all. "I think the gang's all here, judging by my count."

"Yes, they are by mine, too," Periwinkle added. But she seemed distracted and did not smile, and she kept turning this way and that in a not-so-subtle manner.

Suddenly—and without any doubt in her mind about it—Maura Beth realized what was going on and gently took Periwinkle by the arm. "I almost forgot. Weren't you going to give me your recipe for these delicious mini-quiches of yours? I just can't stop eating them. I'm not this big for nothing."

Periwinkle frowned for a second with a tilt of her head. "Was I? Was I going to do it in person or e-mail?"

"In person, remember? We said we'd take care of it today when I came." Maura Beth pointed toward the kitchen door. "Let's just run in there real quick. Nobody will know

we're even gone. I just can't go another day without it, and
I'm sure Parker can play host while I go in and write it all
down."

"Sure I can," Parker said, standing nearby. "You Free
Sample Sisters go right on ahead and do your thing."

"We will," Maura Beth said, smiling. "We always do."

At the kitchen counter, Maura Beth took Periwinkle's
hand while speaking softly.

"Now I want you to listen carefully to me. We've been
friends for so long, I think I can read your mind. You can
trust me with this, so don't try to cover up. It's your mother,
isn't it?"

Periwinkle couldn't seem to look Maura Beth in the eye
as she took a deep breath that seemed to take everything out
of her. "Yes, I sent her an invitation against my better judgment. I was hoping against hope she would come. Fifteen
more minutes and this thing'll be over. But I know in my
heart she's not coming. I guess I knew she wouldn't when I
licked the envelope and put a stamp on it. You know, everyone else I sent an invitation to came today. Book club people,
my best customers, anybody that has ever meant anything to
me. But not my mama."

Maura Beth was briefly conflicted, but she knew she had
to rule out any possibility of telling Periwinkle that Mama
Kohlmeyer had asked about the baby's color in a tone of severe
disapproval and judgment that would cut to the bone. It was
toxic information and should never be repeated to anyone. It
was only for Mama Kohlmeyer herself to say such words to
her daughter and suffer the consequences.

"I'm so sorry she's still turning her back on you and Parker.
I'm sure it hurts, but the important thing now is to become a
family, even if it means moving on without her. You've done

everything you can to reach out to her. If she won't communicate, there's nothing more you can do."

Periwinkle finally caught Maura Beth's gaze with a grateful smile. "Now, how on earth did you know I had my mama on my mind out there in the middle of that crowd of sippers and see-ers? Is that even a word?"

"Probably not. But it's just one of those Free Sample Sisters things, as far as I'm concerned. When you've shopped 'til you've almost dropped with another woman, there are no secrets. I also think pregnant women share a bond that no man will ever understand. It's an experience we have all to ourselves, no matter how empathetic they are, and it's meant to be that way. The men have their gifts and strengths, but everything comes through us women; and without us, no gifts or strengths are possible for anyone on the planet."

Periwinkle dabbed at the tears she had been working up over her mother's no-show and sniffled once or twice. "My, my. You librarians sure can turn out a speech. Bet you did some research for that one. But then you have all those books out at the lake to help you."

Maura Beth gave her a peck on the cheek. "I certainly do." She pulled back and smiled. "And you're right. That did sound a little like a speech or even a lecture. It's probably from hanging around Elise too much. Sometimes I even think I should be taking notes when I'm around her."

"That's funny. I know exactly what you mean." Periwinkle drew herself up and gently clasped her hands together. "You know, I really like Elise. She's like me in that she's her own woman. She's made her choices and stood by 'em. I can respect that. I built The Twinkle up from my divorce settlement with Harlan, but it was me who did all the work, and that can never be taken away from me. I hope it all turns out well for Elise in that same way."

"So do I."

"But as for me," Periwinkle continued, "I wouldn't even want to try to raise a baby alone. I've got Parker, and I know he's gonna pitch in and do his part. So, you're right. Once and for all, I need to accept the fact that my mama's not gonna come around. She just hasn't got it in her. I'm sorry about that, but there'll be no more invitations to anything. Parker's right about me not setting myself up for rejection time and time again. If she should show up at our door one day and ask to come in and be part of our lives, I think Parker and I'll find it in ourselves to forgive her and say, 'Come on in!' But we won't be holding our breath now. Parker's already laid down the law big-time about me worrying about what she thinks."

The two women hugged as best they could with Maura Beth's girth getting in the way. Then Maura Beth said, "Well, are you ready to join our friends again now that we've wrapped up this phony recipe mission?"

"Sure enough. And, hey, we don't wanna miss any new expressions Denia comes up with, do we?"

"Absolutely not."

Alex had been keeping an eye on what Elise was eating during the sip 'n' see, and at the right moment sidled up to her with two more mini-quiches on a small plate. Without giving it too much thought, he was continuing to pursue his favorite aphorism of food as the ultimate common denominator and icebreaker among human beings.

"Another refill?"

She swallowed a sip of her fruit punch and considered. "You talked me into it. I was thinking seriously of quitting, but with a friendly waiter like you at my disposal, I've changed my mind." She took the plate off his hands and thanked him.

"That little girl is just beautiful, isn't she?" he said, but it didn't sound much like small talk. The sincerity of his remark came through clearly. Or maybe it was Denia's irresistible appearance that had infused all conversation with a total lack of pretense. Disarming was often a good thing.

"I think everyone would be grateful to have a baby like that," Elise told him. "What a life changer she'll be for Periwinkle and Parker. And the wonderful thing is, she'll be growing up in a time when the world will be so much more open to women and people of color. The old prejudices are fading fast, or at least I hope that's true."

"I'm sure we'd all like to think so," Alex said, taking a sip of his wine.

Elise finished off a quiche and leaned in, looking somewhat skeptical. "You don't think so?"

"I don't want to sound like a pessimist," he began. "But I teach at the high school. This is still the Deep South. I know what goes on, and I hear about certain students being called into the principal's office for misbehavior. Now don't get me wrong. A lot of it is nothing—just pranks and silliness and boys and girls cutting up in class. You'll never get rid of that. But there are still a few who call names, and it's racist in nature. This is a part of a new generation in the millennium we're talking about. The fact is, some people are still out there trying to fight the Civil War, and they pass that on to their children here and now. I'm not saying that progress hasn't been made—because it certainly has. But perhaps I'm just a little more realistic on the subject at this point."

Elise seemed a bit taken aback. "Do you think I'm being naïve?"

"Not necessarily. I would point out that your academic environment at the university is somewhat elevated, though. You're there teaching students who want to learn the fine points of living successfully in our society. It seems to me that they have reasonably open minds. Am I right?"

"Yes, you are. That's exactly the way I'd put it."

Alex studied the expression on her face and noted that it had changed from somewhat skeptical to something resembling admiration. Was he making slow but steady progress with her?

"So you're telling me that the N word has definitely not been put to bed?" Elise continued.

"Not by a long shot, unfortunately." Alex hesitated, wondering if he should open up further to her, but decided not to hold anything back in the end. He had come this far. "And just last semester, we had a female student who was raped but had the guts to report it so that justice was eventually served. The boy's parents fought it every step of the way, but they didn't prevail. They tried to use that old 'she brought it on herself' defense. I bring all that up because of your comment about a new world for women. I hope I haven't made you think it's all hopeless out there and that tons of bad apples are just waiting to pounce, but I do think we have to be very vigilant about how people are treated."

"You're absolutely right, of course." Elise finished the last of her mini-quiches with great satisfaction. "I'm glad you told me all this. You hear all the time about academics like myself being detached from the real world in our ivory towers. Maybe I've been guilty of that from time to time. I know I've lectured my family enough about everything under the sun. And yet, here they all are supporting me when I need it most. What I've chosen to do has changed me in ways I never expected."

"And that's a good thing, right?"

"Yes, it is. This has been a most enlightening sabbatical so far. It's turning out to be about much more than pregnancy."

Alex let a healthy swig of his wine course through his veins. "I can't help but think that we'll be turning out one helluva book now. I know your academic credentials will count for a lot when the editor looks over our manuscript. I don't think there's a base we won't have covered."

Jeremy came over with some urgency and held up his cell phone. "Leesie, Maura Beth and I both just got a text from Dr. Lively saying he wants Maura Beth to come up to Memphis tomorrow to induce labor. You might want to check yours real quick and see if he's left you the same message."

"Oh, right," Elise said, retrieving her phone from her purse. "I've had it turned off because I didn't want to disturb the Sip 'N See."

When she turned it on, the same message was indeed waiting for her. "Can you believe it? Looks like Dr. Lively really is going to get two for the price of one from the same family. Where's Maura Beth? This is prime bonding time."

Hearing her name called nearby, Maura Beth joined them quickly. "Guess we better run home and pack for the big event. I think we should go up in tandem. Jeremy can drive me up, and Aunt Connie and Uncle Doug can drive you up. Won't we be something?"

"What are the odds of this happening?" Elise said, rising from her chair with some help from Alex. "But what a good story it'll make years from now when Celice and Liam are old enough to understand. It should create a special cousinly bond."

Alex turned to Jeremy and patted his shoulder. "I'd go with you if I didn't have class tomorrow, but I know we can keep in touch with our phones."

"Sure. I'll text you, and you won't miss a thing."

"Hey, I might even drive on up to Memphis after class," Alex continued. "I'd love to be a part of this and lend my support."

"How sweet of you," Elise said, and there was genuine warmth in her voice.

Then they all told Periwinkle and Parker the news and made their manners, full of the hope and energy that comes with knowing new lives would soon be coming into the world.

14

Double Delivery

There was a lingering suggestion of déjà vu for Connie McShay about the Memphis Children's Hospital waiting room and the role she was now playing. Nearly two years earlier at Cherico Memorial, she had functioned as the liaison between Justin Brachle's doctors and nurses and his concerned book club friends when he had suffered a heart attack. Her considerable skills and training as a long-time, though retired, ICU nurse had kicked in, and she had kept everyone informed thoroughly while Justin was being stabilized and then ambulanced to Nashville, where he could receive first-rate care and eventually fully recover. That particular event had disrupted a regular meeting of The Cherry Cola Book Club and set a precedent for many that had followed.

On this late-January morning, however, when both Maura Beth and Elise had presented themselves to Dr. Lively and staff for induced labor, there was only one other person waiting for the outcome in the hospital—Connie's husband, Douglas. Everyone else was tucked away down in Cherico with their cell phones on alert while sending all their positive energy and an occasional text northward. There had been no parade of Greater Chericoans heading up on the Natchez Trace Parkway in this instance.

But the big surprise was that Connie wasn't going to be Elise's coach in the delivery room, as the two of them had been planning for months. Connie had walked in with confidence to confer with Dr. Lively and been given a decidedly different set of marching orders.

"It doesn't quite fit the definition of an emergency, but Elise is going to need a C-section, Dr. Lively told me just now," Connie said, sounding both concerned and disappointed.

Douglas rose from his chair urgently as his wife stood in front of him with the news. "Has something gone wrong? Do we need to worry? I know you. Level with me, please."

"No, it's nothing like that. Dr. Lively just thinks it's the safer procedure right now. Turns out Elise's hips aren't that wide, and it could be a tight squeeze for the baby going down the birth canal. You don't want to risk injury to the brain. C-sections are done all the time, though, and that's the reason I'm out here with you and not in there. By the way, Dr. Lively will be doing the C-section, but Maura Beth's getting a cohort of his, Dr. Drake, to deliver her baby."

"So Maura Beth's having a conventional birth, then? Everything's okay with her?"

Connie brightened somewhat. "You bet. Jeremy's gone in with her now to the delivery room. I imagine he'll soon be telling her to *push, push, push* in the grand Lamaze manner he practiced so diligently. And we'll soon be greeting two new little citizens of Cherico. I'll be texting Susan and Paul and all the rest of the gang in just a minute."

Douglas chuckled. "You make it all sound so easy and clinical."

Connie could not let that one pass and lightly rapped her knuckles on his bicep. "Now, you know better than that. You always hope and pray everything that goes on in a hospital will go down easy, but you have to be vigilant and never let your guard down. Elise will be having general anesthesia in this case, so she won't be aware of what's going on. There shouldn't be a problem, but I've always erred on the side of cautious optimism."

Douglas sat back down and beckoned his wife to join him, putting his arm around her as he spoke. "As much as Elise has invested in all this emotionally, I'd hate to see anything go wrong for her now. As single-minded as she is, I wonder if she could take it."

"Let's don't think about it that way. Dr. Lively seemed very certain that this was the best option to get the baby here safe and sound. I'm sure we'll look back on this in an hour or so and wonder why we ever had any concerns. In fact, I forbid you to have any negative thoughts."

Douglas gave his wife a quick peck on the cheek. "I just remembered how wound up I was until they let me in to see Lindy—and then you, of course. Just like that old country classic, I was walkin' the floor over you. Both of you."

"We were a pair, weren't we?" she said, kissing him back and then tending to her texting duties.

He couldn't help winking at her. "Definitely keepers. You still are."

Elise was hearing voices, but she recognized none of them. Here was a snippet of a high-pitched female voice. There, the basso profundo of a male. But only once. It never returned after booming. There was no steady stream of conversation to be interpreted, however. Just those disjointed snippets. Then a little silence for a while. Then more snippets.

Where was time? She had no sense of it. She didn't even know where she was. Wherever she was, it was not altogether unpleasant. It was rather dreamy. Was she dreaming? It didn't feel much like a dream of hers. For one thing, there was no plot. All of her dreams had plots. Big plots. With dialogue and lots of action that she frequently remembered upon waking.

"That could be a movie," she would often find herself saying when she got out of bed and began her day. "I wish I could remember every detail."

She also dreamed in color. There was no color surrounding her, however. Nor any black and white, for that matter. There was just confusing sound, suspended in . . . space.

Now there were beeps. Consistent, steady beeps. More female-voiced snippets.

They seemed to be floating high above her. Then they seemed to swirl down near her ears. Then in and out of her ears. Maybe like pesky insects in the backyard on a hot summer night. She felt faintly entertained by whatever was going on. It was like a picnic of the mind.

Finally, a series of words broke through. "She's coming around," a female voice said. "I believe she's back with us now."

More sentences began to form that she understood. She felt as if she were coming down out of clouds into bright light. The light was somewhere above her. It was intensely brilliant. It made her squint. There was no relief from it. A couple of faces were hovering near her. Gradually, they came into focus. They were sweetly smiling faces. They were . . . nurses in blue scrubs. The faces seemed very much alike—smooth and placid—but the voices were different. The accents weren't the same. One voice sounded distinctly Southern; the other from the Midwest—maybe Illinois, maybe Ohio—it was hard to tell exactly. Only that the voice was not likely south of the Mason-Dixon Line.

The Southern voice said, "Thay-uh, she izz." There was a peekaboo quality to the phrase, as if the voice were playing with a baby.

"Miz McShay?" the Midwestern voice said. There was a kindness and patience present in the intonation of those two words that could not be dismissed.

Elise could barely gather the strength to grunt in acknowledgment. She was still so foggy she didn't even want to try.

"Miz McShay," the voice continued, sounding almost musical, "your C-section went very well. You are now the mother of a beautiful, seven-pound, nine-ounce little girl. Congratulations."

Elise's brain wouldn't quite let her focus. She needed a few seconds more. And then everything fell into place.

"Am I?" she said. "Am I . . . really? Where is she?"

"They'll bring her to you in a few minutes," the Midwestern voice said. "We had to let you wake up first. You're in the recovery room. You'll see her when we get you back to your room."

"How long . . . will that take?"

"Not too long," said the Midwestern voice. "You'll be up there in no time resting with your baby right next to you. But we need to observe you a bit longer. Then we'll wheel you on up."

"And everything is okay with my baby?"

"Perfect. We counted the fingers and toes for you."

"No extras?" Elise said, finding some humor.

"None. We double-checked."

Elise's onslaught of wit kept on coming. "You never know when an extra might come in handy. We're not lizards, you know."

"Dr. Lively said you were . . . well, a lively one," the Midwestern voice continued. "Would you like a sip of water, sweetie?"

Elise told her she did and was soon sipping through a straw.

"Is my baby beautiful?" Elise said after she had slaked her thirst.

"All babies are beautiful in my book," the Midwestern voice said. "But I think yours is gorgeous."

The Southern voice agreed. "Puhfickly gaw-jus. She's a Miss America in the makin'."

Elise looked like she was getting ready to float up to the ceiling. "I can't wait to meet her. I have such big plans."

"I'm sure you'll be a terrific mother," the Midwestern voice said. It almost sounded like she was singing her comment.

Although Jeremy was finding the Push-a-Thon more than stressful, he was determined not to show it. After all, it was his Maurie who was trying to squeeze the equivalent of a bowling ball out of her body into the real, live world. Then, too, he was beginning to wonder if she was growing tired of the sound of his voice. It seemed he was only capable of two utterances: *Push!* and then *Keep pushing!*

Well, wasn't that what he was supposed to say? Wasn't that why he was in the room in the first place in scrubs and a mask with sweat dripping down his back into the crack of his rear end? No Lamaze practice in the world could possibly have prepared him for this stress test. Nor the screams coming from his beloved wife and sweetheart. What had he done to her? And when her screams weren't filling the room and drowning out the telemetry, there were great gasps of air and visceral grunts the likes of which tennis pros seldom emitted in the midst of a furious rally at Wimbledon. Male or female.

He chastised himself mentally for being such a wimp. She was the one doing all the work, leaning forward with all her might, straining and bearing down with her face on fire, so his only choice was to man up and pretend to be as strong as she was. Because he couldn't imagine what it must be like for his Maurie to be giving birth. He hadn't even passed a kidney stone in his twenty-something life, and those men who had passed them insisted that it was probably the closest a man could come to feeling the pain of childbirth. Perhaps after this was all over and his son was born and they had all settled into their cottage on Painter Street as a family, he could forsake drinking enough water and making enough pit stops during his high school routine to instigate a kidney stone himself, just for the empathy of it. Wouldn't that be the ultimate gesture and balancing act?

"The baby's crowning right now," Dr. Drake announced calmly, as Maura Beth let out a scream for the ages.

Jeremy steeled himself and drifted away for a brief moment or two. *If I tell her to* push *one more time, she is going to stick a knife into my back when we get home. I just know it. And I wouldn't blame her.*

But he didn't have to say it again. Suddenly, Maura Beth released her precious cargo, and everything proceeded at a breathtaking pace. Jeremy was mesmerized by it all—the length of the umbilical cord, the delicate covering of blood on flesh, the severing, the cleaning up, the first cry. He watched it all unfold with the word *miracle* on his mind. There was no other way to put it.

Liam was here with them. In the world. Surrounded by air instead of amniotic fluid. His Maurie fell back, exhausted and covered in sweat, and he leaned down and kissed her forehead gently.

"He's here," Jeremy told her. "Our son is here."

"I know," she said, catching a breath. "I know."

"You are an unbelievable woman," he said. "I know *how* you did that, but I just don't know how you did *that*."

"Stop being an English teacher and playing with words."

He laughed; then he stopped abruptly when the nurse presented their son to them. Peeking out of his blanket, his little head was incredibly pink, wrinkled, and bald. His features seemed abstract, a lot of lines that some deranged artist had sketched together. But his parents saw nothing but delicate, indescribable beauty in the composition. They were indeed the only beholders that counted, and their expressions were nothing but joy to the highest order.

"Hello, Liam," Maura Beth said, kissing his forehead so gently that the kiss seemed made of something lighter than air.

"Hello, little son," Jeremy said, admiring his child as if he were a sparkling diamond. "This is where it all begins."

When Alex entered Elise's room later that afternoon, she did not try to hide a hint of a pleasant gasp. There he was again, living up to his word, living up to his fascination with her and her baby and everything that came with it. He had come all the way up from Cherico after his classes, and that indicated determination and true concern, if nothing else. The pertinent thing was, she was really glad to see him. Something worthwhile and unexpected had kicked in regarding their unconventional, semi-professional relationship—or whatever it was. And she would soon be springing her grand surprise.

"Connie texted me that everything went well," he told her, standing at the foot of her bed. "It was tough concentrating on my classes all day. One of my students pointed out that I actually got the date of the firing on Fort Sumter wrong. Even wrote it on the blackboard wrong. And here I'm supposed to be such an expert on Southern history. Go figure."

Elise's smile was genuine. "I'm sure it wasn't a big deal. I wasn't even able to make a mistake today, since I was under the spell of la-la land, of course."

"That's cute."

"Hey, I manage to get off a good one once in a while."

Alex was surveying the room anxiously. "Is the . . . uh . . . where's your baby?"

"In the nursery right now. You can go and see her when you leave here. She's beautiful, of course. No daughter of mine would be anything else." There was an awkward pause. "I . . . appreciate you coming up to see me."

"I wouldn't have missed it. It's such a big event in your life. Same for Maura Beth and Jeremy. I just came from visiting with them. They're beyond the delirious stage. It'll take a while for them to come down to earth."

"I know," Elise said, tilting her head back and forth in amused fashion. "Aunt Connie has been in and out keeping me posted. The first cousins are doing just fine. I really like the feeling of family that's come out of all this."

Alex seemed at a total loss for words for a brief period, managing only an awkward smile.

"Did you want to say something?" Elise said, trying to rescue him. "You looked like you wanted to."

"It was just that . . . I was wondering how much longer you'll be staying down in Cherico with your aunt and uncle. How soon will you be going back to Evansville to start teaching again?"

Elise sat up in bed a bit straighter and cleared her throat as if she were about to launch into a lecture. "Well, I've still got three months on my sabbatical. I really think I'd like to spend it with Aunt Connie and Uncle Doug at the lodge. They've really made me feel so comfortable and welcome there. And I'd like to talk to Maura Beth about getting Celice and Liam together from time to time. I think we both really want them to have a true relationship growing up. It's never too soon to get that under way, so we'll put our heads together."

Alex stuffed his hands into his pockets like a nervous little boy and shifted his lips to one side. "That's a lot of territory to cover in two months."

"Probably. But it needs to be done." Then Elise caught his gaze intently. "Alex, I've been giving things a lot of thought.

Before you came in today, I had a long conversation with Aunt Connie and Uncle Doug about you."

"About me?"

"Yes."

"Seems like an odd trio, if you don't mind me saying so."

Elise took a moment to rehearse in her head. "It'll all make sense if you just hear me out. We discussed something very important, and it's probably something you've never even thought about regarding Celice. I'm not sure I'd been giving it much thought either until Aunt Connie brought it up. It's not the sort of thing that was ever a priority of mine before, but Aunt Connie has a way about her. What can you say about someone who's fixed your meals and looked after you during most of your pregnancy? When she says something, you sit up and listen."

Alex looked intrigued and took his hands out of his pockets. "Please, go ahead. I can't wait to hear this."

"We came to the conclusion that you deserved this," she said. "I've already okayed it with Uncle Doug. I promise you he doesn't mind one bit, just so you know. He's a pretty cool guy."

"Enough with the suspense and dragging this all out forever. Exactly what do I deserve?"

Elise gave him her best smile as she looked him straight in the eye. "We would like for you to be Celice's godfather. Aunt Connie will be her godmother. As I said, Uncle Doug doesn't mind at all, and I never put much into the whole concept before. But it just seems like the right thing to do. What do you say?"

Alex moved to her side and took her hand. The warmth that flowed between them emboldened him to get at the truth. "I'm flattered that you'd think of me, of course. It's quite unexpected but still an honor. But am I reading between the lines when I say that this is my consolation prize? Is my being

Celice's godfather all that's going to be possible between the two of us?"

She withdrew her hand and gently wagged a finger at him. "O ye of little faith. It's exactly the opposite, as a matter of fact. This is my way of keeping you in the loop. You can come up to Evansville to visit us anytime you want, and sometimes I can come down to Cherico to visit you, Maura Beth and Jeremy, and the rest of the family. You don't even need a reason. Just call me up and tell me you'd like to do something with us, and we'll all take it from there. For the first time in my adult life, I won't have everything programmed like a syllabus. That'll be a healthy change of pace for me, I think. I'll learn to be a bit more spontaneous. I have a feeling that motherhood is going to be the ultimate spontaneous experience."

The look of relief on Alex's face was unmistakable. "So you're saying the door is still open?"

"Yes, it most certainly is. That's the best I can do for now. I hope that's good enough for you."

Alex's relief blossomed into outright celebration, and he pumped his fist. "It sure is. Besides, I hear the best relationships take time."

"And we don't need to explain anything to anybody. They'll figure it out as soon as we figure it out."

Alex lifted his chin with a distant look in his eye. "It sounds like a great adventure to me."

Elise adopted the same pose. "I'm sure it will be. This whole thing I've chosen for myself has been nothing but an adventure from the beginning. Why should it stop now? I think what I've realized by going down to Cherico and living with my aunt and uncle is that you truly don't have to do things alone if you don't want to. Including people who love you is always a good idea."

"You're a much more romantic person than you realize," Alex told her, taking her hand again.

"Am I really? I don't see it. I always thought I was practical and realistic more than anything else."

"You are, though," he said, giving her hand a gentle squeeze. "There's something else beneath the surface. I saw it bubbling up when we started working together on the book."

She laughed brightly for the first time since he'd entered the room. "Bubbling up? You make me sound like a cauldron out of *Macbeth*."

"I didn't mean it that way," he said, returning her laughter. "Maybe it's the passion you have for your studies and theories. You believe them because you want the world to be a better place, not just for women but for everyone. You want it to be a better place for Celice and Liam and Denia and all the other babies who are being born as we speak. You can't keep that kind of goal hidden, and it's contagious in the best sense of the word. I'll say it again—it's a romantic view of the world."

Elise leaned back against her pillow and sighed. "That was a wonderful speech, Alex. I don't think I could have said it any better myself. I'm halfway tempted to have you address one of my classes when I return. I'll introduce you to them by saying, 'Here is a man who totally gets it.' And I'd be telling the absolute truth."

"I'd gladly take you up on that offer if I can work it into my schedule," he told her. "It's hard for me to get time off."

"Well, we can both work on it."

"I'll make it a priority of mine."

Then, Elise felt the moment approaching. It was bubbling up in the manner that Alex had described so impressively a few moments ago. For the first time since she had known him, she wanted to kiss him. Not on the cheek. Not in some casual, professional way she might have done when they were working on the book and playing around. But on the lips with an emotional kick to it. She wanted that to happen, and without saying one word to Alex, it did.

He leaned in smoothly, and she sat up a bit so she could accommodate him. Their lips met warmly and stayed connected long enough to convey a sense of continuity. There was no question that they would explore all of this further and see where it led them. When they pulled apart gently, they were content to gaze at each other fondly, saying nothing, with their smiles still firmly in place.

15

Strolling Down Memory Lane

Maura Beth considered her latest Cherry Cola Book Club brainstorm to be her greatest yet, and she was certain it would never be equaled no matter how long the club existed. Okay, perhaps it was too cute for words, even corny, some had been rumored to say. But it was now April in Northeast Mississippi, and spring was eager to get under way with its first display of yellows and light greens on the branches of trees. It was time for the renewal of life and the rising of sap and the thriving of little babies recently born into the world.

So most people thought it was an adorable idea to line up Liam McShay, Celice McShay, and Denia Place in their strollers with their proud parents on the stage of the library's mini-auditorium for the club's most original idea to date. Nearly everyone who had ever attended a meeting of The Cherry Cola Book Club was there—even the head honcho of Cherico, Councilman Durden Sparks, with his wife, Evie—for it would be politically unseemly for him to stay away and not put in his two cents. Wasn't kissing babies the ultimate political cliché?

It was true that it would be a good while before any of the trio of infants could read a book, much less review one.

But that was beside the point. This particular meeting of The Cherry Cola Book Club was a joyous celebration more than anything else, and everyone was onboard, including children's librarian, Miriam Goodcastle, standing on one side of the stage dressed as Mother Goose, to open the program officially. Long-time front desk clerk and director's assistant, Renette Posey, stood on the other side, costumed as the Old Woman Who Lived in a Shoe.

"Ladies and gentlemen of The Cherry Cola Book Club," Miriam began after tentatively tapping the mike, "we have here before you the future of our library, as well as the future of all libraries. Mothers and fathers, entrust your children to me so that they will soon have their noses in books instead of technology. I say give them rhymes and it will give them reasons to read on. In continuity there is always great strength."

Then it was Renette's turn for a brief moment in the sun. "Fairy tales have their place as children grow up, but if these babies learn as much about the real world as I have working here with Maura Beth, they'll do just fine. So now, without further ado, we call upon the parents of these babies to introduce to all of you the Second Generation of the Cherry Cola Book Club."

Maura Beth and Jeremy smiled and pointed toward Liam in his stroller as planned. "This is Paul William McShay, and this is his official initiation into The Cherry Cola Book Club," they said together. "May Liam read all the books in the entire world worth reading."

Everyone laughed and applauded simultaneously.

Next, Elise gestured toward her little daughter's stroller. "This is Susan Constance Celice McShay. Celice, I've decided to call her; and even though we'll be leaving soon for Evansville to resume our lives up there, whenever she visits Cherico with me, she'll be in this library reading something, I have no doubt. And that alone will make her an official, bona fide member of The Cherry Cola Book Club. A love of literature and good food sums it all up."

After another round of applause, Periwinkle spoke up for herself and Parker, glancing down quickly at her notes once or twice. "Ardenia Bedloe Place, meet your Cherry Cola Book Club family. You were named for your wonderful grandmother, and she loved being a part of this amazing group. You'll find everything you need to know about the world here, including the meaning of acceptance by truly good people. We can't wait for Denia to get to know all of you personally."

Another round of healthy applause followed—and then a surprise. From stage left on cue, the Brachles entered, with Justin holding their son, Markie, in his big, muscular arms. The little tyke was a few months away from his terrible twos, and his parents had decided it was best to keep track of him by not letting his wandering little feet touch the ground.

"Don't forget about us," Becca said. "We're a bit ahead of the other three, but we can't wait to bring Markie to his first story hour in the not-too-distant future. We know it will be something special."

James Hannigan of The Cherico Market popped up after a final burst of applause and said, "I guess I'd better start including baby food in my free samples on Wednesdays and Saturdays. Whadda y'all think?"

"I'll be there," Becca said.

"And I speak for The Free Sample Sisters when I say that you've got a winner," Maura Beth added in the midst of all the laughter and buzzing that spread throughout the auditorium.

Then it was time to retire to the break room and the potluck buffet everyone had brought to catch up on the latest news. Fortuitously, all four of the second generation had been perfectly silent angels throughout the brief ceremony. But that did not stop at least one of them from coming to life, spitting out a pacifier, and crying now and then as everyone moved along the line with their plates and appetites on hand.

"I think you outdid yourself today," Councilman Sparks told Maura Beth as he helped himself to a couple of slices of smoked turkey breast. "I didn't think you could top what you've done in the past, but Evie and I agree, this was a pretty special idea. Looks to me like Cherico will never be without The Cherry Cola Book Club with all these little newcomers."

As she had often in the past where Councilman Sparks was concerned, Maura Beth decided to be gracious, overlooking the years of calculated opposition she had faced from City Hall regarding both the old and new libraries she had directed to the best of her ability. "Thank you, Durden," she said, taking a huge spoonful of broccoli and cheese casserole. "I'm very proud of my legacy, and I know you'll never mind greeting new taxpayers."

"Hey, that's a good one. And I'll be the first to admit it," he continued. "I was wrong about a lot of things. So maybe I did think libraries were a thing of the past at one time. Live and learn, right?" He offered yet another of his trademark, re-election smiles that had worked so well for him over the years, along with that dashing touch of gray at his temples.

Maura Beth flashed her teeth at him a bit too broadly. "Oh, yes, indeedy. Got to learn from those mistakes."

"And I've been meaning to compliment you on how fast you regained that cute little figure of yours," he said, stepping back just a bit for a quick once-over while Evie gave him a look of disapproval as she stood behind him.

That remark gave Maura Beth pause as well. It echoed much too uncomfortably that awkward stretch when Councilman Sparks seemed bound and determined to get rid of her library directorship in order to get her to come to work "under" him. He had even fired his loyal, long-time secretary, Nora Duddney, to set up the sequence. Maura Beth had, of course, figured out what he was up to fairly easily and maintained her distance, and Nora had later come to her aid in forcing City Hall to come up with the money to build a millennium-worthy library. Of all the women in the world Charles Durden Sparks had gone to bat and set his cap for, Maura Beth Mayhew McShay was surely his supreme strikeout.

"Let's don't go there," Maura Beth said, wrinkling her nose at him. "I'll settle for the library legacy compliment, if you don't mind."

Councilman Sparks knew better than to antagonize her and quickly changed the subject as the two of them moved farther along the line. "Well, I can't wait to dig into this delicious food."

"Yes, Durden, let's concentrate on the potluck, shall we?" Evie said, nudging him vigorously.

Then Maura Beth shut the conversation down with a smirk. "Yummy sums it all up, doesn't it?"

Would wonders never cease? Mamie Crumpton had finally given in and accepted the fact that her once-subservient sister, Marydell, had gone to work for Maura Beth as a front desk clerk over a year ago and seemed none the worse for wear. The Crumpton Family name had not been besmirched one iota by one of its scions doing low-paying work, serving the general public and even liking every minute of it. No one thought less of the Crumpton sisters of Perry Street because one of them no longer sat on settees all morning and afternoon ordering servants around and having them wait on her hand and foot. What Mamie had insisted was so very far beneath a Crumpton had actually given Marydell a brand-new life away from her domineering sister, getting her out of the house for a breath of fresh air and much-needed perspective.

Gradually, Mamie had realized that she was never going to get the toothpaste back in the tube. Once Marydell had tasted the freedom of making up her own mind, she was not about to give it up. Well, at least Mamie had been a library user all along—attending the meetings of "Who's Who in Cherico?" that Voncille Nettles Linwood had supervised for so many years. To Mamie's way of thinking, it was not as if Marydell had gone to the extreme and become a fast-food worker at a drive-through or one of those robotic greeters at a big box store. How would the aristocratic Crumpton name ever live down that sort of thing?

For her part, Marydell no longer gave a hoot in a handbag what her sister thought. She had said only *yes* and *no* so politely to her for so many decades, staying in the background while Mamie paraded around Cherico in her one-size-too-small gowns and drooping pearls, that she was determined to make up for lost time. She now had opinions about everything from politics to religion to fashion to food; and, furthermore, she had turned out to be a very helpful front desk clerk because of that. Eclectic had become her middle name, and Mamie had decided to find something else to complain about and to try to control.

"That little initiation makes me wish I had had children," Marydell was saying to her sister as the two of them sat at one of the break room tables indulging in bites of turkey with cranberry sauce.

Mamie stopped just short of cackling. "You live in such a fantasy world, sister dear. As if doing a cutesy, little, fifteen-second skit onstage is all there is to bringing up a child."

"For heaven's sake, I know that's not all there is to it. You completely misunderstood what I meant," Marydell said, narrowing her eyes. "It's the continuity I'm talking about. The fact is, the Crumpton name will be dying out with us."

But Mamie continued to keep the amusement in her voice

while the wheels turned in her head. "Why on earth are you being so morbid about it? Have you been fooling around in the library's genealogy room again? That comment sounds like something Voncille Linwood would say to us. I can just hear her now in that superior, schoolteacher tone of hers, 'Ooh, after being one of the first families of Cherico, there will be no more Crumptons to trod the hallowed sidewalks of Perry Street. Isn't that a terrible shame? However will we get along?'"

Just at that moment, Maura Beth passed by on her way back to the buffet line, and Mamie got her attention. "If you have just a minute, we need your advice and counsel, Maura Beth."

"I'm always at your service," she said, stopping in her tracks with her gracious, librarian smile.

"Here's what we've got going. Marydell seems to bemoan the fact that we are the last of the Crumptons in Cherico. Now this is your chance to lighten her load and show that her coming to work for you was absolutely the most brilliant move she could ever have made." Mamie folded her arms expectantly. "Go right ahead. I can't wait for your response."

It took Maura Beth only a second to come up with a reply. "May I remind you both that the Crumpton name is emblazoned on the façade of this magnificent library? It will forever be known as The Charles Durden Sparks, Crumpton, and Duddney Public Library. The more than substantial contribution that you two made from your family fortune enabled this facility to get off the ground in the first place. Yes, Councilman Sparks saw the light of reason and finally chipped in, and Nora Duddney rounded out the trio of major contributors. But this incredible building will stand for many generations to come long after all of us are gone, and as a result, the Crumpton name will never die out. How's that?"

Instead of applauding, Mamie was frowning. "Well, I didn't expect you to have an answer like that, Maura Beth. Good God, you ought to go on *Jeopardy!* with the way you think on your feet. Do you have a buzzer hidden on you somewhere?"

"Thanks for the lovely compliment, but you probably shouldn't have asked me in the first place."

Marydell had the most impish grin on her face, and she was not about to let it go. "I told you she was the most wonderful boss in the world to work for. She always knows what's going on and what to say to everybody who walks in."

Mamie seemed more resigned than anything else. "Yes, I suppose you two were meant for each other—a match made for all those stacks. In the meantime, you're right, Maura Beth. The Crumpton name on this building is a pretty nice accomplishment if I do say so myself. I'm quite sure our parents would have approved of the way we spent their money."

"There you go," Maura Beth added. "That's the right way to look at it. And I promise you if Marydell ever gets tired of working tirelessly at the front desk without complaining even once, I'll gladly let you take her place for the exact same salary. When it comes to the Crumpton family, I'm an equal opportunity employer."

"Don't push it," Mamie said. But her tone was not really snarky. Like Councilman Sparks had realized some time ago, she knew she had met her match.

Locke and Voncille Linwood had finished eating and making the rounds, paying their respects to all the babies in the strollers and to squirming little Markie Brachle as well. His attention span was waning by the second. Now, they were sitting at one of the tables in the midst of a pleasant conversation with Maura Beth and Jeremy, catching their breath.

"You don't think The Cherry Cola Book Club will ever start reviewing children's books, do you?" Voncille said, pointing to Liam's stroller and the other ones across the way.

Maura Beth laughed and then took a sip of her cherry cola lime punch, the club's staple drink. "That would be Miriam Goodcastle's department. In a way, her story hours do that at the beginner's level. But our club will stick to what the adults like to read—and what they like to cook and eat."

"Do you think your library will ever allow an adult beverage or two into our meetings?" Locke said, making a gesture with his hand of tossing one back. "There are times when I've wanted a good, stiff drink to go along with all the back-and-forth and such the club brings out in people. Are there any laws on the books that forbid spirits on the premises, so to speak?"

"I'll have to look into the fine print."

Voncille gave him a playful nudge. "Now, Locke, you don't want to get our Maura Beth into more trouble, do you? After all, she's been through quite a lot since she came to Cherico seven or eight years ago. We're so lucky she just didn't up and leave town and go back to New Orleans for good. She was put through the mill by Councilman Sparks and his cronies."

Locke seemed to be reviewing the recent past in his head before he spoke. "That's true. All those ultimatums you got from City Hall, fighting to keep the old library open, all that thunderstorm damage to the roof that came along, scrapping to get the new one built, and then picketing from that crazy church group last year when it finally opened. A lesser woman couldn't have made it through all that. You've sure earned your keep here in Cherico, Maura Beth."

"She sure has," Jeremy said, coming to his wife's defense. "But thank goodness it looks like everything's finally calmed down, and the future looks bright for us and the entire town. We just finished talking to Ana Estrella over at the buffet table, and she said the Spurs 'R' Us plant out at the industrial park will be opening up in another month. Those cowboy boots'll be flying out the doors to the whole world and truly putting Cherico on the map. Maurie and I are looking forward to raising our children here, no matter what." He paused to let that sink in to the Linwoods and added, "Oh, yes, we're going to have more than one, believe me."

"I think that's wonderful," Voncille said, clasping her hands together. "Maybe big families will be making a comeback in the millennium. When I was growing up as a Baby Boomer, it was never in question, but things seemed to have slowed down a bit recently."

"We're planning on at least two, maybe three," Maura Beth added, looking at Jeremy affectionately. "I was an only child, and I didn't particularly like it. I remember specializing in imaginary playmates. My mother even had the *Times-Picayune* print an account in the social column of a birthday party I had for one of my imaginary friends. I think I named her Mrs. Figgie Newton, and she was turning five, as I recall. Not that that was a bad thing, you understand, but I do want to try the sibling arrangement and see how that works out for us."

"Sometimes it works, sometimes it doesn't," Jeremy said in somewhat of a monotone while averting his eyes.

"You and Elise, for instance?" Maura Beth said.

"On the whole, I think it's worked out now that we're all grown up with our family responsibilities. Doesn't really matter how we got there. The point is that we both finally grew up and left our sibling rivalry behind. It's really something that's been long overdue."

"At any rate, we're going to try for more than one," Maura

Beth told them, sounding completely carefree. "That Second Generation of The Cherry Cola Book Club is going to be something special, I'm happy to tell you."

Over on the other side of the room, Elise and Alex were having a quiet little conversation with Connie and Douglas while Celice was cooperating splendidly, sleeping quietly in her stroller.

"We sure are gonna miss you," Connie was saying between bites of broccoli and cheese casserole. "The old lodge just won't be the same without you and the baby. Sometimes I felt like I was back working in a hospital again—but without any emergencies or meds to administer or telemetry to monitor with a vengeance. Without the possibility of a flat line, it's all good."

Elise reached over and patted Connie's hand affectionately. "Well, you did make sure that I took all my vitamins every single day. But you have no idea how much your kindness and TLC has meant to me." She included Douglas with a quick glance his way. "You've both practically been saints over there in The McShay Home for Wayward Mothers."

Laughter broke out around the table, and Douglas said, "That's funny, but you know you've just been family to us."

Elise nodded enthusiastically. "Yes, I have to say I've learned a thing or two about how that really works."

"How much time are you spending with your parents before you go back to your classes at the university?" Connie said. "I know Susan and Paul are really looking forward to seeing you—and not just for a random weekend. You really do owe them that much."

"I promised them a solid two weeks so they could get to spend more time with Celice—and me for that matter. I guess they really have gotten the short end of the stick so far. So we'll be bunking it together in Brentwood after we leave here. I fully expect to be spoiled the way you spoiled me down here in Cherico, but that might take a little doing."

Then Connie couldn't resist being a little nosy, catching Alex's gaze. "By the way, a little birdie told me that you might be planning to go visit Elise and the baby up in Evansville sooner rather than later. Am I right?"

"We're working on it," Alex said, reassuring her with a wink. "As soon as I'm through with this semester out at the high school, as a matter of fact. We have a few dates circled."

"And I might come down here from time to time," Elise added. "One of the things that Maura Beth and I agreed upon a while back when we were eating our way through our pregnancies was that it's hard to quit this little town of Cherico. It has staying power when it comes to making good friends. And The Cherry Cola Book Club is something else."

"Douglas and I are so glad we retired here from Nashville. We've never regretted it for a second," Connie said. "The important thing to remember is that Cherico is always here waiting for you anytime you miss it."

Elise snickered. "Greater Cherico, right?"

"I've asked around, but nobody seems to have the vaguest notion who invented that particular term," Connie said. "But it sure did stick, and everybody loves the implied ambition behind it—like everyone is still convinced that Cherico will amount to something one day. They can have their faults, but the truth is, sometimes the smallest towns are the greatest places to settle down."

An hour or so after the Second Generation celebration and potluck had ended and everyone had gone their separate ways, Maura Beth and Jeremy found themselves out at the deck railing of the library, looking out over the lake. They each had a hand on Liam's stroller, as he was "down" for the moment. It was a calm April afternoon with no hint of the unpredictable blustery weather that so often came to Cherico in the spring and frequently wreaked havoc for as long as it cared to remain. At the moment, several bass boats had ventured out on the water to try their luck but seemed to be having not a bit so far.

"Not a single fish hauled in since we've been here," Jeremy was saying, shaking his head. "But they're probably out there just for the pure relaxation of it. I know I would be."

"My office relaxes me the same way," Maura Beth said. "The smartest thing I ever did was to have the architect give me those big windows right there on the water. Just call it the ultimate director's privilege. When I shut my office door, I'm in my own little universe."

"Fess up, and I think I already know the answer to this one, but have you ever taken a nap?"

"The answer that would keep me out of trouble would be that it comes with the territory. Renette has woken me up more than once with a buzz from the front desk. She can vouch for the occasional snort and unintelligible grunt she hears at the other end when I pick up."

They both laughed, but the conversation lapsed for a while. It was enough to savor Lake Cherico on a day like this. It was enough to stand on the deck of the vision in Maura Beth's head that had materialized after years of struggle in a hopelessly outdated building that was an embarrassment to Cherico. In fact, the old, ex-tractor warehouse of a library on Shadow Alley had since been razed to make way for a downtown parking lot, a far better use of that small patch of real estate, which ironically had never featured any parking for patrons.

Memories of what had gone on there for so many years remained, however; particularly of that first meeting of The Cherry Cola Book Club that had begun the transformation of Cherico into a community that had finally learned how to get things done and look after one another. And one feisty young librarian had made all the difference.

Maura Beth and Jeremy turned away from the water together for a moment to smile down at their sleeping Liam.

"Second generation," she said, almost in a whisper.

Then they returned to the lake and its placid surface, which stretched all the way to the horizon.

The Complete Cherry Cola Book Club Cookbook

With the popularity of all of the recipes that have graced the end of all of The Cherry Cola Book Club novels, we thought we'd round them up and put them in one place for interested readers. They're all here—from tomato aspic to hot tamales to crème de menthe wedding cake to Chicken on the Sofa. Toward the end of this compilation, you'll find a batch of new recipes for *Book Club Babies.* They are a tribute to the Sip 'N' See chapter in which Periwinkle Place invites her friends in for light fare and drinks to see her precious new baby.

For the most part, all of these recipes are easy to fix and perfect to trot out anytime for entertaining on any occasion. What's more, when Ashton Lee has traveled all over the country working with libraries and book clubs on talks and signings, he's found that many of these dishes have been waiting for him and the patrons and members to sample. What a thoughtful readership he has!

If you have a book club that would be interested in hosting Ashton Lee, you can contact him on his Ashton Lee, Writer, page at facebook.com/ashtonlee.net to work out the details. And thanks for being a reader of The Cherry Cola Book Club series: in order, *The Cherry Cola Book Club, The Reading Circle, The Wedding Circle, A Cherry Cola Christmas, Queen of the Cookbooks,* and *Book Club Babies.*

From *The Cherry Cola Book Club* (Book 1)

Becca Broccoli's Easy Peasy Chicken Spaghetti

Ingredients you will need:

1 whole chicken
1 package of thin spaghetti
1 stick of butter
1 chopped onion
½ cup chopped green pepper
1 cup chopped celery
1 large can of mushroom soup
1 can of diced pimentos
2 cups of grated cheddar cheese
Salt and pepper to taste

Cook chicken in salted water until tender. Remove chicken and dice the meat. Use chicken broth to cook spaghetti until tender. Saute butter, onion, green pepper and celery until onions are translucent. Add veggies to pasta; then add large can of mushroom soup, chicken and pimentos; pour into casserole dish and sprinkle cheese over top. Bake at 350 degrees Fahrenheit until golden bubbly.

—Courtesy Mrs. Rose Williams Turner, Natchez, Mississippi

Connie McShay's Frozen Fruit Salad

Ingredients you will need:

8 ounces cream cheese
½ cup sugar
1 cup mayo
1 cup white raisins
½ cup chopped nuts (walnuts or pecans)
1 can fruit cocktail
Poppy seed dressing

Mix cream cheese and sugar; add mayo, raisins, nuts and fruit cocktail; pour cocktail into twelve lined muffin tins and freeze; package in large Ziploc bag. (For additional flavor, add two tablespoons of poppy seed dressing upon serving.)

—Courtesy Alice Feltus, Lucy Feltus, and
Helen Byrnes Jenkins, Natchez, Mississippi

Periwinkle Lattimore's Baked Sherry Custard

Ingredients you will need:

2 tablespoons sugar
1⅓ cups whole milk
Dash of salt
3½ teaspoons sherry
1½ teaspoons vanilla
3 egg whites
1 additional tablespoon of sugar

Combine the two tablespoons of sugar, milk, and salt in a pan; cook on simmer to low heat until sugar dissolves—approximately five minutes; remove and then add sherry and vanilla together.

In a separate bowl, combine the egg whites with the additional tablespoon of sugar; whip or beat into soft-peak stage; and add the milk mixture slowly. Use sieve to strain the entire mixture into a two-cup baking dish; place dish in a baking pan with water bath (usually halfway up the sides) and bake at 325 degrees Fahrenheit for about an hour. If toothpick comes out clean when inserted in middle of mixture, custard is done. Serve warm or cold.

—Courtesy Helen Louise Jenkins Kuehnle,
Natchez, Mississippi

Becca Broccoli's Cherry Cola / Lime Punch

Ingredients you will need:

1 liter any chilled cola beverage (do not use diet variety)
1 liter any chilled ginger ale beverage (do not use diet variety)
1 jar maraschino cherries
3 limes

Pour cola and ginger ale into large punch bowl and stir. Add jar of stemless maraschino cherries and one half the liquid. Cut limes in half and squeeze juice into mixture. Stir everything together and serve.

—Courtesy Lauren R. Good, Memphis, Tennessee

Periwinkle Lattimore's Tomato Aspic
with Cream Cheese

Ingredients you will need:

2 cups tomato juice (or V8 juice)
½ cup chopped onion
2 chopped celery ribs
1 envelope unflavored gelatin
¼ cup cold water
2 tablespoons lemon juice
Dash of hot pepper sauce
Dash of Worcestershire sauce

Boil tomato juice, onion, and celery for about twenty minutes, or until veggies are tender; drain tomato juice and set aside. Soften gelatin in ¼ cup cold water and add to tomato juice; then add lemon juice, pepper sauce, and Worcestershire sauce.

Ingredients you will need for cream cheese filling:

8 ounces cream cheese
2 tablespoons mayo
1 teaspoon grated onion
Salt and pepper to taste
Paprika (optional)

Make small balls of filling ingredients; put at the bottom of individual mold or at the bottom of a casserole dish and cut into squares. Pour tomato aspic liquid over the cheese balls; after everything has congealed, serve chilled. For additional flavor, top with dollop of mayo and sprinkle paprika over that for color.

—Courtesy Mrs. Rose Williams Turner, Natchez, Mississippi

Maura Beth Mayhew's Chocolate, Cherry Cola Sheet Cake

Ingredients you will need for the batter:

2 cups flour
Dash of salt
2 cups sugar
1 cup any cola beverage
⅓ cup oil
1 stick butter
3 tablespoons dry cocoa
½ cup buttermilk
1 teaspoon baking soda
2 teaspoons vanilla
3 tablespoons maraschino cherry liquid
1 jar of finely chopped maraschino cherries
2 eggs

Mix flour, salt and sugar in bowl. In separate pan, bring to a boil the cola drink, oil, butter and cocoa. Add hot liquid to the bowl and beat heavily; then add buttermilk, baking soda, vanilla, cherry liquid, cherries and eggs and continue beating. When well-mixed, pour into sheet cake pan sprayed with non-stick spray and bake for twenty-five minutes at 350 degrees Fahrenheit.

Ingredients you will need for the icing:

1 stick butter
3 tablespoons cocoa
6 tablespoons whole milk
3 tablespoons maraschino cherry liquid

1 pound confectioner's sugar
2 teaspoons vanilla
1 cup finely chopped pecans

Heat the butter, cocoa, and milk until the butter has liquefied; add the remaining ingredients and beat well. Pour icing onto cake while it is hot or still warm for ease of spreading; cut when cake has cooled.

—Courtesy Marion A. Good, Oxford, Mississippi

Mr. Parker Place's Lemon / Lime Icebox Pie

Ingredients you will need for the crust:

1 7.05-ounce box of Carr's Ginger Lemon Creme Tea Cookies
2 tablespoons of butter or margarine

Empty box of Carr's Ginger Lemon Crème Tea Cookies into food processor and pulse until crumb consistency is reached; or, empty box of cookies into Ziploc bag and pound/roll with rolling pin until crumb consistency is reached.

Pour crumb mixture into a 9-inch aluminum-foil pie pan; melt butter and then drizzle into crumb mixture; mold mixture into crust, adhering to pie pan; set aside.

Ingredients you will need for the filling:

1 can fat-free condensed milk
3 eggs
4 limes or 4 lemons

Note: Using limes will give the pie a tarter taste; using lemons will give it a sweeter taste.

Pour can of condensed milk into large mixing bowl. Crack three medium eggs and separate yolks from whites (if you wish to save whites for omelets, etc., do so; otherwise discard.) Put yolks into condensed milk and stir thoroughly until well-blended.

Juice four limes or four lemons (do not use reconstituted lemon or lime juice); add juice into condensed milk-egg mixture in small portions and mix in thoroughly each time until all juice has been added and blended.

Pour mixture into pie pan and bake at 350 degrees Fahrenheit for about twenty-five minutes; overbaking will make the texture of the filling mealy. Cool before cutting and serving. Serve at room temperature or chilled. Serves up to six.

—Courtesy Mr. Parker Place (Joe Sam Bedloe, Cherico, Mississippi)

And finally: Stout Fella's Instructions for "Islanding" Ice Cream

Ingredients you will need:

1 tablespoon (fresh and hot from being cleaned in the dishwasher, if possible; if not, blow on metal until warm)
1 gallon of previously untouched, unopened ice cream, any flavor

Take ice cream out of freezer; put it on counter, and yell at it to hurry up and soften just a tad bit. Open the hatch or the top and begin testing the edges; start scraping on all four sides; keep going deeper until you have reached the bottom and created an "island," or your wife comes in and screams at you to "Stop, you'll spoil your appetite for dinner!" whichever comes first; repeat, if she goes away; and rinse (the spoon).

—Courtesy Justin Rawlings "Stout Fella" Brachle, Cherico, Mississippi

From *The Reading Circle* (Book 2)

Mr. Parker Place's Egg Custard Pie

Ingredients you will need:

4 eggs
1 cup sugar
1 ½ cups half-and-half
1 tablespoon vanilla extract
½ tablespoon almond extract
1 whole nutmeg grated
1 deep-dish pie shell
1 tablespoon butter

Beat eggs well. Slowly add sugar while beating with mixer. Add half-and-half, vanilla and almond extracts, and grated nutmeg. Beat on medium speed for 1and ½ minutes; pour into pie shell (may be raw or slightly baked). Slice butter and lay super-thin slivers all over top of pie; place on cookie sheet with a deep lip. Add water under pie and bake in 350-degree Fahrenheit oven for 1 hour or until brown crust has formed over pie. Allow to cool and refrigerate. Best if made a day ahead.

—Courtesy Abigail Jenkins Healy, Natchez, Mississippi

Periwinkle Lattimore's
Easy Banana / Cranberry Bread

Ingredients you will need:

2 very ripe bananas
1 cup Stevia sweetener
1 box Chiquita Banana Bread Mix
⅓ cup water
1 egg
1 cup dried cranberries

Mash bananas well. Add Stevia, banana bread mix, water, egg, and cranberries. Spray loaf pan with cooking spray; then pour batter into pan. Bake at 350 degrees for 50 minutes, allow to cool, then turn out onto paper towel. May be stored in refrigerator or breadbox. Good cold or toasted with jelly.

—Courtesy Abigail Jenkins Healy, Natchez, Mississippi

Mr. Parker Place's Clam Canapes

Ingredients you will need:

1 package (8 ounces) cream cheese
1 small can minced clams, drained
3 teaspoons Worcestershire Sauce
1 teaspoon minced green onions
Salt to taste
Dash of red pepper
Paprika (optional)
Parsley (optional)

Whip the cream cheese with a fork. Add clams and mix well; add other ingredients and whip well. Place in refrigerator in covered dish until ready to bake. Spread on plain Saltines and bake at 300 degrees for 20 minutes. Sprinkle with paprika or parsley and serve.

—Courtesy Helen Byrnes Jenkins, Natchez, Mississippi

Periwinkle Lattimore's Cashew Cheese Log

Ingredients you will need:

1 pound yellow cheese
2–3 ounces of cream cheese
1 cup of cashew nuts, salted or unsalted
2 cloves of minced garlic
Paprika

Put yellow cheese through meat grinder or in blender. Whip softened cream cheese. Put cashew nuts through grinder or in blender. Mix all ingredients except paprika; shape into log about 1 and ½ inches in diameter; then roll in lots of paprika. Wrap in waxed paper and refrigerate. To serve, slice very thin and place on round crackers; log may be frozen for later use.

—Courtesy Helen Byrnes Jenkins, Natchez, Mississippi

Mr. Parker Place's Chicken Gumbo

Ingredients you will need:

1 whole chicken, boiled, deboned, and chopped
2 large bags of frozen baby okra
1 cup of any cooking oil
3 onions, chopped
1 celery stalk, chopped
1 large green bell pepper, chopped
2 large cans of chopped tomatoes
2 cups flour
3 large bay leaves
Salt and pepper to taste
Hot sauce to taste

Boil, debone, and chop chicken meat; refrigerate meat and strain cooking stock. Grind the frozen okra. Cook ground okra in oil slowly until okra is bright green; add all vegetables and cook slowly for about 2 hours. Add in silted flour a little at a time and mix; add more oil if needed; cook about 40 minutes or until everything is well-mixed and smooth. Add the stock from the chicken a small amount at a time; add chopped chicken (or seafood such as shrimp, oysters, or crawfish, if you prefer.) Add salt, pepper and hot sauce to taste. Serve as is or over rice.

—Courtesy Mrs. Rose Williams Turner, Natchez, Mississippi

Periwinkle Lattimore's Hot Fruit

Ingredients you will need:

1 orange
1 lemon
2–3 tablespoons light brown sugar
8-ounce can of apricots
8-ounce can of pineapple pieces
8-ounce can of sliced peaches
8-ounce can of pitted Bing cherries
Nutmeg to taste
1 container of sour cream

Grate the orange and lemon rind; add the zest into the brown sugar. Cut the orange and lemon pulp into thin slices, removing seeds and as much of the white membrane as possible; mix these slices in with the rest of the fruit pieces and make a bottom layer of it in a baking dish; sprinkle in zest and sugar mixture and a dash of nutmeg. Repeat layers until all has been used up. Heat in a 300-degree oven for 30 minutes. Top with cold sour cream before serving. Bon appétit!

—Courtesy Helen Byrnes Jenkins, Natchez, Mississippi

From *The Wedding Circle* (Book 3)

Periwinkle's Chicken Salad

Ingredients you will need:

1 half-pound fryer
2 tablespoons seasoned salt
2–3 ribs of celery
¼ onion
¼ bell pepper
5 lemons
4 eggs
Dash of salt and pepper
1 cup of mayo (preferably Hellmann's)
Dash of paprika (optional)
Lettuce (optional)

Cover fryer with water and simmer until tender; add seasoned salt, celery ribs, onion, and bell pepper. Continue simmering until vegetables have softened. Remove fryer and cut 4 cups of chicken using kitchen scissors. Remove vegetables. Cut celery ribs into 2 cups of chopped celery. Finely chop onion into 2 tablespoons—more if desired. Finely chop bell pepper into 1 tablespoon. Juice 5 lemons and set aside. Boil 4 eggs. Finely chop the eggs. Mix chicken, all veggies, all seasonings, lemon juice, egg, and 1 cup of mayonnaise together. Best served chilled. May add dash of paprika on top and a leaf of lettuce on bottom.

—Courtesy Helen Byrnes Jenkins, Natchez, Mississippi

Periwinkle's Artichoke Party Dip

Ingredients you will need:

1 can artichoke hearts (buy variety with hearts only, no leaves)
1 cup mayonnaise (preferably Hellmann's)
1 cup grated Parmesan cheese
1 pie pan or Pyrex dish
Paprika
Corn chips

Drain and mash artichoke hearts. Mix in mayonnaise and cheese. Spoon into pan or dish and bake at 350 degrees until bubbly. Remove from heat, dust with paprika, and serve with corn chips.

—Courtesy Lucianne Wood, Natchez, Mississippi

Mr. Parker Place's Crème de Menthe Cake

Ingredients you will need:

1 18-ounce package white cake mix (may substitute yellow,
   if desired)
2½ tablespoons crème de menthe liqueur or flavoring
1 16-ounce can chocolate syrup
8 ounces fat-free whipped topping
1½ tablespoons crème de menthe liqueur or flavoring
5 or 6 hard peppermint candies (optional)

Prepare cake mix per package instructions, but stir in crème de menthe instead of water. Bake in 13 x 9-inch pan according to instructions. When cake is done, remove and immediately poke holes throughout cake top with toothpick; pour chocolate syrup across top so that it will seep into the holes. When cake is cool, mix whipped topping in bowl with 1½ tablespoons crème de menthe liqueur or flavoring and spread over cake. Refrigerate until ready to serve; also may freeze, if desired.

Optional: Pulse 5 or 6 hard peppermint candies in food processor until in shard or powder state; dust shards or powder over top of cake.

—Courtesy Lauren Good, Mobile, Alabama

Periwinkle's Crazy Caprese Salad

Ingredients you will need:

1 12-ounce can roasted red peppers
12 slices fresh mozzarella cheese
12 slices ripe tomatoes
25 leaves fresh basil
Olive oil
Salt and pepper

Julienne can of red peppers and arrange in any pattern on platter as a base for the salad. Layer slices of cheese next; atop that layer, place tomato slices; final layer should be basil leaves. Splash olive oil, salt, and pepper to taste. Serve by scooping up portions of all layers per person.

—Courtesy Marion Good, Oxford, Mississippi

Periwinkle's Super Crazy Caprese

Ingredients you will need:

All of the Crazy Caprese ingredients in previous recipe, plus:
1 ripe avocado
Worcestershire sauce
1 container (regular size) roasted red pepper hummus
(preferably Sabra)

Prepare Crazy Caprese salad according to previous recipe; then julienne avocado and add slices of ripe avocado atop basil leaves. After olive oil and salt and pepper have been added, splash Worcestershire sauce over all ingredients. Atop each serving of salad, place a generous dollop or two of red pepper hummus.

—Courtesy Marion Good, Oxford, Mississippi

Mr. Parker Place's Frozen Key Lime Pie

Ingredients you will need:

1 8-ounce tub whipped topping
1 can condensed milk
½ cup key lime juice (fresh squeezed is best)
Prepared graham cracker crumb pie shell

Mix together whipped topping and condensed milk in bowl. Add in lime juice slowly until all is thoroughly mixed. Pour into pie shell; freeze. Pie is best if allowed to thaw for about 5 minutes and then served still frosty. Do not overthaw, as pie will become runny. Garnish with mint leaves or fruit of any kind, if desired.

—Courtesy Sissy Eidt, Natchez, Mississippi

From *A Cherry Cola Christmas* (Book 4)

Fat Mama's Homemade Tamale Recipe

Ingredients you will need:

2 pounds beef
2 pounds pork
2 tablespoons garlic, minced
1 cup yellow onions, chopped
Salt
Black pepper
Red pepper
10 cups masa harina (corn flour)
3 cups lard or shortening
Corn husks

Making tamales is a labor of love and is time-consuming. Please keep in mind that it will require 5 to 6 hours from start to finish. So take off your instant gratification hat. The meat and masa (dough) are prepared separately, then combined to make the tamales. We suggest you invite friends and family over when making tamales so it is as much a social event as it is a good day's work in the kitchen!

MEAT MIXTURE

Ingredients (from the above) you will need:

2 pounds beef
2 pounds pork
2 tablespoons garlic, minced
1 cup yellow onions, chopped
Salt, black pepper, red pepper to taste

Combine beef, pork, 2 tablespoons of minced garlic, 1 cup of chopped onions, and salt, black pepper, and red pepper to taste in a large pot and cover with water. Bring pot to a boil, then reduce heat and simmer for 3½ hours. After 3½ hours, remove pot from heat and allow to cool. Once moderately cool, remove and strain meat from liquid and shred. Be sure to keep the strained liquid for use in your masa later. Once you have shredded the meat mixture, place in refrigerator to cool.

DOUGH (MASA HARINA)

Ingredients (from the above) you will need:

10 cups masa harina (corn flour)
3 cups lard or shortening
1 tablespoon salt
1 tablespoon black pepper
Red pepper to taste
Seasoned water that meat was cooked in

Mix your 10 cups of masa harina, 3 cups of lard or shortening, 1 tablespoon of salt, 1 tablespoon of black pepper, and red pepper to taste in a large container. Slowly add the hot strained liquid from the meat mixture and mix thoroughly. We suggest that the masa have the same consistency as thick cornbread. Allow to cool once masa has reached desired consistency.

CORN SCHUCKS /HUSKS

Wash the corn shucks under running water, removing the corn silks, and then soak in a big pot of hot, but not boiling, water for at least 3 hours in order to soften the shuck so it is easy to handle. This step can be done while the meat is cooking. Once the shucks are pliable, you can lay them out to be filled with the dough and meat mixture. Spread the dough (masa harina) on with a knife; then spread the meat mixture over the masa. The meat mixture will be heavier and thicker than the masa mixture. Once the masa and meat are applied to the shuck, the narrow end of the shuck is folded up and the shuck is then rolled up from side to side. Tie the tamales in bundles of six with a string prior to the final step.

FINAL STEP

Once the tamales are all bundled, place them in a steam basket and cook them over water. It is important that the water is not completely steamed away at any time. Keep the steamer full of water so the tamales do not dry out. They are best served hot right out of the pot. Suggestion for libation: ice-cold beer.

—Courtesy David Gammill, Natchez, Mississippi

The Twinkle, Twinkle Café's
Baby Kale, Spinach, and Blueberry Salad

Ingredients you will need:

15-ounce bag or package of baby kale (do not use mature
    kale)
15-ounce bag or package of baby spinach
Dried dill weed
1 11-ounce package of fresh blueberries
2 ounces Feta cheese crumbles
Balsamic vinaigrette dressing (any bottled brand)

Wash baby kale and spinach leaves; place in very large salad
bowl. Sprinkle dried dill weed throughout. Wash blueberries
and distribute throughout salad. Sprinkle Feta cheese throughout; drizzle dressing to taste. Toss everything together lightly,
but do not bruise or crush blueberries. This recipe serves up to
six. Halve ingredients, except dill weed and cheese crumbles,
to serve two or three. An excellent light dinner party selection
and a cool accompaniment to any hot tamales being served.

—Courtesy Marion Good, Oxford, Mississippi

From *Queen of the Cookbooks* (Book 5)

Mrs. Frieze's Cheeze Ballz

Ingredients you will need:

2 eight-ounce boxes of Philadelphia (Original) cream cheese
1 envelope Hidden Valley Ranch Seasoning
2 tablespoons garlic powder
2 tablespoons onion powder
2 cups shredded cheddar cheese
1 can Hormel ham
1 package chopped pecans

Mix first six ingredients together thoroughly and then roll mixture into balls. Roll cheese balls in the chopped pecans until completely covered. Refrigerate for at least 2 hours. Best served with crackers.

—Courtesy Mignon Pittman, Director,
Calloway County Library, Murray, Kentucky

Aleitha Larken's Chicken
on the Sofa (Chicken Divan)

Ingredients you will need:

2 cups cooked chicken, sliced or large pieces
1 package dehydrated onion soup mix
1 pint sour cream
2 packages frozen broccoli, cooked
1 cup heavy cream, whipped
1 tablespoon Parmesan cheese

Bake chicken breasts or dark meat—whichever is preferred, or use both. Slice chicken into large pieces. To make sauce for cooked chicken, add soup mix to sour cream and beat with rotary beater until well blended. Arrange cooked broccoli in shallow casserole dish in a single layer. Spoon half of sauce over broccoli, then add layer of chicken. Fold whipped cream into remaining sauce and pour over chicken layer. Bake at 350 degrees for 20 minutes or until bubbly. Sprinkle Parmesan cheese and brown under broiler. Recipe serves 4.

—Courtesy Margaret Trigg Kuehnle, Natchez, Mississippi, and Margaret Kuehnle Fulton, Lake Concordia, Louisiana

Ana Estrella's Pigeon Peas Cake

Ingredients you will need:

1 cup *gandules* (pigeon peas) (if using canned *gandules,* which
    come in a 15-ounce can, drain the *gandules* first and use 1
    cup for this recipe; save the rest for a savory dish)
¼ cup coconut milk
¼ cup 2% milk
1½ sticks unsalted butter, softened
2 cups granulated sugar
1 teaspoon vanilla extract
2 large eggs
2 cups cake flour
½ teaspoon baking soda
2 teaspoons ground cinnamon
½ teaspoon freshly ground nutmeg
1 tablespoon Maxwell House International Café Hazelnut
    Flavor powder
3 ounces baking dark chocolate, coarsely chopped

In a small food processor, mix the *gandules* with both milks and
process until it is puréed. Set aside.

In a large bowl, beat the butter and sugar with an electric
mixer until creamy. Add vanilla and eggs, one at a time, and
mix.

In a separate bowl, combine cake flour with baking soda, cinnamon, nutmeg, and International Café Hazelnut powder and
sift once. Remove about 2 teaspoons of this flour mixture and
set it aside. Gradually add the rest of the flour mixture to the
butter mixture, mixing well.

Add *gandules* mixture to the batter, mixing well.

In a small bowl, mix the chocolate chunks with the 2 teaspoons of flour mixture that was set aside and fold into cake batter.

Pour cake batter into a greased and floured Bundt cake pan and bake in a preheated oven at 350 degrees for about 25–30 minutes or until a toothpick inserted into the cake comes out clean, without crumbs.

Once cake is done, remove from oven and let cool inside the pan for 10 minutes; then invert cake onto a cooling rack. Let cake cool completely. Once it has cooled and is ready to be served, sprinkle with confectioner's sugar. Slice and enjoy with a cup of *café con leche! Buen provecho!*

—Courtesy Ana Raquel Ruiz,
Atlanta, Georgia, and San Juan, Puerto Rico

Maribelle Pleasance's
No-Sugar-Added Cherry Cake

Ingredients you will need:

1 can pineapple tidbits in own juice
1 can cherry pie filling (no sugar added)
8 ounces walnuts (or pecan pieces)
1 box yellow cake mix (no sugar added)
1 stick real butter

Preheat oven to 325 degrees. Combine pineapple tidbits and cherry pie filling, and stir together in an ungreased pan. Do not drain pineapple tidbits. Layer nuts on top of fruit. Add cake mix dry. Do not stir in, just level out. Melt stick of butter and then spoon over dry mixture. Bake for about 45 minutes until brown on top.

—Courtesy Marilyn Cadle Holkham,
London, United Kingdom

From *Book Club Babies* (Book 6)

These are the drinks and appetizers that Periwinkle Place served at her sip 'n' see in the novel. They could also be used for general entertaining purposes.

Periwinkle Lattimore's
Sip 'N' See Knockout Punch

Ingredients you will need:

1 12-fluid-ounce can of frozen orange juice concentrate
3 cups water
1 46-fluid-ounce can of pineapple juice
1 liter ginger ale

In a punch bowl, combine orange juice, water, and pineapple juice; chill. Stir in ginger ale just before serving.

—Courtesy Leslie Price Burrell,
Traveler's Rest, South Carolina

Periiwinkle Place's
Blush Punch or Pink Beeritas

Ingredients you will need:

1 12-ounce can of frozen pink lemonade concentrate, thawed
3 12-ounce bottles of light beer (NOT DARK), chilled
¾ cup vodka, chilled
Ice
Fresh cranberries, strawberries, or other fruit (optional)

Combine all ingredients; garnish with fresh cranberries, strawberries, or fruit of your choice.

—Courtesy Kate Barron Rosson, Oxford, Mississippi

Periwinkle Place's
Cucumber Tea Sammies

Ingredients you will need:

2 cucumbers
½ cup ranch dip (premade is fine)
⅛ cup cream cheese, softened
1 teaspoon Greek seasoning
1 teaspoon garlic powder
½ teaspoon dill
1 loaf of white bread

Using a mandolin, slice the cucumbers thin and place each slice flat on a paper towel to drain excess water. Place paper towel on topside of cucumbers to also drain top excess water. While cucumbers are drying, mix ranch dip and cream cheese, seasoning, garlic powder, and dill until smooth.

Using a biscuit cutter (or knife if you don't have one), cut out bread into round, square, or triangle shapes. Layer spread on both pieces of bread, then place cucumbers on bread. (Make sure to use a little of the spread in between the cucumbers to help "glue" the cucumbers and keep them from sliding.) Close the sammie. Serve right away, or it can be made ahead of time and placed overnight in an airtight container with a dry paper towel to absorb moisture.

—Courtesy Kate Barron Rosson, Oxford, Mississippi

Periwinkle Place's Pimento Cheese

Ingredients you will need:

2 cups white sharp cheddar cheese, shredded
¼ cup Parmesan cheese
1 cup Duke's mayonnaise (or other favorite mayo)
6 ounces roasted red peppers or pimentos, diced
¼ cup chopped green onions
¼ teaspoon hot sauce
¼ teaspoon Cajun seasoning
¼ teaspoon Worcestershire sauce

Combine all ingredients. Serve with Wheat Thins.

—Courtesy Kate Barron Rosson, Oxford, Mississippi

Periwinkle Place's Zucchini Squares

Ingredients you will need:

4 eggs, beaten
½ cup oil
1 cup Bisquick
½ cup Parmesan cheese, grated
½ cup chopped onion
3 cups zucchini, sliced thinly with skin on
½ clove garlic chopped
½ teaspoon salt
½ teaspoon seasoned salt
½ teaspoon oregano
10 dashes Tabasco sauce

Beat eggs; add oil, Bisquick, Parmesan cheese, and onion. Mix well. Add remainder of ingredients and stir together. Pour into a 9-by-13-inch greased baking pan and bake uncovered at 375 degrees for 30 to 35 minutes until golden brown. Cut into squares and serve either hot or at room temperature.

—Courtesy Marion Good, Oxford, Mississippi

BOOK CLUB BABIES

Ashton Lee

ABOUT THIS GUIDE

The suggested questions are included to
enhance your group's reading of Ashton Lee's
Book Club Babies!

DISCUSSION QUESTIONS

1. Do you think Elise and Alex will eventually get together and bring up Celice together?

2. Do you think Periwinkle's mother, Mama Kohlmeyer, will ever come around and accept her grandchild and her daughter's marriage to Parker Place?

3. What did you enjoy most about Maura Beth's development as a woman and librarian throughout the series?

4. Is Councilman Sparks still the character you "love to hate," or has your perception of him shifted?

5. For women: How did your pregnancy compare with those of the women in this novel? Discuss similarities and differences.

6. For men: How did your wife's pregnancy and your experience as a "pregnant father" compare with Maura Beth's and Jeremy's?

7. Some readers have indicated that they would like to live in a town like Cherico. Would you? If so, why? If no, why not?

8. How is the place you live like or unlike Cherico?

9. How do you picture Maura Beth and Jeremy ten years from the ending of this novel?

10. Is the racism depicted in this novel getting better or worse in the world?

Connect with

Us

Visit us online at
KensingtonBooks.com
to read more from your favorite authors, see books
by series, view reading group guides, and more.

Join us on social media

for sneak peeks, chances to win books and prize packs,
and to share your thoughts with other readers.

facebook.com/kensingtonpublishing
twitter.com/kensingtonbooks

Tell us what you think!

To share your thoughts, submit a review,
or sign up for our eNewsletters, please visit:
KensingtonBooks.com/TellUs.